BETWEEN *us* AND THE *moon*

BETWEEN
us
AND THE
moon

REBECCA MAIZEL

HARPER TEEN
An Imprint of HarperCollinsPublishers

HarperTeen is an imprint of HarperCollins Publishers.

Between Us and the Moon

Library of Congress Cataloging-in-Publication Data
Maizel, Rebecca.
  Between us and the moon / Rebecca Maizel. — First edition.
    pages cm
  Summary: Just before spending her sixteenth summer on Cape
Cod, Sarah's boyfriend breaks up with her and, as a scientist whose
focus is on winning a scholarship through her study of a comet, she
designs an experiment to become more like her older sister to see if
she, too, can be popular.
  ISBN 978-0-06-232761-1 (hardcover)
  [1. Popularity—Fiction. 2. Dating (Social customs)—Fiction.
3. Experiments—Fiction. 4. Sisters—Fiction. 5. Astronomy—
Fiction. 6. Family life—Massachusetts—Fiction. 7. Cape Cod
(Mass.)—Fiction.] I. Title.
PZ7.M279515Bet 2015   2014034847
[Fic]—dc23   CIP
                                                             AC

Typography by Torborg Davern
15 16 17 18 19   PC/RRDH   10 9 8 7 6 5 4 3 2 1

First Edition

To Brooke Darcy Nordstrom, Aviva Fink Cantor, Zoe Houldsworth LoPresti, Leigh Ann Razza, and Katie Caramiciu, my childhood friends—now and always.

This is my love letter to you.

BETWEEN *us* AND THE *moon*

JUNE SCHEDULE

IMPORTANT DATES:

June 19th—Last Day of School. See ya later, losers! Here's to being a junior.

June 20th—Leave for Cape Cod

LOOKING AHEAD:

June 26th—BIRTHDAY! 16!

July 3rd—Comet Jolie reaches perihelion

TO DO: IN ORDER OF IMPORTANCE

Organize for Waterman Scholarship: due date August 8th

☐ Application (16 pages, snail mailed in to scholarship board)

☐ Online registration—due June 26th (Birthday!)

☐ Comet data, compiled in duplicate

☐ Letter of recommendation from the East Greenwich Observatory

☐ Personal essay (ugh)

☐ Write thank-you note to Headmaster Winston. Make sure to <u>thank him</u> for the rousing yet embarrassing speech about being the top of the class.

ONE

"WHAT'S THE POINT OF DOING ALL THIS MATH JUST to track a comet?" Scarlett says and squints through the lens of my telescope. "It's a fuzzy white speck."

"The whole point is to use pen and paper to predict the comet's perihelion."

"Perry-what?"

"It means the comet's closest position to the sun."

"But you have your school computer," Scarlett says. She motions to the SUMMERHILL ACADEMY loaner laptop that's open on a small collapsible table.

"I program the telescope with the computer. That's it," I explain.

"I would *definitely* cheat."

It took ten minutes to get Scarlett out here, so now that she is, I want her to look through the telescope and see exactly what I see. I want her to know how hard it is to project its coordinates *every single night*. I've been working on this experiment since the Comet Jolie first streaked into our skies eleven months ago.

"The math is what makes it precise," I explain. "Any old computer can be programmed to take a guess."

"I suck at math," Scarlett says. Her deep red lipstick is so pretty. If I wore that tonight, I'd get it all over Tucker and probably my clothes. I'm not graceful, not like my sister.

"When it finally reaches its perihelion and streaks into the Northern Hemisphere I will have tracked it over forty million miles."

"*Northern . . .*" Scarlett stands up and sounds out the word. "*Hemisssphere.* Doesn't that sound epic?"

"Well, yes, technically speaking the Northern Hemisphere has the most land. Two-thirds of the Earth is actu—"

Scarlett laughs and laughs.

"You have zero perspective, Bean," she says with a flip of her hair and turns back to the house.

"This comet is the brightest comet to pass by the sun in a hundred years," I say, but I am talking to her back. The moon is waxing crescent tonight, so it's a sliver, but still, Scarlett's blonde hair glimmers down her back. I swear, every year Scarlett gets more and more beautiful, like a freak of nature or something.

"I want to do this old school," I add. "You know, Galileo style. Okay, not quite as old as Galileo, but pen, calculator, anti-vibration, internal GPS, hi-res optics style."

She glances back at me before disappearing into the house.

"It's definitely cool," she says, though it's clear she is just try-ing to be nice. I'm doing fine! Besides, it's easy for her to say—all Scarlett cares about is ballet. "But you need to get your head out of the stars once in a while."

"Bean!" Mom calls. "Tucker's here!"

Took him long enough. The forecast predicted rain after eleven. No clouds yet, luckily. I run a hand over my Stargazer. In under one month the Comet Jolie streaks across the sky and we can see it without a telescope.

I lay my nightly coordinates sheet down on the ground on top of my favorite blanket. When Tucker gets here he can see how complicated it was to locate and identify the comet's position in tonight's sky. I know how intricate it is, but it's nice to have my best friend, my *boyfriend*, who happened to score six points higher than me on the PSATs, see what I am capable of doing.

I wait for it—there's a *squeaksqueak, squeaksqueak* as Tucker makes his way through the living room.

Our old Victorian has mismatched floorboards. Most are original which means they creak *loudly*.

"If you ever sneak out," Scarlett once told me, "avoid the red Oriental rug. All original floor. *It squeaks,* you know what I mean?" At the time, she stopped and shook her head. "What am I talking about." She flipped her hair over her shoulder. "Little Miss Stars and Planets? Sneak out?"

Scarlett passes by Tucker and says, "Tell Trish to call me when she gets home. No excuses." Scarlett points at him and he nods.

Trish is Tucker's sister and Scarlett's best friend. Inseparable—well, until now.

Tucker has to dodge a tower of brown and red suitcases piled high next to the kitchen table. There are six: one for Mom, one for Dad, one for me, and three for Scarlett. On top of Scarlett's sit two pairs of pointe ballet shoes. The thick satin laces lie across the suitcases and unfurl onto the floor. He walks past Dad, who, as usual, is reclining in his leather chair in front of the TV. He's watching a show on the Discovery Channel. Gray wisps of his Einstein hair stick up and point in every direction.

"Every year you guys bring more and more stuff to the Cape," Tucker says and comes off the patio to join me in the backyard. His voice clips in his usual singsong way. It makes everything he says sound like a joke he's not quite finished telling.

"Tell that to Miss Ballerina," I say. "Juilliard's dance program will never see so many hair ties, perfume bottles, and pink tank tops ever again. The onslaught is coming."

"You'd be surprised," Tucker says, but there's an edge to his tone that sticks to the air. He looks different tonight. I can't place it. I lean forward and he kisses me on the lips. He pulls away before I can reach out to him, link my hand behind his head, and go in for a deeper kiss. Like the one we had last week. Out of nowhere, Tucker held his arms around my back, pulled me close, and kissed me so deeply that for a moment, we weren't just Tucker and Bean, best friends for nine years, boyfriend and girlfriend for one year.

I wanted more than polite kissing.

Now, when he pulls away, Tucker digs his hands in his

4

sweatpants pockets. Hmm. Hands in pockets, curved back, and eyes to the ground. I've known Tucker too long—something is up. Neither one of us are excited about me going to the Cape, even though it's unavoidable.

"You're *driving* up in two weeks!" I say, trying to make him feel better. "It's better than having to wait until August for Scarlett's going-away party."

I link my arms around his waist and he leans his body weight into mine. It is familiar now, his body and my body, close together.

"I don't know if they'll give me the car," he says quietly.

"Trying to get out of coming? I don't blame you. I wouldn't want to be in the same house or even the same state as Aunt Nancy if I didn't have to."

He laughs but it's soft, like a private joke between us.

"Your great-aunt isn't that bad."

I raise an eyebrow.

"Okay, she's the worst," he admits.

His chest shudders when he laughs and I can feel it, he's pressed so close to me.

"I don't want to go almost two months without seeing you," I say.

"We did it last year."

"Yeah, but that was before you fell madly in love with me."

I kiss his nose and pull back to ready my coordinates and show him all the varied equations and procedures I used to track the comet tonight.

"Either way, I'll see you at Scarlett's party," I add. "It's all Nancy has been talking about for *months*."

He nods. Something about him *is* different. I can't place it.

I'd better get down to business. He'll cheer up eventually. *I need more time than you to express how I feel,* Tucker has said about a dozen times this year. I should remember that sometimes it takes some people longer to express themselves.

I throw my hair behind my shoulders and wave the coordinates sheet. This should raise his spirits. The sight of mathematics and equations usually gets a smile and a lift of his eyebrows over his dark eyeglass frames.

"Now," I explain, "the perihelion isn't projected to be until July 3rd, but it's amazing, I'm telling you. Even with light pollution this comet is the brightest I've ever seen."

I punch in the coordinates to my school computer.

I run a hand down the telescope like Vanna White. I'm careful not to move its position. "Look at this baby. Eight-inch mirror. Highest magnification possible."

Tucker nods but doesn't say anything.

"Ready?" I say.

"Steady," he replies, but our usual call and answer tradition sounds hollow. I have kept this information a secret on purpose. He knows this. Way to be a buzzkill.

Whatever. I push on; his bad mood isn't going to change mine. Tucker *wanted* to see this. He said so this morning as we cleaned out our lockers at school.

The computer beeps, starting to record the images from the Stargazer.

"This baby was worth 7,562 pizza orders," I say about the telescope. "Good-bye Pizza Palace for almost two whole months." I sit down on the blanket, cross my ankles over each other, and pop a mint. I'm not opposed to making the first move.

He peers through the lens.

I make room for Tucker on the blanket.

"You did it," he says with a small lift to his voice. His deep tone is gentle, like he doesn't want to talk too loudly. "You're gonna win that scholarship." The slice of the moon above his head outlines him in a pearly glow.

"You look really good right now," I say. "Standing next to my Stargazer. It's sexy."

I laugh, but Tucker's cell phone vibrates. He reaches into his pocket and silences the buzzing.

"So what do you think? You're being quiet."

I know I'm being impatient, but this is bizarre.

"Come out to the front yard?" he asks, and the word "yard" kind of fades away. Crap.

His quiet voice is *not* a good sign. This is the same tone he took when Trish rode a motorized Barbie car over my rock polisher when we were twelve. The same tone he used to tell me his Nana Patrick died. He barely spoke for two weeks, except for Mathletes when he could recite equations. "Please," he adds.

"Did you get a B on a final or something?" I ask.

He shakes his head.

Tucker should be asking me what coordinates I have, what constellations the comet's trajectory passes through, and what phase of the moon is best to achieve optimal viewing conditions. What does he mean, follow him to the front of the house?

Tucker's wearing his Summerhill Academy sweatpants and

a blue T-shirt. He nudges at the grass with his toe. Someone should document this. Mr. I Always Bring My Day Planner Everywhere left the house without Converse sneakers? He's wearing flip-flops. Tucker pushes his glasses to the bridge of his nose.

He takes a step away from the Mason jars for our iced tea and the fuzzy blanket he kissed me on three days ago until my jaw was sore.

"I don't want to talk about this here," he says.

"This?"

He sighs.

Now that I focus, his sandals are familiar. They're the same kind all the guys on the Summerhill Academy baseball team wear. The jock guys that Tucker makes fun of at lunch.

He walks around the house to the front yard with his shoulders hunched to his ears.

"Can you just tell me what's going on?" I say and follow behind.

Tucker stands in the street at the front of the house. He still has his hands in his pockets.

"I'm—" Tucker mumbles.

"*What* is going on with you?"

"I—I want to break up," he finally gets out.

My stomach swoops just like when we drive twenty miles an hour over the huge hill on Overlook Drive. Me and Tucker. We do that in his Volvo all the time.

"Break up. Bean."

I shake my head. Shake. Shake. Shake.

"I want to," Tucker says again. It sounds like he's pleading with me.

"I'm sorry," he says and slides his glasses up to the top of his nose. "But I want to."

"No, you don't," I say, but my voice isn't strong anymore. It breaks.

I focus on Mom's oak tree, where Tucker and I used to climb when we were little kids. I don't care about his knobby knees or the messy strands of his blond hair. "No, you *don't*," I say again. "We have green grass, a starry night—hell, I can see Rasalgethi, even with the lights from the house. This is a romantic moment, Tucker, not a breakup. You're supposed to check my coordinates." My voice is squeaky. I *hate* when I sound like this.

"Please don't yell at me, Sarah," he says.

Oh my God. His tone; it's not begging or pleading—it's pity.

I make a fist and dig my nails into my palm. I release and repeat the motion.

Tucker won't look up from the ground.

"What about last week? When you—" My cheeks warm. "When you *touched* me?" I ask. I don't need to remind him of the play-by-play.

One hand caressed the small of my back. Tucker pressed his chest to mine. His tongue met mine and he ran his fingers over my breasts.

Tucker keeps his chin close to his chest and his hands are still deep in his pockets. The phone vibrates a second time, but he gets to it quick.

"I remember touching you," he says. "But I stopped us from going any further. I didn't want to push it until I was sure."

"You hooked up with me and you were *debating breaking up with me?*"

I can't help yelling again.

He takes a step toward me and holds out his hands. "No, that's not what I mean." When I don't take them, he brings the heels of his palms to his eyes and sighs. "I'm not good at this. I don't want to hurt—" His phone buzzes yet again. He silences it for the third time, but it fumbles from his fingers to the grass.

I snatch it and hand it over. Becky Winthrop's name is on the screen.

"Tell her she'll have to wait until you're done breaking up with your girlfriend to plan your tutoring session tomorrow."

He slips the phone into his back pocket.

"It's Friday night," he says. "Don't you want to hang out with your friends? Ettie? Or the Mathletes?"

"*We* were hanging out . . . weren't we?" I ask.

"I have plans with someone else tonight."

I gasp and hate myself for it.

"There's someone else?" I whisper.

He steps closer to me. I can't say no. I don't have the words to stop him from holding me.

Tucker runs a hand over my hair and a shiver runs down my back. He slides his hands around my waist. He squeezes me and I hate the touch of his hands.

The warmth of his body against mine is unfair. He will pull away and whatever we are now will be—an after.

Tears burn my eyes.

I will not cry. *Periodic table. Recite the elements in alphabetical order. No crying.*

Actinium. Aluminum. Americium. Antimony.

Okay. This is working.

Argon, arsenic, astatine.

"Remember?" he whispers. His nose sounds stuffed and he doesn't let go. "When you were seven I tricked you into thinking that was a piece of the moon?" He gestures to the Zuckermans' boulder on the lawn of the house across the street.

"I would have believed anything you told me," I say with a sniff. Tucker pulls away. The heat between us threads away and dissipates, to become part of the world again.

He kisses my head and says, "I've got to experiment. Or I'll stay the same."

"Who wants to change?" I ask. We meet eyes for one split second, but my bottom lip quivers like I'm five.

He looks away, shifts his posture, and his spine slouches.

These are all expressions of guilt.

Why would he be guilty? Because he's hurting me? Because he gave me no indication this was coming?

"So who is it? Who are you going out with tonight? Pi Naries, *again*?" I ask, referring to our math club.

"I'm taking a break from the Pi Naries," he admits.

"You *created* the group. You went to the principal. You . . ."

It's not worth it. Tucker keeps making excuses about needing a social life and I turn to walk back around the house. I don't know if I can bring myself to go inside. It's pathetic, but I'm purposefully walking away so he'll call me back.

"You're just really logical, Bean." This stops me and I freeze. I hear Scarlett in my head: *you need to get your head out of the stars once in a while.*

I face Tucker again.

"You watch the world. I'm not even sure you live in it," he says.

My gut stings. Tucker stands before me in a blue T-shirt and Summerhill sweatpants; he isn't dressed in his usual Polo button-down and jeans. It's not just the flip-flops—it's so much more.

Last week, we were drafting my Waterman Scholarship application checklist. He's right, two days ago I wanted him to take my bra off, but he stopped me.

"Haven't you noticed I've been hanging out in the junior parking lot? Or that I'm not at every single Pi Nary meeting?"

He keeps rambling, but nothing he says is what I want to hear.

"I'm different. I am. And you haven't even noticed."

My bottom lip keeps quivering so I bite at it to try to make it stop—doesn't work. I ache right beneath my ribs. I place a hand over my stomach.

"I'm sorry," he says. A sob catches in his throat; it makes his voice thick. He spins on his heel and heads down the street.

His apology is his good-bye.

The moon backlights him as he passes by the Zuckermans' house and their idiotic oversized boulder.

The light flickers from a room upstairs in our house. Scarlett's angular features watch me from her bedroom window. Her face in the moonlight is porcelain. She drops out of the window frame, leaving behind a view of the blue comforter on her bed.

You watch the world.

I try counting elements, but nothing seems to work. I make it all the way to the middle of the alphabet twice, but my face is still wet and puffy.

Neon. Neptunium. Nickel. Nobelium.

A breeze moves the branches above my head. Somewhere on the street, a baseball game on TV echoes through an open window. Yet, still, my uneven breath is the loudest sound around me.

The streetlight in front of our house spotlights the ground—a crack zigzags up and down right on the pavement where Tucker had been standing. In fact, its shape mimics Cassiopeia, a constellation that is supposed to look like a queen chained to her throne.

The garage light flickers on, and I make sure to keep my back to the house. I wipe my cheeks and smooth my ponytail.

"Bean? Is that you?" Mom rolls the recycling bin to the end of the driveway.

"Yeah," I say, and clear my throat so she can't hear the thickness in my voice.

"I didn't know you were still out here. Tell Tucker good night and come inside. We're leaving tomorrow right after graduation, and everything needs to be ready to go."

I listen for the sound of her flat sandals to head back to the house and eventually shut the door. I guess I've been out here for a while because Cassiopeia has moved westward across the sky.

"Good night, Tucker," I say to the empty street and go inside.

TWO

THE TEN O'CLOCK NEWS ECHOES FROM THE living room. I don't want to be in my bedroom, where pictures of Tucker will be staring at me from various mirrors and frames. Sleep is clearly not an option so I have the Waterman Scholarship application out in front of me on the table. I tap my pen against the top of the page on the spot where it says the scholarship prize money: $34,000 dollars.

I slip my backpack from the floor to my lap and unzip. Right at the top are a couple photographs from when I cleaned out my locker earlier this morning. I slide them out and they sit in my hand: Tucker and I at the Summerhill winter formal right after we got together; the time I got first place at the science fair.

There's a few more of Ettie and me, but of course, the bulk of the images are of Tucker and me doing anything and everything to do with science. In each of the photos he wears his ratty Converse with the numbers of Pi, written on every available white space.

In my bag are brochures from lectures, planetarium tickets, and—

I slide out the first notes he ever wrote me after we decided to make it exclusive a year ago.

Thinking of you all day today.

Can't believe we're doing this, Bean.

I crumple the tiny pieces of paper into my hand as hard as I can. When I release, the muscles in my palm ache. The moon moves through the clouds, but still—the sun will rise and it will be a new life without Tucker, for the first time since kindergarten.

I hate my books. I hate this dumb scholarship. I smack my pen to the floor and it skids across the kitchen tiles. I freeze, but Mom and Dad don't seem to hear anything over the television in the other room. The *last* thing I need is for them to see my eyes, ask why I am crying, and push until I finally cave.

I sigh—the truth is, I don't hate my books or the scholarship. I hate that I love them both and it's exactly what Tucker doesn't want.

"Oh my God," Scarlett's voice cuts through the air. She sits on the porch steps on her cell phone. "Summerhill graduation gowns are hideous. Mine is swimming on me," Scarlett says to someone on her cell phone. Her blonde hair flows down her back in beachy waves. "Yeah, we have to leave for the Cape right after.

Believe me, I bitched about the timing."

There's a car horn from the front of the house.

"Mom!" Scarlett yells. "Trish is here!"

Ten thirty. Good, now that Scarlett's gone I can call Gran and have her all to myself. In San Diego it's seven thirty.

I get up and hold the note from Tucker in the palm of my hand. I hesitate over the trash can and turn my hand over ever so slowly.

"I don't want to just be friends anymore. Don't you think it's pointless?" Tucker's got me cornered in the bio lab. One hand rests on the wall near my head, the other in his pocket.

"What do you mean?" My heart thuds so hard I'm surprised he can't hear it.

"I've been in love with you since we were nine. Since you tripped over my stupid dog and fell flat on your face in the front yard."

Tucker brings his face to mine, his lips hover so close I can feel his breath. I want to kiss him; I've never seen him so close, never felt his body heat.

"I've known you since kindergarten," I say.

"That makes it better."

I shake my head from the memory and inhale lingering aromas of pasta and sauce from dinner. The crunched pieces of paper cling to my skin, but gravity always wins out. My hand hovers for less than a second and Tucker's notes fall into the can joining chicken carcasses, old eggshells, and orange peels.

Gran will make sense of this.

Mom and Dad sit in the living room, but now they're watching a special on global warming.

I want to make this call without having to explain why. I tiptoe behind their loungers, trying not to make too much noise.

Everything's cool, no one's moved. I'm almost to the back porch. I take another step over the red Oriental runner and a floorboard squeaks.

"Beanie?" Mom says.

Damn.

I stop short, hip checking a coffee table, and send the car keys to the floor.

"Just being graceful over here," I say and pick them up.

"Make sure you make a copy of the Waterman Scholarship application in case something happens to the original at Aunt Nancy's."

Waterman Scholarship. It's all Mom can talk about since she was laid off from East Bay High, a school in the city. They fired everyone because kids weren't passing the public school standardized tests. I'm not sure how all of the teachers, even ones like Mom, who went to conferences and ran after school programs, deserved to be fired.

"Make an extra copy of the work you've done so far. Just in case," she adds.

"My research?" I ask.

"Back that up too," she says.

"I already have backups," I say.

"Back up your backups."

"Right," I say with a slouch of my shoulders. "I'm gonna call Gran first."

Without this scholarship, Mom and Dad will have to ask

Nancy for money not just for Scarlett's college but for my last two years of Summerhill, too. I pass by six cardboard boxes of Dad's research on my way to the porch. They are stamped with the initials: WHOI, Woods Hole Oceanographic Institution. They're piled high next to our suitcases. I usually go with Dad to work every summer and help him catalog or research specimens. I hope I have as much time with all the work I have to do for the Waterman Scholarship.

"Tell Gran to have fun on her retreat," Dad calls. "What is it again?"

"Silent meditation," Mom replies.

I close the door to the screened-in patio and plop on our ancient blue couch. I pull the curly coil wire so the kinks are almost straight, and dial Gran.

Someone picks up in the middle of the second ring.

"Coriander, Gracie. Coriander. It's tikka masala not brisket, for Pete's sake."

In the background Gracie says, "I would put coriander in a brisket; I bet it's good."

"If you want to vomit," Gran counters.

"Gran!" I say.

"Bean!" her voice sings at me. "Sweetheart, would you put coriander in a brisket?"

"Coriander is an Indian spice," I reply.

"Right, you're not crazy. Get the red wine, Gracie," Gran says. Gran and Gracie have been together forty years, since they were twenty—two years after Dad was born. Gran says Dad is the best and only decision she ever made with a man. Even still, Grandpa

Henry died four years ago and Gran led his memorial service.

"Tucker dumped me," I say.

Silence.

"Gracie, finish the tikka. Gotta put out a fire," Gran says.

"Oh no," I hear in the background. This makes my eyes burn from tears. Again. I take a few deep breaths. I look up to the ceiling because somehow this makes it easier not to cry. My eyes burn anyway and my nostrils flare. I'm gonna need a tissue any minute.

"What happened?" Gran says and she exhales. I can see her on her porch too with the blue-and-white-checkered cushions and the wicker furniture. She's probably settling into her favorite chair next to her famous ferns. I bet she brushes the leaves with the tips of her fingers as she talks. Gran and Gracie are wild for ferns.

"He told me that I watch the world. I guess he wants someone more exciting."

"What's more exciting than someone who knows how to track a comet? Hogwash. How the hell does he know what he wants? He's sixteen!"

"I'll be sixteen in a week."

"Honey, Tucker Jackson has been chasing you around since you were a little kid with your chemistry set."

"That's just it," I say, gesturing to the empty porch as though Gran were standing here with me. "It's not like him. We're serious and logical. It's the best part about our relationship. It's like he got a new personality." I pick at the familiar frayed fabric of the seat cushion.

"Aren't you going to the Cape tomorrow?" Gran asks, but her words are stern.

"Yeah," I croak.

"Aren't you going to be tracking that comet of yours and winning some fancy scholarship *and* winning the Nobel Prize for astronomy?"

"Physics," I say.

"Well, hell, Gracie that's some naan!" With a mouthful of Indian bread Gran says, "Beanie, I love you more than my luggage. Tucker's going through some alien boy phase and while he's E.T. Tucker you remember what you love and what you have to do."

She's already making me feel better. Gran's right. *Right*. I don't care about Tucker. I don't.

I sigh.

Because I do.

"Go to the beach, go to Woods Hole with your dad and hang out with the *Albert*."

"Alvin."

"Exactly," she says, referring to a deep-sea submersible. It's a submarine that's been as deep as the *Titanic*. "Go see that hunk of metal, kiss on it, and you'll be good as new."

"You know why I love the *Alvin*, Gran."

Gran recites as though she's a robot reading from a textbook, "The *Alvin* has the capacity to see life-forms at the bottom of the ocean that would be analogous to life-forms on other planets."

I laugh though tears still linger on my cheek. I *hate* crying.

"I love you, Gran."

"Aw, kid. I love you. Don't let Tucker get you down. Do what *you* love. And don't let my sister make you wear anything ridiculous or force you to go to any Daughters of the American Revolution parties."

Her sister is Aunt Nancy.

"You know she will," I say. "Or else she'll threaten to stop paying my tuition."

"Don't I know it."

Gran explains the purpose of the silent meditation retreat that she and Gracie are going to at the end of the week. The retreat is to remind her to stay true to herself as long as she can "cut away all the excess noise of culture."

"Enjoy the tikka and your silence. Tell Gracie I love her," I say.

Gran offers me some extra money for the summer, though I say no. She doesn't have enough to send to both Scarlett and me. I know she'll send me more than she has for my birthday. I always tell her to spend her money on a plane ticket instead. By the time we hang up, I exhale and sit back into the seat. I do feel better. Even if it's only for a little while, even I know Gran's spell is only temporary.

Because I am clearly a sick person, I step out to the front of the house and sit on the edge where the lawn and street meet. Sometimes, after Tucker goes out with some of the Pi Naries to the Pizza Palace, he comes over. I do work out here on the curb until I see his lanky frame at the end of the street. He sits down, and we talk. It's that easy.

In the fantasy version of my life, he comes to meet me for our tradition. He walks down the street in his familiar Converse and jeans. He has his hands in his pockets and takes those long familiar strides toward me.

He sits down and looks over my coordinates.

"They've been consistent for eleven months," I say out loud to the fictional Tucker. "The optics on the Stargazer are hi-res, antiglare," I add.

"I knew you could do it, Sarah," Fantasy Tucker tells me. "Did I mention I'm falling in love with you?"

I blink away the fantasy to the empty street.

Little moths flicker in circles in and out of the streetlight. He is not coming. He is never coming. He won't buy the chips and I won't hear the debate team gossip.

A car zooms down the street and stops before the house. My head snaps up—Trish's blue Fiat. Scarlett gets out and her ballet flats walk up the grass to me. Her pink jeans crop at the ankles and she wears a tiny gold anklet. She stops and sits down next to me. I stare out across the street to the Zuckermans' front lawn.

"Trish told me what happened. I called your cell, like, nine times."

"How long?" I ask, and my cheeks warm. I will not cry anymore. "How long did you know?" The strain from not crying sends a throb through my neck. I finally meet my sister's blue eyes. Periwinkle, Gran always says.

Her voice drops when she speaks and she picks at the grass, "I didn't know. I wish I did."

I am not sure if I believe Scarlett. Trish had to know, and she tells Scarlett everything. Trish also knows everything about everyone in school, so why wouldn't she know that her own brother was going to break up with me?

"You need to brush it off," Scarlett says.

"Brush off my best friend and boyfriend breaking up with me?"

"Yeah. You've gotta get a stronger backbone or people will walk all over you."

I stand, leaving my sister on the lawn. I am a few steps from the house but stop.

"Don't say anything," I say without looking back at my sister. "Please."

THREE

OUT THE BACK WINDOW OF OUR STATION WAGON, the trees change from the maples and oaks on my street to twisting pitch pines. We're getting closer to Cape Cod. The bark is so bleached it's as though all the salt in the ocean has crept into the trunk and up to the leaves. In the way back are the suitcases as well as my state-of-the-art Stargazer 5020.

I face front again.

Scarlett would never notice the different types of trees. She is too busy staring at me. Her eyes are blue slits and her mouth purses—staring. The bun on top of her head is in a tighter coil than usual, making her neck seem extra long. Mom always says Scarlett has rose petals for lips. No one ever says this about me.

"What?" I say.

"Nothing," she says but keeps her gaze fixed. I'm sure Scarlett is counting the moments until she leaves for Juilliard's dance orientation. She's never been gone so long before. When she comes back from New York the first week in August we'll say good-bye with the famous going-away party.

Scarlett raises her legs toward the air so the tips of her toes graze the top of the car ceiling. Her toes are gnarly bunions, blisters, and oozing pus. Her toenails are bubble gum pink. I don't know, maybe it's because she points her toes, but they look like bruised works of art. I lift my knees so they rest on the back of the passenger seat. I've never painted my toes.

"Sarah, you're digging your knees into my back," Mom says. She only calls me Sarah when she needs to tell me something important, usually to do with school or the money we don't have. This means I must be annoying Mom so I drop my legs.

"Ettie also called you last night," Scarlett says and stretches her hands to her toes. "I wonder what she wanted to talk to you about?" She raises her eyebrows in a knowing way.

"Shut up," I whisper so no one can hear but Scarlett.

Scarlett stretches her legs up to the car ceiling again while wearing that stupid smug smile. I rub the hem of the Pi Nary T-shirt.

"Tell Mom. She's going to find out from Carly eventually and then she'll want to know why you didn't tell her," she whispers.

I ignore Scarlett and lean forward so my face is between Mom's and Dad's seats.

"So will the *Alvin* be there when we get to Woods Hole?" I ask.

"In transit from off the coast of Martha's Vineyard, on a ship back to Woods Hole. It'll be going through some major renovations this summer," Dad says.

I would love to be there when they take it apart. That way I can see exactly how it works. It's amazing to think of the precision and technology necessary to protect the marine biologists inside, like Dad. The water pressure outside the *Alvin* would kill on impact.

I open my mouth for my next question: What is the maximum amount of time I can avoid Aunt Nancy? But Scarlett interrupts.

"Why do you always wear stuff that's two sizes too big?"

"What are you talking about? Everything fits me with moderate and appropriate comfort."

I'm wearing a baseball hat, my Math Club T-shirt, and my usual khaki shorts. Very offensive.

The truth is that I don't know what looks good and what doesn't. One time last year I put on one of Scarlett's dresses, a black, short one. It looked pretty good even though the straps kept falling off my shoulders. She walked in and screamed at me to take it off until her voice cracked, and she had to whisper for the rest of the day. All the girls at Summerhill dress exactly the same. They have identical chemically highlighted hair, too. Maybe I should put some product in it like Scarlett does in the morning.

"My clothes are not baggy," I grumble.

"You wear whatever Mom and Dad give you and lame baseball hats from your algebra club."

"Excuse me. Our name is the Pi Naries and we are an advanced mathematical award-winning team. So what that means is we do math. Math involves *numbers*. You can add, subtract . . ."

"Whatever, Bean. Maybe that's why Tucker broke up with you."

Mom spins around in her seat.

"When did that happen?" she asks. Mom's eyes are a stormy blue—same as Scarlett's.

"Thanks a lot, traitor." I groan and cross my arms over my chest. I refuse to look at Scarlett. I know that face, the face of victory in relation to my immediate shame.

"Are you okay? When did that happen?" Mom asks. I hate the worry in the angle of her eyebrows and the grip of her slim fingers on the armrest.

"I'm fine. I would be even better if we could disinvite Tucker from Nancy's party?" I ask.

Mom's mouth parts. In her eyes is an apology. "You know I can't do that to Carly."

Mom haphazardly slaps Dad on the shoulder.

I shove Scarlett in her bony shoulder when Mom isn't looking, but she shrugs. "What? You might as well get it out in the open," she says.

Mom slaps Dad a second time; he jumps in his seat.

"What's happening?" he asks.

"Tucker and Bean broke up," Scarlett says. With a crane of her neck, she tries to meet Dad's eyes in the rearview mirror. I rub the hem of the Pi Nary T-shirt again. Didn't I ask her *not* to say anything? Whenever she is the littlest bit offended, she turns on me.

27

"What did Bean break?" Dad asks.

Mom shakes her head, "Forget it, Gerard."

"Who's broke?" Dad asks. His long hair sticks out so far on his head it comes out on both sides of the headrest. It's like he put his finger in an electrical socket.

"Tucker and Bean," Mom says. "They broke up. I have to call Carly."

"No, you don't!" I say. "You don't need to tell Carly everything."

"She's my best friend, Bean. She might already know."

I want to bang my head against the window.

Mom's cell phone pad makes little annoying tones as she hits the keys.

"While you two are discussing my break up, maybe you could casually mention the party. That way Tucker doesn't have to come if he doesn't want to," I offer. "You know, give her an out."

I wouldn't be in this situation if it wasn't for Scarlett opening her big mouth.

"I invited Carly and Bill to the Cape for Scarlett's going-away party months ago. They already got Tucker a tux."

"Oh yes," I say with a groan and sit back in my seat. "I know. I was there."

"It's not like I asked for the party," Scarlett says.

My sixteenth birthday is a week away and I'm not getting a big party. I wouldn't want one, especially without Gran; she and Nancy don't exactly get along.

"I have an idea for you, Mom," I say, turning my head to

my sister. "Why don't we let Scarlett make the call to Carly and Tucker? She's apparently an expert on my love life."

Scarlett rolls her eyes at me. "Don't flatter yourself, Bean."

I clench my jaw.

"Can we *not* talk like that to one another, please?" Mom says. The beeping on her cell phone keypad continues.

"Actually," I say, crossing my arms over my chest, "I didn't get a chance to break up with *him* first, but it was my idea."

The shame of the lie burns and I try to hide my face by turning away to the window. I know my cheeks must be red. I don't like to manipulate the truth. Science is the search for absolute truth, but this is different. I've had enough criticism over the last two days.

Scarlett nudges me with the tips of her cold feet. I don't look at her. She nudges me again.

"You are the worst liar," Scarlett whispers. "I saw your face last night."

I lean my head back and keep my eyes away from my sister. The massive Bourne Bridge looms ahead. I can't wait to get out onto the beach and track my comet. Tucker thinks he has a shot at the Waterman Scholarship too. Hell no. I'll win the scholarship and get my tuition paid in full at Summerhill for junior and most of senior year. Summerhill Academy, the place where guilt was born. Because Aunt Nancy has had to pay for it since eighth grade when I transferred from public school. I scoot down in my seat. I hate admitting it, but this shirt is from eighth grade.

"I don't know, Mom," Scarlett says, responding to something

I didn't hear. "Why do I have to know everything? I have my own life to worry about."

I press the button for the window and it slides down. The rushing of the wind drowns out the chatter about my breakup.

I slide my cell phone out from my back pocket. No calls from Tucker.

It's weird not texting him from the car or hearing the ding of his messages. The wind whips my hair around my cheeks.

I can't help wondering if Tucker misses me. Maybe if Mom does tell Carly that Tucker doesn't have to come, he'll come anyway, just to see me. I roll my eyes at myself. It's best not to wish for something that won't happen.

Why didn't I see it? I blink a few times, my vision going all fuzzy. *It's the tear ducts obstructing my view.*

Crying = death. I will not cry two days in a row.

Especially not in this small space where Scarlett can watch my tears fall. I take a deep breath and hold it in—I'm not going to cry. I know what to do. I'll recite the elements backward this time.

Zirconium. Zinc. Yttrium. I will not cry. Ytterbium. I will not cry. Xenon . . .

"Bean, Bean, Bean, look at you. All that cleavage just showed up in a year!" Aunt Nancy somehow thinks that because she is sixty-something she can say whatever she wants to me. She smothers me against her white Chanel suit.

I pull away from her overzealous embrace and cross my arms. I'm pretty sure I will stink like Dior for the rest of the day.

"I see you brought your little gadgets," she says and raises an eyebrow at the Stargazer. It sits next to the car along with four catalogued boxes of comet-tracking equipment.

"It's my Stargazer 5020."

"Just make sure you put it up in your room where it can't stain the carpet."

"It's a telescope."

Aunt Nancy hated the rock polisher I brought along last summer and the portable microscope the year before that. There may have been a *small* incident when I was transferring some algae to the slides, but it ended up being *fine*. That part of the carpet was cut out and replaced.

Looming above us is Nancy's four-story, light gray, shingled monstrosity, our home every single summer since before I was born. A plaque over the five-car garage reads: Seaside Sanctuary. Or as I like to call it: Seaside Stomachache. Scarlett calls it Seaside Shit Show, but I don't tell anyone that. Once, when Scarlett and I were little, we carved our initials into one of the shingles on the back of the garage. I should see if they're still there.

"You are a vision!" Nancy says and basically mauls Scarlett. "Your hair is like gold. Look at you!" We just saw Nancy over spring break, but she fawns over Scarlett like she's Miss America.

I roll my suitcase into the front entranceway and haul it up the main stairs to my usual bedroom on the third floor. I should think about the comet every time Tucker's "apologetic" face comes into my head. I'll track the comet, write my essay, and win that damn scholarship. I'll go to the reception lunch at Brown University, where I've heard they serve nineteen different kinds of cake.

By the time I reach my door on the third floor, I'm out of breath. I open up to the familiar bedroom. Nancy might be hell to deal with, but she keeps my room the same every year. She doesn't even let guests stay in here when someone comes to visit.

As a kid, I picked this room because of the massive skylights. I wanted to watch the stars when I lay in bed.

I throw my shoulders back and lift my chest up. "Stand tall and proud," Gran always says. I do, even though I don't feel very proud. The summer away from Tucker will help. It doesn't matter if he comes to the party or not. Without Tucker, I won't have any distractions from my scientific observations on the Comet Jolie.

I've spent eleven long months tracking its movements—132 hours at the Frosty Drew Nature Center & Observatory, 149 hours of backyard gazing, 82 hours of research in the library.

I can't give up now. I'm so close.

FOUR

WHEN I CALL ETTIE THE NEXT MORNING, SHE doesn't even say hello. It rings once and she says, "First, I cannot believe you told me about this breakup via text. And second?" She takes a deep breath and her tone softens. It's enough to make me cry. "He's a bastard."

"I know."

"You're not alone in your summer of woe. Your summer of *pain*," she cries.

"Wow. We're dramatic today, Ettie."

"I didn't even see you before you left," she says.

I sit in Nancy's oversized Adirondack chair and make a visor with my hand. The sun sparkles high on the bay in the distance.

I can just make out the path to the harbor beach below, but it's hidden by green leafy trees and purple hydrangea.

"Aunt Nancy still smell like Bergdorfs?" she asks. There's a wet click as Ettie removes her retainer. "Because band camp still smells like band camp except now they pay me to wash down the lake boats instead of being forced to ride in them. Thank God for day camp; I hate playing the cello for these brats."

I appreciate that she is trying to keep the conversation light.

Silence.

"Well, it's only eight weeks. I didn't even get to Hilltop for a chocolate frozen yogurt blitz before I left. I feel cheated," I say.

"Yeah . . . ," Ettie says, but it's guarded.

"What?" I ask.

Silence.

"Ettie?" I press.

"IsawhimtwonightsagoatHilltopCreamerywithBecky-Winthrop. I'msosorry"—gasp—"Itriedtocallyoulikeninehundred-times—"

"What was he doing tutoring her at a creamery?"

"Um . . ."

"I know he likes Hilltop," I say, "but that's kind of ridiculous. He could have at least brought me an ice cream before breaking up with me." Might as well be glib.

Silence again.

"Hello?"

"Bean, they were kissing," Ettie says.

"Becky Winthrop? Yeah right. Kissing. Sure."

"I know what I saw."

"Tucker is not dating Becky. *Please.* He was her—"

"Tutor all May," Ettie interrupts.

"Yes, but it was purely academic!"

Now that I think about it . . . Tucker did spend every Saturday morning tutoring Becky at the East Greenwich library.

There's no way Tucker is *with* Becky Winthrop. Becky freakin' Winthrop is the only sophomore on the varsity cheerleading squad. She broke up with Kyle Lennon, the hottest kid in East Greenwich, Rhode Island. *She* broke up with *him*.

"They were there at, like, seven; they weren't even having ice cream. I guess he used his fancy biodiesel project to fuel her old junkie car. They had this huge crowd," Ettie explains. "All the baseball players."

"He was showing off with the biodiesel project that we made together for AP Chem?"

I helped him break down the parts of the car engine. I went to disgusting junkyards for weeks.

"My biodiesel?" I ask again.

I'm different, Tucker had said. *I just—am. And you haven't even noticed.*

Ettie is still talking, going on and on with excuses and plans of action.

Tucker . . . *cheated* on me?

I imagine Tucker with Becky, surrounded by all the popular kids at school. They have funny inside jokes, Tucker's the ringleader with his fancy biodiesel, and I'm at home, working on the comet, waiting for him to come over. I shiver and rid myself of the image. Tucker couldn't have changed that much, *that* fast . . .

could he? I thought he looked guilty, and I was right.

You watch the world.

I'm sloped forward and it takes a lot of effort to sit up straight. *Tall and proud* isn't an option right now. I want to crumple in on myself.

"I'm sorry, Bean," Ettie says in a tone that gives away she really is. She's probably sitting on her bed, cello leaning against the wall, with her black hair pinned up above her ears. "They're losers," she adds.

They aren't the losers.

I am.

As I set up my desk, or "comet headquarters," I can't stop thinking about Becky Winthrop and Tucker. I see them in my head on a loop, kissing at Hilltop before he even broke up with me. How long was it going on? How long did I ignore the signs?

I toss the last pen so it rolls off the desk and onto the floor. I don't even pick it up before heading downstairs.

"Well, *Town and Country* wanted to take pictures, *again*," Nancy says from the living room. She's explaining that her house is still "the talk of the town" because it sits on a peninsula at the very end of Shore Road.

Apparently this means that everything in Nancy's house needs to be white. I mean, WHITE. White lighthouses perched on white mantles, ivory-colored couches and off-white wall paint. Interspersed with all the sea-shelled toilet paper holders, napkin rings, and scalloped shell doorknobs are miles and miles of white carpeting. This mansion is like a seashore cottage that's been pumped up with steroids. Since the algae incident, I'm not allowed to drink anything colorful unless standing outside on the porch.

"Beach!" Scarlett yells. I'm in the living room and she crosses in front of me toward the front door.

She's in a blue sundress and hoists a beach bag over her shoulder.

"I'll come too," I say. I could use some time on the beach. I might even tell Scarlett about Tucker and Becky Winthrop. Or maybe she already knows.

"No, Bean," she says, putting on white sunglasses.

"Why not?" I ask.

"I'm meeting Shelby and Allison at the second lifeguard chair."

"I can't be at the second lifeguard chair?"

"I need some girl time. I haven't even seen them yet."

I come to a stop and the door closes hard behind Scarlett. She knows what happened with Tucker; the least she could do is invite me to the beach. I plop down on a white lounger that faces the back patio. Mom is in the kitchen, unpacking some items into the refrigerator. I'm surprised one of Nancy's cooks isn't trying to help.

"Want to help me with these groceries?" she says.

The sunlight sprinkles over the gentle harbor and the wooden dock at the base of Nancy's beach.

"Sure." I help Mom organize some of our normal items, like Dad's favorite Babybel cheese. "It's not like we're friends at home, but she at least invites me to the mall sometimes," I mumble. "Of course, it's when she's going alone, but still . . ."

"You always tell her no," Mom says and puts away the grapes in the fridge. "You go with Ettie to the observatory or do your work. You don't even like the mall."

"We've gone for lunch loads of times," I explain. I hate feeling like I have to justify what I choose to do with my time. It wasn't a problem before.

All the Summerhill girls go to the mall. For *Becky Winthrop* it's a Friday-night ritual. I don't feel the need to hang out with gaggles of girls for fun. I mean, I guess I haven't ever done that before, so I can't empirically say for sure.

Mom's brown hair falls out in wispy brown strands from a bun at the back of her head. She stands at the counter, packing the rest of the groceries into the white wooden cabinets. With the exception of the stainless-steel appliances, everything in here is white too. I hand Mom some of the cereal boxes. Nancy demands every year that her chef make all the meals, but Mom insists that we retain some normalcy at breakfast.

"Anyway," I say, "Scarlett gets to go to the beach, and I have to help with the groceries."

"This is Scarlett's last summer. She should spend some time with her friends," Mom says.

"But I want to go to the beach too."

"So go," she says.

"I don't want to go by myself. Normally, I don't mind single-person activities, but given my present situation . . ."

"I'll go with you," Mom says, and I don't need to explain anymore. The wrinkles around her eyes deepen when she smiles.

She does want to take me to the beach.

"Okay," I say, helping to pack away a box of Sugar Crunch.

"We'll go put our feet in the water in a while. Your sister is leaving for a month. Let her get some fun in."

"Doesn't Scarlett always get her fun in?"

Mom throws her head back, laughing. When she does that, openmouthed, hand on her stomach, she is identical to Scarlett. Even the way her neck cranes back just so.

"Help me with the milk," she says and hands it to me. "Then we'll go."

Turns out Mom has to take Nancy to pick up her heart pills.

"Might as well make yourself useful," Nancy says as they are walking out the door. Mom's cheeks redden and I can't tell if it's from anger or embarrassment. When she's mad she purses her lips, and she isn't doing that now. "Maybe we can find a *Providence Journal* while we're there, help you find a new job. Lord knows you didn't bring one with you."

After the door closes, I decide that

1. I hate Nancy and

2. I should busy myself by getting started on my scholarship application and essay. August 7th will come quick.

I trudge up the stairs, past Scarlett's closed door on the second-floor landing. Heaven forbid I set foot in there. I plop down at Comet Headquarters. On a calendar above the desk my birthday is circled in blue—it's also the registration date for the Waterman Scholarship. The online form has been saved and filled out. I need to reread it at least two times and spell-check before sending in the registration.

Tucker said, "A computer checks the registration. No one cares if you spell-check it."

I'll send it out on my birthday. That way I can spell-check one extra time just to prove a point.

I get to work and scroll through and stop where I always do: the dreaded essay question.

> Please explain in 1,000 words why your experiment successfully represents who you are as a scientist and how the execution of your experiment reinforces your educational goals.

I rest my chin in my hand and tap my pen on the desk.
You watch the world.

The sunlight streams in from the skylight onto my hand and warms the skin.

I wish I had gone to the beach. I don't have anyone to call to go with me. I just haven't made a lot of friends here. Scarlett has. I've been with Dad in the labs, or the people my age that I have met over the years only stay a couple weeks at a time. Not many people come back summer after summer.

I put the pen down. Scarlett is a little like Becky. Popular, well liked, confident, and funny. Everyone is always laughing when they are around Scarlett. She knows who she is and she's got boyfriends all the time. They don't dump her for Becky Winthrop. She always knows exactly what to say to other people her age. I don't. I always trip over my words and overthink *everything*.

Until I can figure out why Becky and Scarlett get all the guys, it's going to eat away at me. There are people who can just talk to other people—they can socialize and it's not hard for them, it's no big deal.

I get up and pace.

I can study that specific behavior. There has to be a set of parameters, something concrete that both Scarlett and Becky have in common. Since I can't study Becky, who I might throttle to death if I saw in person, I can watch my sister. Scarlett does and says specific things that make people want to be around her all the time. Just like Becky.

There has to be a direct correlation between Scarlett's specific behavior and style to the number of people who revere her and want to be her friend. If I figure this out, maybe I'll get Tucker to see who I am—that I'm not "watching the world."

I put my pen down. I can wait to write the essay. If I do this before Scarlett goes to orientation in a week or so, it'll help me figure out what Becky Winthrop does that I don't.

I'm going to the beach. I open the bureau and slip on my red one-piece. It's what I wore for swim lessons and it's comfy. I'm going to get my fun in too—in a different way. I snatch my journal and slide it into my backpack. The walk to Nauset Beach is .75 miles.

"I'm not logical," I say aloud, and when I get outside, I hike a beach chair into the crook of my arm. "And I don't watch the world!"

FIVE

WITHIN TEN MINUTES, I'M ALMOST AT THE entrance to the beach. The beach chair keeps slipping out from under my arm and I adjust its position. Nauset Beach already has a line of cars ten deep from the tollbooth.

A group of boys in a Jeep Wrangler drive by and stop at the end of the line of cars waiting to pay and park. Sitting in the backseat is a blond guy who has his arms out resting on both of the empty seats beside him. His back is very defined. Maybe he's a swimmer? He turns his head to me, but he's wearing Aviator sunglasses so I can't verify if he's looking at me. It's possible he's interested in the various foliage growing on the roadside. That kind of guy would check out Scarlett, not me. I walk a bit but keep pace with the slow creep of the Jeep. He keeps glancing over and smiles.

I shoot forward, tripping over a rock. The chair flies out of my hand, my arms pinwheel, but I steady myself. The chair clatters to the ground. These dumb flip-flops. The guys made it to the tollbooth and the driver talks to the guard. The blond in the back is still laughing. He calls, "Are you okay?"

"It's just the rock sediment!" I say and reposition the chair.

"It's the what?" he calls back.

The car revs past the tollbooth and speeds into the lot.

Rock sediment? What the *hell* is wrong with me? This is why I am dumped for people like Becky—because I bring up the stinkin' rock sediment.

When I get to the lot they're nowhere to be seen. Good. I've humiliated myself enough in front of cute guys for one day.

Okay, so, if I'm observing Scarlett then I need to compile a short list of concrete observable behaviors and go from there. The world is an equation. I just have to fill in the right factors to find the answers. I can't be a ballerina, but Scarlett's social interactions are at least worth a look.

I need to be far enough away from the second lifeguard chair but close enough so no one can recognize me. There are four possible boardwalks. I walk up the first one and when I get to the end, I try to stay near groups of people. The second lifeguard chair is one hundred yards away. There are about five hundred people in my immediate view, so I should be camouflaged. I have to get closer to see Scarlett. I walk along the edge of the beach and the dunes that run all the way to the parking lot. I can hurry back to the first boardwalk if necessary.

I don't see her. She's not at the—

Holy crap.

Scarlett stands up about twenty feet from me and pulls a blue strapless dress over a zebra-print string bikini top. I drop the chair and turn my back to my sister, pretending to riffle through my beach bag.

A few couples and their beach umbrellas separate us. I hunch my shoulders up as though somehow that will hide my face.

"I love that suit even more on you than when we saw it in the catalog," a girl says. I recognize her but don't know her name. Scarlett made friends with a lot of local girls, but I have only met them out on Main Street when we've bumped into them on our way to dinner. She even hangs out with them when she visits Nancy throughout the year. Except for the summer, I've never been to visit.

"It's so cute, right?" Scarlett says and adjusts the triangle cups. "Definitely an eye catcher."

They pass by me and once they turn onto the boardwalk I hurry behind.

The sand sinks beneath me as I haul ass the way I came. I slip in my flip-flops, burning the underside of my feet on the sand. The silver bar of the chair is slicked with my underarm sweat and the thong of the flip-flop is killing the skin between my toes. This sucks.

Boardwalk. Thank the beach gods.

Once I get to the end, I walk slowly because the sound of a person running on the planks will travel. Scarlett and her friends are already past the third boardwalk entrance and near the beach headquarters, which sit just before Liam's, the best clam shack in existence.

I leave the chair by the showers and follow their path car by car.

Scarlett and her friends hold their bags, pass by Liam's, and keep walking. I scoot to a car nearby, but stay hunched over and out of sight.

"Well, well. If it isn't my true love, Scarlett Levin."

I peer around the side of the car. The driver of the Jeep gets out and walks toward Scarlett and her friends. The Jeep Wrangler idles near the entrance to the outer beach. The blond guy who laughed at me secures a cooler with a bungee cord. They seem to be packing to go somewhere.

The driver says something I can't hear. Scarlett laughs and it chimes out over the parking lot. I don't laugh like that; I snort.

"You coming to the outer beach?" he asks Scarlett.

"I wish," Scarlett says. "My aunt is having some kind of welcome-back dinner."

She lets her hands linger on his chest. The blond guy keeps working on the cooler. "Tate, you want to let the air out of the tires?" he asks the other guy riding in the Jeep. His hair is so blond, it's almost white.

Oh, they're going four wheeling. You can't go out on the beach unless your tires are at a lower pressure. It makes it easier to drive on the sand.

"Drive me home first?" Scarlett says. "You won't make me walk, will you?"

How can Scarlett just ask them for something like that? These guys were about to go out on the beach and she gets them to stop their plans, drive her home, and *then* come back. Does she have some kind of special power? Some branch of science that hasn't been discovered: a boy manipulation molecule?

"I'll see you tonight. Main Street," she adds.

The girls jump in the car and Scarlett sits in the front on the lap of the guy with the white blond hair. Her friends cozy up next to the guy who talked to me. The Jeep screeches out of the parking lot. The girls scream and fall into fits of laughter.

As they speed away, my guy, the one in the back, tips his chin to the sky as if he were more interested in the warmth on his face than the girls sitting by his side.

I can respect that.

After dinner, Scarlett walks to town to join her friends. I follow a little later, but she doesn't know that. It's better than sitting in this house, fielding calls from Ettie about band camp.

I walk past the town pier, turn onto Main Street, and there it is: the Seahorse shell and gem store, the best store in the world. Every August, when we pull out of Nancy's driveway to head home, I calculate how many hours I have to work during the school year so I can buy whatever catches my eye the following summer.

Scarlett is down in the Silver Lining, a jewelry store she loves. Mom, Dad, and Nancy are at home, and I have a good hour or two before it's optimal viewing conditions for the comet. Plenty of time to observe Scarlett in her natural habitat. The street smells the same as it always does: like the thick marinara from the pizza place, the sugary sweet cotton candy from the ice-cream store, and of course the ocean, because it's never too far away.

I take one step off the main drag and into the Seahorse. Inside, everything sparkles: rare rocks and gems, fossils as big as my Stargazer. There are bins of shells, and twisting mobiles made of rocks and starfish. I don't know where to go first. My eyes fall on a blue agate stone tied to a leather strap, under glass in a display case. It's a slice of a geode, a hollow rock that's been crystalized due to volcanic heat and water. Anyway, it's *really* sparkling there under the store lights.

"Those look so good with the shape of your face," a voice says.

Toward the back of the store are three girls, each trying on different kinds of sunglasses. One of them has long black hair that falls to her mid-back. She poses for her other girlfriends and they take pictures next to the turnstiles of sunglasses.

"Let's find the boys," says one of the girls, who has a short pixie-cut hairstyle. They put the sunglasses back and, hand-in-hand, the girls form a chain and file out toward the store exit. The one with the long black hair stops next to me and points at the geode necklace.

"Oh my gosh, are you getting that? It's so pretty."

"Definitely," I say, trying to channel my inner Scarlett. "When I get the cash."

"Right?" she says. The other girls peek at the glass case. "I want everything in here."

They remain in their chain and continue out onto the street. I turn, watching them go. I have never done that, made a chain of hands with my girlfriends. I never wanted to, but it looks fun.

I am about to take one step to see where they are going, maybe even see if I can hang out with them, when Scarlett's voice echoes from outside. Right. I almost forgot the reason for being on Main Street in the first place. Through the open French doors of the shop, I see Scarlett toss her hair over her shoulder. I hide behind a wooden turnstile holding dried sand dollars and conch shells. I peek around.

As Scarlett walks, her blonde hair swishes behind her in wavy lines. She goes into Pleasantries, a clothing store I know she can't afford. I step out of the Seahorse and follow slowly, close enough to hear but not so close that she'll see me. I stop next to a busy restaurant and pretend to look for someone coming down the road. From where I am standing, I can see Scarlett walking inside the store. A familiar Jeep Wrangler idles at the nearest intersection and I recognize the driver. He runs into the store after Scarlett and playfully carries her outside.

The girls follow behind and Scarlett laughs, holding on to the guy's sculpted arms as he grasps her waist. I would give anything to be there too. I know from their dark tans in June that these boys are either locals or lifeguards. I don't see the blond guy from the beach earlier today, and surprisingly I'm disappointed about that.

I stand across the street, hidden by the crowds of people window-shopping and planning their dinners.

"Hello to you too, Curtis," she says. He puts her down and kisses Scarlett right on the mouth. He even dips her. He's tall, with shaggy hair that would have been dark had it not been lightened by the sun. The way the boys look at Scarlett and her friends you'd think they were hungry or something.

She pushes him back with a laugh. "Get off!" she says. "Don't even. I am not slumming it this summer, Curtis." Scarlett saunters away from the boys, but Curtis, the brown-haired guy, grabs her hand and pulls her back.

"I'm only joking, Miss Scarlett. Come to Lighthouse Beach; we're starting a bonfire."

Scarlett runs a hand through her hair so it fans out on her shoulders and back. She does that all the time and especially loves to do that when her hair has been up in a bun. It gets *tons* of looks from guys. I've seen it. Okay, so I guess I need to excessively play around with my hair.

Scarlett looks to her friends, who I can see even in the reflection of the window, are dying to go with Curtis and his friends. Hell, I am dying to go and I'm across the street. Her friends look at Scarlett, eyes wide, waiting for her to make the executive decision.

"Okay. Fine. But do not bring that crappy light beer again. I'm strictly drinking vodka this summer." Scarlett side glances one of her friends. "I need to watch my calories," she adds with a shrug. Okay, good. This is a clear, observable behavior I've seen Scarlett do. If I act like I don't care, or show disinterest when I am actually interested, people will think I am even more interesting.

This is complicated.

Curtis agrees to grab some vodka and runs into the liquor store a few buildings down from where we stand.

This gives me time to find a different vantage point before she crosses the road to where Curtis's Jeep is waiting.

The side street that runs down to Main is very steep. I turn the corner and run up so I am looking down on Main Street, just where Scarlett is standing. A couple of ladies head into the diner, the Bird's Nest, which is next to Pleasantries.

I lean against the building and keep checking for Scarlett and her group of friends to cross the intersection to the Jeep.

I slip out a flip notebook from my pocket. I scribble down some Scarlett observations underneath those from the beach earlier today:

1. *Scarlett's confidence seems to be the biggest influence. Zebra bikini. Asks for boys to tote her around because she knows they will say yes.*
2. *Toss hair around.*
3. *If you act like you're not interested in people they will actually be more interested in you.*

Scarlett can just throw her shoulders back and not care what people think. I'm only confident when recounting things like the complex theories of black holes.

A red truck pulls up the side street from Main and stops just beyond me at the top of the hill. A sticker on the back of the rusted bumper says, "If the Doors of Perception Were Cleansed, Everything Would Appear to Man as It Is—Infinite."—William Blake.

Who the hell is William Blake?

"I thought you were paying!" Scarlett's voice carries up the hill.

Curtis must have come back with the vodka. They are going to pass before me any second. I tuck deeper behind the Bird's Nest Dumpster and peek around to look down the street. I guess this vantage point isn't so great after all. A door closes from the pickup behind me and a familiar frame gets out of the car. I think—I think it's the blond guy from the beach? The one who laughed and smiled at me. He carries a shirt or a team jersey in his hand.

The guy ties the arms of the shirt around the tree so it seems to be hugging the bark. It's not that dark out with the street lamps, but I have to squint. He presses his palm onto the tree trunk and after a moment bows his head and brings his other hand to cover his eyes. His back shudders.

It clicks—he's crying. I immediately put away my notebook. It's *wrong* to be watching this. This is a very private moment and I should not be here. I step out from behind the Dumpster to hurry down Main Street, away from this guy, and leave him to his privacy. The damn flip-flops crunch on something and echo loudly in the little alley. I try to make a run for it, but my foot shoots out from under me and I grasp onto the side of the Dumpster so I don't fall. I cry out, the back of my heel scrapes on the asphalt.

The guy at the tree looks in my direction. Great.

I brush off my heel and pretend I was just oh so casually coming from the back alley of the string of shops and restaurants.

"You okay?" he asks and walks down the hill toward me. Before he gets close enough he wipes his eyes on his shirt.

"Fine." I groan. *I'm a stalker, but I'm fine.* "I think I contracted E. coli from the dirty ground," I add.

Maybe I could explain my reason for being here? Maybe he would get it?

When he gets close to me, he steps into the light. His eyes aren't too red, but they aren't dry either. He wears a thin T-shirt that is ripped a little on the chest. His tan skin peeks through.

He looks down and grins sheepishly. "Oh. I just got out of work."

Oops. Caught.

"That's twice you've fallen today," he says.

"I'm really much more stable than this," I say. I need to get out of this alley. I head down to Main Street. He keeps pace with me down the hill. I try not to meet his eyes. He's cute. His hair is a little long and he is much taller than me too, 6'3"? Maybe 6'4"?

"I didn't fall," I stress. "I had a gravitational issue."

He laughs. My cheeks have to be redder than Gracie's tomatoes, as Gran would say.

His shoulders are defined too. He probably plays football at his high school. He also doesn't seem the type to say "gravitational" on the regular.

"Hey—" he says, stopping next to the Bird's Nest Diner. "Thanks. I needed that."

Needed what? I want to ask, but I don't know how. It seems oddly personal and I know it's connected to the jersey tied around a tree trunk. Maybe I should act disinterested and pull a Scarlett. I am about to do Scarlett's hair-flipping routine when about five hundred yards down the block Scarlett and a gaggle of people parade in my direction. I spin the other way and hurry to the lawn of the library nearby.

"Hey—wait!" the blond guy calls after me.

"I gotta go!" I cry.

"Andrew!" Curtis calls. "Andrew! You're late!"

I run to the library. I don't even look back. I can't. I'm in the shadow of the side of the building when I stop and peek around the corner. Andrew has joined the group. He looks back once more in my direction, and under the streetlights, he is tanned, tall, and his structured features are proportionate. He's hot.

"What are you looking for?" Scarlett asks Andrew.

"I was talking to this girl. But she's gone," he says. "She ran off."

"Okay—weirdo," Scarlett says with her same derisive laugh. They move as a group down the street and I don't want to follow. Not anymore. I'm a weirdo who runs off when handsome guys talk to me because I have no idea how to interact with people. Tonight's attempt at observation and conversation was a complete bust. I head for home to check the comet's coordinates on Nancy's beach. Where it's safe. Where I know who to be.

Where I can be alone.

SIX

"LETTERS OF RECOMMENDATION?" DAD SAYS TO me a couple days later. He loves to do this when he hasn't checked in on my application in a while. The marine biologist in him can't help it.

"Completed two months ago."

"Transcript?"

I lift the blue folder I have designated for the Waterman Scholarship.

"Application?"

"Just need to fill out the general info."

"Registration forms?"

"Completed but not sent. They're due on my birthday, Friday."

"Essay?"

"Ugh," I reply. "You know I'm not a creative writer."

Dad gently holds his hands over mine so I can't fidget.

"You'll do it," he says. Dad's hands are warm and big. I think about Scarlett's laugh on the beach and the girls running in a linked chain of hands out the door of the Seahorse. I can't fake enthusiasm. I'm fine with that usually—but maybe there's something wrong with me? A legitimate reason Tucker prefers Becky, and I haven't bothered to make tons of friends here every year.

"Do you—do you think I'm merely logical and devoid of emotion? You know, a weirdo?" I ask.

Dad frowns at the table. As I verified with Tucker, avoidance of eye contact means guilt or omission of truth.

"No, Beanie," he says, making sure to look me in the eye, which is assuring. "Who said you were devoid of emotion?"

"No one. Just curious."

"Was it that idiot? Tucker?"

I meet Dad's eyes and he has his "serious face" on, which I don't see very often. I sit up straight in my chair.

"Maybe I am," I say, not wanting to admit that yes, Tucker is absolutely the reason for this conversation. "Scientists need to be objective about their work and honest with themselves about the validity and success of their hypotheses. But maybe I need to be devoid of emotion to be good at what I do. Maybe to excel you need to be callused so your emotions don't get confused with the results."

Dad squeezes my hand. He doesn't touch me that often or hug me too much so I don't move away.

"I wish your gran was here." He takes a deep breath. "Listen to me; you are loving and smart. And being smart tends to mean you stand on the outside, observing."

"Like watching the world?"

"Maybe."

I groan. This is not what I want to hear.

"You're just different than most kids your age. You have more important things on your mind than boys and clothes."

"Yeah . . . ," I say, but the last part is untrue. I do care about boys and clothes. Just not to the same extent as my sister.

"Gerard!" Nancy calls.

"I don't want science to be all of who I am," I say quietly. "I want to be more like Scarlett sometimes," I add, but I don't think Dad hears because Nancy squawks again:

"Gerard!"

I want to be able to care about clothes and boys, but be good at science, too. I want to be both.

"You'll find your essay," Dad says, and his hand lifts from mine. He winks at me before getting up to cater to Nancy.

I grab my application checklist. Loneliness blows. Scarlett wasn't alone last night. *You need a backbone or everyone is going to walk all over you.* Easy for her to say.

I head upstairs but stop at the second floor when Scarlett laughs from her bedroom. I stop outside the door and listen, making sure to hold on to the collection of application papers tightly so they don't rustle and give me away. The door is cracked just a little. She is doing her morning stretches, which means she is going to practice soon. She is doing a wall stretch.

Her leg is lifted and flushed against the wall. She brings her head to her knees and leans into it. How she can do this and balance a cell phone at the same time is some kind of a rare talent.

"Curtis kissed me last night," she says. "God! He is ridiculously hot."

She laughs and changes legs so the left leg is now pressed against the wall.

"He has a scar on his collarbone." She hesitates. "And I licked it."

I can hear Trish's cackle through the phone. Trish Jackson. Tucker's sister. I don't want to listen anymore. I head up to my room. I can stand outside Scarlett's door watching and follow her around Main Street, but it's not going to solve the problem. I'm a scientist. Tucker is right. Scarlett is right too. I watch the world so I can understand it.

Yes, it's true that I don't know how to just casually be in conversation with a guy without blowing it. It's not like I can just wake up confident like Scarlett.

Wait . . . I hesitate on a stair.

Why can't I use what I know about science and Scarlett to change my life?

Observation is reductive. I've had fifteen years to research my sister. If I pretend I am like Scarlett, dress like her, talk like her, and behave like her, I will live the life I've always wanted. I'll have friends and a boyfriend who is nothing like Tucker. It's a set of very specific parameters to follow. It's genius!

I won't ever be humiliated again.

I hesitate again in the middle of the stairwell.

First step before you conduct an experiment? Formulate a question.

Okay. Will I ever have fun, be comfortable, and look mildly normal, maybe even hot like Scarlett? Scarlett *never* has problems with guys or with what she wears.

I move up the stairs toward my room but stop again.

Step two? Do field research. Observe.

Okay fine. I've been doing that for as long as I can remember.

Once I get to my room, I stand above my suitcase with my hands on my hips.

Step three: formulate a hypothesis. If I wear Scarlett's clothes and behave like Scarlett I will:

1. Attract attention that does not involve complete and total humiliation.

2. Attract a hot guy who is different than Tucker in every way and who would never cheat on me.

3. Make new friends who are exciting and think I'm special. If the experiment is a resounding success, I'll be put-together, popular, and finally live the life I want.

Inside my suitcase are neat, folded shirts, pressed shorts, and accurately angled socks. I dig to the bottom and pull out the red one-piece from the beach the other day. I hold it up to the light. There are a few holes in the stomach. I groan. The translucent material could split right in two from eons in the ocean and pool. I wouldn't even know what to buy if I went to the shops in town.

This suit is the reason. This papery, ruffled suit is why Tucker broke up with me. A big freakin' metaphor for my whole life.

It is time for another experiment but this time, one that I can use for myself. This is a *life* experiment.

The Scarlett Experiment.

I want to start the Scarlett Experiment now. But I need to wait until Scarlett's downstairs practicing. That takes at *least* four hours and gives me plenty of time to look through her things and prepare my experimental setup.

It takes her highness an hour to organize and get downstairs. Once classical music echoes up the stairwell, I know she's practicing.

I make my way to the second floor and stand outside Scarlett's bedroom. Nailed to the front of the door is a sign with Scarlett's name scrawled in cursive over an image of a pair of ballet slippers. The sign has yellowed, but Scarlett leaves it on the door out of respect for Nancy. I place my palm on the brass knob and hold it tight so it won't squeak. I learned that trick from Scarlett when she came home late one time. Nancy is taking a nap on the first floor on the opposite side of the house. Regardless, she has a tendency to scream my name at the top of her lungs for the smallest, most ridiculous reasons. Mom is job searching in the kitchen and Dad is at WHOI.

I hesitate at the door while it's half open and half closed. Scarlett's room is the one room that I am forbidden to go into unless she accompanies me. There are Scarlett's things and Bean's things, *my* things, items that for some reason, my sister never seems to want to borrow. Scarlett's sweaters, perfumes, and makeup are so much more interesting than mine. I don't need science to figure this out—it's fact: Scarlett's stuff is better.

I dip a toe into her bedroom. I slide through and step into the room.

Tiny string bikinis, short shorts, T-shirts, and patterned dresses drape over the sides of the open suitcase. In a pile by the window are four or five pairs of pointe shoes along with some thread and a needle. Scarlett sews her ribbons into her shoes when she's breaking them in. She wants the pointe shoe to mold to her feet *perfectly*. When the shoes are stiff, hard, and wrapped together, she hasn't broken those in yet.

I squat down—careful not to touch the shoes or she'll know I was in here—and start digging through. I push some socks out of the way, some tops, leotards, and tight pants. More lycra.

A white star stares at me from the bottom of the suitcase. I pull out one long string attached to two triangular tops. It's an American flag print string bikini. I hold it up to the light filtering through the window onto Scarlett's floor.

Bean . . . this is the right choice. Doooo it, the tiny bikini whispers to me.

It's very demanding.

My fingers graze the strings. The bikini cups have soft padding.

This bathing suit is what I should wear first.

There's a full-length mirror on the back of the door. I hold the suit over my body. It might fit . . . I've got wider hips than Scarlett and she's, like, two inches shorter than me, but maybe it will fit. I take off my T-shirt, letting it fall on the floor next to my feet, and cup the triangles over my breasts. I don't think the sides of my boobs are supposed to be coming out on both sides, but it covers my nipples and that's all that matters anyway with these kinds of suits. I take off my shorts and underwear and slip the bikini bottom over me.

I have never worn anything like this in my life.

My smile in the reflection fades. In my mind, Tucker stands in the light of the street lamp. Becky Winthrop's name flashes on the screen of his cell phone. "I need to do this experiment." I say Tucker's words to the mirror. "Or else *I'll* stay the same."

I put my hands on my hips. I guess Aunt Nancy is right; everything did kind of show up in a year. I raise my neck in the air and my brown hair trickles down my back. It isn't me in the mirror, that girl with the wide hips and trim waist. My hair isn't blonde or bone straight like Scarlett's. My skin is powdery white from the year in the bio lab, but that can be fixed with some quality beach time. Who is this person in the reflection? I cock my head to the side. I look . . . well, I look *good*.

Scarlett's bathing suit has made me beautiful. Just as I projected!

I turn to the side to check myself out and have to pull the tiny triangle tops over my breasts so they're more covered. Eh, I shrug, it's supposed to look like that.

All experiments have various factors. My first variable is this American flag string bikini.

The experiment is a go. The next step is to execute it. I take off the bikini and place it back in Scarlett's suitcase. I bend over to pick up my clothes.

"Bean!"

I clutch my hands over my boobs. Nancy's shriek—can't miss it anywhere.

In the reflection, my knobby knees cross over each other, my arms bend at strange angles.

"Come help your mother and me! We need to start getting this party menu together and we need help with the computer!"

I fumble into my T-shirt and slide back through the door. Before I jump down the stairs two at a time, I sneak one glance back in Scarlett's room. I leave the suitcase as I found it.

Open . . . and waiting.

SEVEN

THE NEXT DAY IT'S BUSINESS AS USUAL FOR everyone but me.

Scarlett Experiment: Day 1.

Scarlett is practicing downstairs by 10 a.m. and the moment I finish my comet calculations, I put on the American flag bikini. I hide it under my T-shirt and shorts. Scarlett announced at breakfast that she was going to practice all day. Good. Plenty of time to get her bathing suit back in the suitcase before she even notices it's gone.

In .75 miles, I am heading past the Nauset Beach guard booth and into the parking lot. Nauset Beach is the kind of place in the summer that smells like onion rings, seaweed, and suntan lotion.

In other words, it is the best place on earth. The parking lot is at capacity again, which is good because I can blend in more effectively. There are six lifeguard stations. I'll go to the fourth one. I nod to myself. Great. I'm nodding to myself in public.

The planks of the boardwalk are hot again. I bring a smaller beach chair than last time and pull it higher under the crook of my arm. Two people with heavy footsteps run up the boardwalk behind me.

"Go! Go! Go!" a male voice yells. A tall guy zips by me and then another.

I whip around just in time to jump out of the way.

One of the guys, in red swim trunks, almost elbows me into the restricted beach grass.

"Sorry!" he calls without a glance backward.

"I could have damaged the dune grass!" I yell. "It's a very fragile ecosystem!"

He turns.

No way. It's the guy from the street the other night. Andrew—I think that was his name. He would be *perfect* for the Scarlett Experiment.

Recognition passes over his face and he jogs back.

When he gets close, he smiles at me.

"You coming down?" he asks and raises an eyebrow. "Or are you going to run away faster than the speed of light again."

"I think, I mean, maybe." I sigh. "Yes," I say, finally getting out something normal to say. Something more like Scarlett. "I am coming down, yes."

"You sure about that?" he says through a laugh and follows

after his friend. He disappears off of the pathway, down the dune, and onto the beach. *Be Scarlett*, I tell myself. *Scarlett wouldn't trip over her words.*

I stand at the top of the boardwalk; Andrew and his friend run toward the ocean. They dump their things in a heap by the shore and dive headfirst into a huge wave. When I can get a good look, I recognize Curtis, the guy that Scarlett likes.

The sand is hot, burning hot. I don't take my flip-flops off until I sit down in my beach chair. I admit, I drop my things near their cooler and towels by the water. One good wave will wet their towels. Bean, without Scarlett's bikini, would stand at the shore and tell these guys that their belongings were dangerously close to being washed away. It's high tide after all. But Scarlett wouldn't do that. Neither will I. Not Sarah.

Not while I am conducting the Scarlett Experiment.

What ensures a properly conducted experiment? Make sure that you change only one factor at a time.

I peel off my shirt first and place it down on the ground next to my open beach chair. I place my hands on my hips. Next, I look left and right. There are people, but no one seems to notice my string bikini top.

Hmm. Tricky.

Observable fact: wearing Scarlett's flashy clothes doesn't mean I'll have someone instantly looking at me and paying attention to what I do. Every great scientist knows that one shouldn't expect instant gratification when conducting an experiment.

When I slip off my shorts, one of the dads nearby peers at me over his book. *Gross. Too old.* Success? Not quite. He gets back to his book. I'm not sure this is the kind of attention the Scarlett Experiment is supposed to generate. I've never seen dads talk to Scarlett. The experiment hypothesizes that I find a guy that *Scarlett* would pick out. That guy looks like my gym teacher at Summerhill.

I plop down in my beach chair.

I have to remain objective. I will analyze the data after leaving the beach and try to interpret what exactly happened while I wore Scarlett's bikini. That way I can formulate the perfect combo of clothes and behavior.

About fifteen minutes later, I am properly SPF'ed and my eyes are closed.

"I've never been so patriotic in my life," Andrew says and sits down on the sand next to me. "Nice suit."

Success. Scarlett's bathing suit is an attracting factor.

He shakes the ocean from his hair and I take that second to check out my legs and stomach. Looks good, no stray hairs. *Okay . . . act natural.*

At the shore, a lot of people walk up and down the edge of the water. Curtis chats with a couple of lifeguards.

"You have seaweed in your hair," I say and sit up. Andrew is sopping wet and toweling off his legs with his T-shirt.

"Get it out for me?" he asks and leans forward. His hair is blonder than I thought. I pick out the long seaweed string and lay it next to my feet. A few icy drops from his head fall onto my thigh and roll down my shin. His eyes are more blue than green, and I think that one of his parents must be blue-eyed because genetically—

"So what were you saying about the dune grass?" he asks. Water drips down his biceps. He must notice my gaze because he looks at his arm and brushes the fleck away with his fingers.

"The ecosystem is endangered. And you almost shoved me into it," I say, meeting his eyes again. I want to cringe because Scarlett would never mention anything about the ecosystem. Andrew loops his hands around his legs and lets the salt water drop on the sand. Even the hair on his legs is blond. "It's important to preserve the natural beauty of the dunes," I add with a flip of my hair.

"Is that so?" he asks with a smile. "What were you doing on the street the other night?" he asks. "Hiding in the dark?"

"What?" I laugh it off. "I wasn't hiding."

"You almost took a digger into the street."

"I just wanted a second by myself."

"So you hid in an alley?"

"I was avoiding someone I didn't want to see," I say, and the truth of the words comes out a bit more serious than I'd like, though I don't think Andrew notices.

"I know what you mean. I wish I could avoid people in town," he says. "I haven't felt much like doing my usual thing this summer. You kind of caught me in a weird moment."

Maybe I should ask him why he was—

"You made me laugh though. I needed that," he adds.

"Oh yes. I'm hilarious," I say sarcastically and try to remember to be cool. *Be Scarlett.* I don't want to pry into his personal life because Scarlett wouldn't. She would keep the conversation flirty. "I hear you," I say with a dramatic, Scarlett-like sigh. "I want to just take it easy this summer. I'm so tired of parties, you know?" I lean back in the chair and cross one leg over the other. "I went to *so* many this—whoa!"

The weight of the chair flings me back and I yelp as my legs fly in the air. Andrew grabs onto my ankle and pulls me forward just before I completely teeter backward. The chair hits the sand and my teeth clamp together.

"Wow, that was close," he says, and his face is red. He's trying hard not to laugh in my face. He dips his head and laughs between his knees. I place my sunglasses back on straight.

"I do that all the time," I say with a scoff.

I want to die. I put my face in my hands. That was *not* Scarlett-like. "*Why* can't I ever be graceful?" I say with a chuckle.

Andrew shakes his head at me, but this time we share a laugh. At least, I *think* he's laughing with me. He squints at me and a little smile lingers on his lips. "Andrew," he says and extends a hand. "Andrew Davis."

I meet his warm palm with mine. "Sarah Levin," I say and immediately tense up.

Oops. He was with Scarlett last night, he has to know her last name. He doesn't appear to have made the connection between Scarlett and me.

"Sarah," he says. "I like that."

I am in no way going to explain that people call me Bean.

He's still holding on to my hand as I *slowly* cross one ankle over the other and curse myself for not painting my toenails bubble gum pink. I bet Scarlett has nail polish I can borrow.

"So how did you become a dune grass expert?" he asks.

His hand is still in mine.

"I'm a scientist," I say. Scientist has a very regal sound. Maybe it can redeem me from the falling incident.

He cocks his head a little. "Really?" he says. "That's cool."

"Do you always shake people's hands for this long?" I ask with a glance at our intertwined fingers.

"Just beautiful, smart scientists."

I lift my chin and try to mimic the many ways Scarlett has done this same behavior. I wonder if this is when I should act like I am disinterested so he'll be *more* interested. Our eyes flicker back and forth from our touching skin to each other. I don't even know how to act like I'm uninterested. "Actually, I'm an astronomer. I'm tracking a comet this summer," I say instead. Being an astronomer is also impressive.

"The only things I track are lobster traps."

We laugh again and he lets my hand go.

The side of his mouth lifts. The rest of his mouth follows, as if something is dawning on him.

"What?" I ask.

"I've never met an astronomer before."

"I love the stars," I say. "They're my whole life."

"That's how I feel about working at the juvie camp," Andrew says. "Right now, I lobster full time. But I work part time with troubled kids out in Brewster. You know, in the part of Brewster you don't see. You go to school for astronomy?"

"Not yet."

I want to ask about the juvie camp, but he keeps throwing questions at me.

"You starting in the fall?" Andrew asks.

A dash of happiness runs through my belly. This boy, with his sun-streaked hair and proud, bronzed nose is so gorgeous and is talking to *me*. I wonder if he has ever broken his nose and why the bump seems to fit him like that. I wonder why I have never spoken to a boy who looks like this in my entire life. The Scarlett Experiment is working! I am a Scarlett-pheromone-wielding phenom who can summon anyone while wearing an American flag string bikini.

"What about you?" I ask, trying to turn the question of school back on him. I figure the more vague I am, the more time I can buy to figure out what I should say.

"I'll be a sophomore at Boston College," he says. "I'm nineteen, but I'll be twenty in August."

I almost blurt out that I'll be sixteen in a few days. He's nineteen? That's not *that* old. Granted, he'll be twenty soon but that's not for a few months.

"What do you study?" I ask, stalling.

"Well, it should be criminal justice."

"Should be?"

He hesitates.

"I just want to make sure that's really what I want to do."

I can smell the ocean salt in the air and I love the way he licks the drops of water off his top lip. He keeps talking, using expressions like "the T," dorms, and Commonwealth Avenue, but I keep thinking: Driver's Ed, PSATs, and the Waterman Scholarship.

"Where do you go to school?" he asks.

Here it is. I can't be evasive forever. I don't want to tell Andrew the truth, that I'm just a high school student whose only friends are the Pi Naries and whose boyfriend just dumped her for the class boobs. I take a deep breath. That is not what the Scarlett Experiment is about. I don't want him to get up and leave. Not after the way he looked at me when I mentioned the comet. Not after he said I was just what he needed last night. No one has needed me to make them laugh. Not until now. He might be just what I need too.

I have to answer. Where do I go to school? How silly. Of course I know where I go to school. The number one school I will apply to in two years.

"I start MIT in the fall. I'm eighteen."

"So you gonna call me? Because I think you should," Andrew says.

We walk up the boardwalk toward the parking lot. Curtis waits at the end of the walkway yelling into his cell phone. All I hear is, "Dude. No way. Beachcomber?"

"I'm here through August," I say, holding the sweaty lounge chair under my arm. Without asking, Andrew takes it from me and holds it with the tips of his fingers.

"Me too; school starts the day before my birthday, sucks huh? Hey, we'll be in the same city," he adds. "My friends and I can show you around."

Oh crap. MIT and Boston College are *both* in . . . Boston. They *both* start in August.

"So it's crustaceans and convicts until school," I say.

Crustaceans and convicts? *Wonderful.* Who even talks like that?

"Yeah, you could say that," he says, but he's smiling so I am taking this as a positive sign.

We stand in the parking lot, and stretching behind Andrew is the street that leads back toward Aunt Nancy's. Cars pull out of the lot in a long line; it's almost four thirty. I can't help peeking around for Scarlett, even though the string bikini is now hidden under my clothes. Not only that, I would have to explain why I am talking to Curtis and his friend, Andrew.

"Dude . . . ," Curtis says now, talking to Andrew. He motions with his arm toward the cars in the parking lot.

"Which one is your car? I'll help you with your stuff," Andrew offers.

He thinks I drove here.

Oh boy. Didn't think about that.

"I walked again but *without* falling this time," I say and gesture to the street running past the guard booth. "I live less than a mile away."

"Let's *go*. Waves in Truro," Curtis says. He still has the cell phone next to his ear. He barely acknowledges I'm there other than a small, "What's up?"

Andrew and Curtis head toward a beat-up red pickup, the same one from the side street next to the Bird's Nest. When he is next to the car, he reaches to the driver's-side tire and pulls out his keys. I point and say, "Your chances of vandalization and/ or theft are much higher with that method of concealing your keys." I immediately want to slap myself with the beach chair.

I am just blowing this opportunity with Andrew left and right.

Andrew bends over and laughs again. He asks for and takes my cell.

"I've never thought about possible vandalization or theft," he says, but he's beaming. "But I will now."

He punches the keys on my phone. When he hands it back, the screen says ANDREW and below it: ten numbers with a 508 area code.

"You should call me, Star Girl," he says with a wink. And just like that, he gets in the car, revs the engine, and pulls past me with a wave out the window. Just like that—he's gone.

EIGHT

RESULTS DAY 1: THE SCARLETT EXPERIMENT

Subject was inconsistent with the variable of behavior. Though there were a couple of positive results, they were, at best, unreliable. Nothing is conclusive yet. Subject was a silly, impulsive twit who fell over in her beach chair. In order for the Scarlett Experiment to execute accurately and for the hypothesis to be proven, subject must employ behavioral tactics of Scarlett Levin.

It's safer up here at my desk where I can shut the door and I don't have to listen to Nancy go on and on about how unlike Scarlett I am. If only she knew that I was better at being like Scarlett than she realized.

Okay, so my first attempt at the Scarlett Experiment wasn't a complete success, but I did employ some variables that yielded partial success!

1. *Andrew liked the bikini.*

2. *He thought I was funny (potentially laughing at me when I flew backward in my beach chair)*

I put my pen down and reread my notes. I just pretended that I was Scarlett and wore her clothes, and it worked. I had a few embarrassing moments when I let my guard down, but repetition is the key to success. Okay, so I lied about my age too, but I don't need to see Andrew again. It's not like we are going to date or anything. It's just one dumb lie. He doesn't even have my phone number.

I will need to find something else of Scarlett's to wear to test out. I'll also need an exact list of Scarlett's behavior to choose from at any given moment. That would prevent anymore Bean moments from sneaking through when I meet someone else.

That evening, after I finish recording my experiment results, I make sure the American flag bikini is washed and deep in Scarlett's bag again. My skin is warm from the day in the sun, and even though I won't talk to him again, I can't help but peek at my phone for that name: ANDREW in big letters.

Dark bulbous rain clouds pass over my skylights. No point in taking out the Stargazer. I can't work on data collection in inclement weather. Even though I could work on the essay. I don't want to work on the application or the comet right now.

I think you should call me, Star Girl.

Dad says Scarlett has been downstairs practicing a solo all afternoon for a Juilliard showcase. I'm not surprised she would miss out on an opportunity to go to the beach on a day like today; Scarlett is as dedicated to dance as I am to my comet. I come down to the kitchen and check to see if anyone's hanging around. I know how much Scarlett loves Nancy's studio. She visits during school breaks just to dance. Nancy buys her whatever she wants so Scarlett can master her routines without "any of us around," or so she says.

I stop at a collection of photographs that sit on a side table near the entrance to the basement. A few of these tables run against the wall next to the glass patio doors. The picture is of two women in bathing suits on the beach, their arms wrapped around each other. It's the 1960s; I can tell from the bathing suits and bouffant hairstyles. I recognize Gran immediately. She's on the left and her long blonde hair runs all the way down her back, like Scarlett's. The woman on her right has straight brown hair that falls halfway down her back, too.

That woman must be Nancy.

Even though we've been coming here forever, I've never seen this photo before. Wow. I really look like Nancy when she was my age. That's slightly horrifying.

I check behind me just as classical music echoes from the open door to the basement. I slide the photo out of the frame and rest it in my hand. Nancy seems almost normal. Gran can't be more than sixteen. I know Nancy is three years older than Gran.

I try to imagine that this image is of Scarlett and me in place of Gran and Nancy. I have no idea who would be who. Their whole lives were ahead of them. How could they know what their lives would be? Who knew Gran would move to California and meet Gracie? Who knew Nancy's husband, Raymond, would die after twenty years of marriage? If they knew then what they know now, I wonder what would be different. I slide the photo into my back pocket and hide the empty frame behind some other pictures.

I squeeze through the crack in the door to the dark basement stairwell. The carpeted stairs cushion the sound of my footsteps. I sit and scoot down a couple of stairs like I did when I was a kid. First stair, second stair, third stair . . . from here I can sit in the shadows.

Through the air, Scarlett lifts her arms and leaps across the floor, one two three, one two three. She does this leap three times in a row, her signature move. *Grand jeté* with the cleanest lines in Rhode Island. That's what everyone says when they come to her recitals. "You have to see Scarlett's jumps."

She stops just as the music finishes and her hands glide back to her sides. With her hair up in a tight bun, her posture is so elegant, like a doll. She brings her heels together in first position and uses a remote control to restart the music. Tchaikovsky begins again.

"Five, six, seven, eight," Scarlett counts aloud and she lifts a leg toward the sky so it's almost parallel to her body. She places it down and flies into another leap. She lands onto the floor without making a sound. I can't move like that, like my body is a ribbon curling and flying through the air. Up and down, Scarlett breezes over the wooden floor. Her body is thin under that pink leotard. "She's so ladylike," Nancy says of Scarlett. I just don't know how to be graceful like that. After today's debacle on the beach, it's painfully obvious that grace is not my strong suit. I need to try even harder than most people to keep both feet planted on the ground.

Scarlett lifts her hand above her head and I try to mimic it in the dark of the stairwell. I curve my wrists like I, too, am pirouetting on my tiptoes. It's not the same. I lower my hands and examine the calluses on the side of my middle finger from writing lab reports. Scarlett's long blonde hair and bubble gum pink toenails seem so vibrant compared to my thick wavy hair and jagged toenails.

Scarlett spins and rises on the tips of her toes. She lifts her chin and appraises herself in the mirror. She comes back down on the flats of her feet and takes a sip of water.

That's what makes her irresistible to guys. That she can lift her chin, throw her head back, and drink with the boys. She can be the best dancer in the whole state and the best person to be around too.

Except when she's with me.

I would never have a picture like the one of Gran and Nancy because Scarlett would never take a picture like that with me.

She presses the music to start again. The routine is better now that she's warmed up. Her jumps longer, her turns cleaner.

I exhale heavily through my nose and sit in the darkness of

the stairs. I never wanted to be a dancer, and I still don't. I just want someone to sit here like I am right now. I want someone, for one moment, to see something special in me that has nothing to do with science. I press on the balls of my feet and inch back up the stairs, one by one until I am out the door again.

By dinner, the rain is lightening up to a patter on the patio outside Nancy's panoramic windows. I spear a piece of garlic broccoli.

"Must we go to the same restaurant every year?" Nancy says.

"I made the reservation at Lobster Pot this afternoon," Mom says, referring to my birthday celebrations. Friday is my actual birthday but we have to make accommodations for the princess; Scarlett has dinner plans on my actual birthday that she "absolutely can't miss." Nancy always comes to my birthday celebrations except that she never bothers with our annual mini-golf tournament. It's "too tiring" after a big meal, or so she says.

Maybe she'll give me some non-guilt-ridden cash instead of a "teen journal" with a pink pen attached by a glittered chain like she did last year, or a makeup kit like the year before that. In truth, I could use the makeup kit now for the Scarlett Experiment. Too bad I gave it to Ettie.

"Okay, Lobster Pot *again* if that's what Beanie wants," she says.

I do love the Lobster Pot and our mini-golf tournament, but it *might* be nice to go to a more upscale restaurant than the Lobster Pot. I don't *have* to do the same things every year. I am tempted to bring this up, but Nancy switches gears.

"So, as for the theme of Scarlett's going-away party," Nancy says, sipping a glass of water. She's dressed in a blue suit and her hair curls on top of her head like a child's doll. Her neck is so large that some of her skin folds over her collar. I can't see the girl from that photo with Gran anywhere. "I was thinking something with a *Great Gatsby* elegance. Wouldn't that be lovely? Maeve, I think that would be lovely," Nancy says.

"Lovely," Mom says, stealing a glance at Dad while taking a bite, and now we're all talking like we're dripping in caramel. "Scarlett, why don't you call your friends and see what kind of theme they would like before we commit."

"Maeve, you don't want to take a teenager's advice, do you?" Nancy asks. "It's hard enough to get Scarlett to bring her friends over," Nancy adds. She, too, takes a tiny bite. "Oh, very well, I guess you should ask your friends. If they exist," Nancy says with a wink to Scarlett.

Scarlett never brings her friends to the house. She always meets them out. One time I heard her say to Trish that she didn't want her Cape Cod friends to meet her "nerdy sister" and her "weird parents." I never told Mom and Dad that.

Either way, Scarlett has to have the party and let Nancy go all out, she knows that.

"We told you, you don't have to throw Scarlett a party," Dad says after swallowing some chicken. He has some sauce on the corner of his mouth.

"Someone in this family needs to show Scarlett off. Juilliard! I just can't stop telling everyone I meet!"

"We can't afford—" Dad starts to say and wipes his mouth.

"I *know* you can't afford it and if you would stop these research jobs, Gerard, and take my advice, you'll bring in some consistent money. If you do your research on the side, or run a few labs, you might be able to pay some bills."

There's a pause and I hope this is a break from the money talk. We each fill our mouths with food so no one has to continue the conversation. "And now with Maeve losing . . ." Nancy stops herself and with a large exaggerated smile says, "Of course, you know I don't have a problem paying for any of it."

Scarlett returns the smile, but it's fake. I hate her white teeth.

I wonder what she is *really* thinking. We all know, the universe knows, that Nancy loves reminding us how much she pays to keep our family afloat.

I need that scholarship.

"So, the party," Nancy continues. "For a *Great Gatsby* theme we can have twenties music, champagne, silk everywhere. It'll be lovely," Nancy gushes.

"What's *Great Gatsby* again?" Scarlett asks. "It sounds familiar."

She just graduated from Summerhill Academy. Didn't she read *Great Gatsby* sophomore year? Or at least see the movie?

"A novel," I say.

Nancy's eyes move down the table at me. Her pudgy face resembles a Persian cat. "Very good, Bean."

Did she just dare to compliment me?

"But why would we have a good-bye party with that theme?"

I am brave enough to ask. "Almost everyone dies at the end of that book."

"Well, not everyone is quite so literary, dear," Nancy replies.

Damn, I have nothing left to shove in my mouth so I can avoid this conversation. All that is left on my plate are a couple of peas. As usual I ate too fast and am finished before everyone else. "What is your focus this summer?" Nancy asks me. "No slimy algae, I see."

"Tracking a comet—" But I don't get to finish explaining because she turns to Mom and Dad.

"She should spend more time with kids her age."

"Most of the kids leave after a couple weeks, or they don't come every summer like we do," I say. This seems perfectly reasonable to me.

"She hasn't a single friend here," Nancy continues like I haven't said anything. "She's spending far too much time with telescopes and computers. I hate to say it, Gerard, but maybe she's spending too much time with her dad in science laboratories."

"I have a job, Nancy," I say as nicely as possible. "And a best friend. And a boyfriend." I know it's not technically true anymore, but Nancy makes me so mad and it just slips out.

"She needs to find some interests outside of science. It's limiting for a young girl." Nancy sighs and continues, "It's exactly why I planned this excursion for her tonight."

"Excursion?" What the hell does that mean?

"Bean needs to be at dances with friends and participate in school clubs. Colleges care about socialization." She glances around my head. "What time is it?" she asks. "It's six forty-five.

Beanie, you need to get dressed for the teen dance."

"I'm sorry—the what?" I say, leaning forward. My voice squeaks.

"Nancy thought it might be good for you to go to a teen thing," Dad says gently. "At the pier."

"You told her no, right? I can't. Not—" I'm already nervous and out of breath. I can barely look at my sister. She must be loving this.

Nancy motions to the kitchen help for our plates to be cleared away. "It's cloudy tonight," she says. "How are you going to track a comet in these conditions? What else are you going to do?"

"Dad, how could you make that decision for me?" My voice shakes.

"We thought it might be nice," he says. I hate that he actually believes that. Does he know me *at all?*

"I hate large groups." I will not cry in front of Nancy and make her case even stronger.

"You need new experiences," Nancy insists.

"Give the dance a try, Beanie," Mom says, taking a bite of carrots. I finally succumb to my sister for help. She isn't smirking like I thought she would be.

She presses her lips together and looks back and forth between Nancy, Mom, and Dad.

"Tell them how lame school dances are," I beg. I haven't ever been to a dance on the Cape, but if it is anything like the dances at Summerhill, I can only imagine. I went to last year's Snow-flake Formal with Tucker and we spent the whole time making fun of everyone. "Please?" I say with my teeth clenched.

"They are kinda lame," Scarlett concedes, and I could hug her and her white, bunny teeth.

"See? Even Scarlett thinks they suck!"

"And everyone who goes is really young," she adds.

"See?!" I accidentally gesture wildly and my palm smacks the table. The silver and glassware shake. "Oops," I mumble.

Nancy's lips pucker tight.

My knee jumps up and down. I stop it by pressing down on my kneecap.

"We thought it would be fun," Mom says, and Nancy breathes heavily through her nose. "You don't need to get so upset. Don't go if you don't want to."

Thank the heavens.

"What about wearing white to my party, Nancy? All white?" Scarlett suggests, and I know she's changing the subject for me.

Nancy takes a second to reply but can't help herself. "We can't have red wine if everyone wears white."

I cannot believe they were going to force me to go to that dance. They think I'm still a little kid. That they can just make decisions for me and I won't even argue.

You should call me sometime, Star Girl.

Andrew didn't think I was a kid.

After dessert, I leave Mom and Nancy in the living room to talk about dress codes and canapés. Dad is working at the kitchen table, and Scarlett was gone before dessert was cleared. I didn't get to say thank you. I reach in my pocket and slide out my cell phone. Andrew's phone number shines in the darkened stairwell.

I think you should call me.

My cell phone sits in the palm of my hand. With Andrew, it was easy to be like Scarlett. Too easy, actually. I was independent; I was cool.

I make it up to my bedroom, shut the door, and lock it behind me. I sit in the window seat and peer down onto Shore Road.

The only lights on the street outside Seaside Stomachache are from Nancy's porch and a couple of street lamps.

Downstairs it's Discovery Channel reruns, party talk, and questions about the Waterman Scholarship. Scarlett is out in town somewhere, having a great time. I wish I were with her, or Ettie, or even the girls trying on sunglasses from the Seahorse the other night.

I wonder what Tucker is doing and grip the cell phone tightly.

I am not going to spend my summer in my bedroom alone while Tucker makes out with Becky Winthrop all over Rhode Island.

Scarlett is living the life she wants. I want to live the life I want. In the spirit of the Scarlett Experiment, I am calling Andrew. It's what Scarlett would do—it's what she would do to have a life outside the walls of this house.

I dial Andrew's number.

Eek! It rings. Once . . . twice. Oh God. Maybe I should hang up?

"Hello?" a voice says through the receiver. There is music and chatter in the background.

"H-hi." I stand up from the window seat. Somehow, I need to be standing for this conversation. A chaos of voices and music echoes through the cell phone. "This is Sarah." I have to raise my voice for him to hear me but try to keep the sound from traveling by turning my back to my bedroom door. "From today? At the beach?"

"Star Girl," he says. His voice is happy, like he's smiling. "What took you so long?"

"So long? We met this afternoon," I say. I note the panic in my voice and clear my throat to cover it up.

He laughs. "I know. I hate all the rules. You should just call someone when you want to call someone."

Rules? What rules? There are rules for calling people? Why didn't I research this? Damn teen dances. My impulsivity clouded my judgment.

"It's loud where you are," I say and expect to hear Nancy's screech throughout the house any second.

"I'm at a bonfire out on Nauset Light. If you'd called earlier I would have invited you. You need four-wheel drive to get out here. Do you have access to an SUV or anything?"

"No, it's um, actually hard to get a car right now. I'm at the mercy of the family this summer," I think up quickly. *Be Scarlett.* "Guess you'll have to pick me up for our date." Wow, that was forward. I hold my breath.

Party chatter echoes in the background for a second.

"Definitely," he says, and I like that there's a lightness in his voice.

I must have been walking in circles because the inertia of my body pulls at me when I stop. I'm smiling big now, and when I glance through the skylight, I'm right underneath the Big

Dipper. I stand here, with facial muscle exhaustion from talking to a boy who is not Tucker. My cheeks hurt.

"When are you free?" he asks.

I nudge my toe into the carpet. "Oh you know, whenever."

"How about Friday night—" There is a crash of something glass in the background and Andrew's laughter echoes out of the phone again. "Wow," he says, "my friends are idiots. Remind me not to introduce you." He laughs again and says, "You can show me these famous stars of yours."

"Great!" I say, rocking on the balls of my feet a little. "We can actually go to Nauset Light. It's the equinox and Jupiter is really bright and—"

He laughs again and it reminds me of a teddy bear, a *big* teddy bear laughing at me through the line.

"Wow," he says. "You *are* smart. Hey, I have to go, Star Girl. Where should I pick you up?"

Damn. Friday is my birthday. I know we're not officially celebrating until Saturday, but I'm sure we're doing *something*. There's no way I'm going to reschedule with Andrew. I'll make it work.

The thought of Andrew coming to the door makes my stomach clench. Mom would insist on saying hello and Dad, too, with his Einstein hair. Oh *God*, and Nancy would want to talk to him just so she can see me interact with someone of the opposite sex. Then, to add insult to injury, someone would call me "Beanie." He would know I'm not eighteen in two seconds.

Even worse? Scarlett would answer the door and Andrew would know we were sisters. He would probably like her better than me.

"I'll be in town so why don't you pick me up in front of the Bird's Nest?" I finally say and add as a joke, "You know, for old time's sake? How about seven thirty?"

"See you there," he says. "Oh yeah, and be hungry."

When I hang up the phone there is a tingling in my chest. Like the moment before the results of an experiment, when all of the elements coalesce. *Coalesceeee*. Scarlett would say that word sounds epic. . . . She *always* knows what to say.

The secret of my date makes me giddy. I nearly jump down the stairs.

In the living room, Mom and Dad watch the end of a Red Sox game. Dad's hair sticks up from over the lounger in zig-zag strands. He snores, which is par for the course at the eighth inning. I slip my phone in my pocket and plop down on the couch next to Mom.

"I'm sorry we didn't tell you about the dance sooner," she says, putting her hand on my back. "Nancy was insisting that you would have a *great* time."

"It's no big deal," I say. "Thanks for letting me stay home." I tuck my feet under the blanket with Mom. I lean my head on her shoulder and fall asleep just like that.

Warm. Comfortable. Happy.

NINE

THE NEXT DAY, DAD DRIVES US TO FALMOUTH.
The *Alvin* is finally at WHOI, so I jumped at the opportunity
to go to work with Dad. As we drive, we pass by the ferry that
takes tourists to Martha's Vineyard and Nantucket. We pass my
favorite restaurant, Allen's, and of course the best coffee shop in
Falmouth, Coffee Craze. The brownies there are the *best*.

Once we get past the tourist area, a string of familiar stone
buildings flank both sides of the street. Woods Hole Oceanographic Institution looks the same every single year no matter
how much time passes. Just the thought of all that marine life,
the tanks of fish, and enormous deep-sea vessels sends a rush of
familiar excitement washing over me.

We park in front of Building 40, our usual WHOI home. I grab some of the remaining boxes that Dad still needs to bring upstairs to his office. Once we get inside, I set them down in the foyer.

At the end of the long hallway are the double doors to the tech shop.

"Can I?" I say.

Dad rolls his eyes with a smile. His hair sticks out from underneath his WHOI hat and he nods as he puts down his boxes too.

I could map out this place with my eyes closed. We walk together down the long hall and into the tech shop, which is actually so big it's more like an airplane hanger. Inside are hundreds of tools hanging on the walls and the satisfying smell of oil and gasoline. Welders' masks hang on pegs in a long row. Below them are crates of gloves, hammers, and batteries of all different sizes.

"Sarah!"

Rodger, my favorite marine biologist, walks from the center of the room to Dad and me. He's the youngest marine biologist at Woods Hole. Behind him, standing in the glow of a spotlight is the *Alvin*. Rodger steps into my view.

"Is that a beard?" I ask and reach up to touch the scruff.

"It's to cover my double chin!" he says and hugs me tightly. He's got a bigger gut than last year, but it looks good on him.

"You're tall!" he says and slips a WHOI baseball hat out of the pocket of his oversized white lab coat. He plops it on my head.

"Thanks!" I like the hat; it fits well and has WHOI stitched in blue letters on the front.

"So? How's it going with the comet? You didn't email me and Nina nearly enough updates."

"Registration is tomorrow. My *birthday*," I say. "Then it's actually official."

"Tomorrow!? Happy Birthday, spud!" he says with a squeeze to my shoulder. He's been calling me that since I was nine.

"Congratulations to *you*!" Dad says with a pat to Rodger's back. "Let's see some pictures."

Rodger digs in his pocket for his phone to show us some pictures of his newborn baby.

I am respectful and look at the tiny newborn with the same nose as Rodger, but I can't help being pulled away by the *Alvin*.

Last year's upgrade makes it look different, more high-tech. It has five viewports now, when it used to have three. It's about as wide as a Suburban SUV but much shorter. No matter how many improvements they make to the sub, it always surprises me how enormous it looks, but how small it is inside.

Rodger hands me his clipboard with all of the newest dimensions on the upgraded sub. It's classified to most people, but I get access.

I run down some of the list and review the new specs:

Titanium Alloy: 6A1-4V Eli.

It's 4.6 inches wider on the inside than the last version of the *Alvin*.

Still cramped as hell in there.

I want to see the new specs and changes myself. I want to

climb up the ladder and look inside. I place the clipboard on the floor next to the base of the ladder and turn to Rodger and Dad.

"Can I look inside?" I ask.

"Sure," Rodger says just as a zoom of a saw revs in the other corner of the shop where some mechanics are working.

"Just off the coast of Martha's Vineyard?" Rodger yells to Dad over the noise. They've moved on to a conversation about Dad's work. It's impossible to stop Dad once he gets going about the barnacles he and his team discovered.

As I climb up, a spray of sparks illuminates from the mechanics in the corner of the room. Their saw revs a second time, making Dad and Rodger yell through their conversation again.

I place one palm on the cool titanium and grip the other over the side of the personnel hatch, where the scientists sit when they explore the bottom of the ocean.

I peer inside. Nearly every space of the wall inside the spherical pod is covered in buttons, switches, and levels. I can't imagine how the pilots know how to work everything. There's space to sit, though a few tall scientists in that pod could make for a really uncomfortable descent.

I imagine myself in the tiny space, maneuvering the hydraulic arms, taking samples, and recording data. I could make a difference in the world by what I discovered.

"Come on, Bean," Dad calls. "We can come back later."

"Okay," I say and climb back down, but not without one last glance in the pod. As I step onto the shop floor, I hand the clipboard back to Rodger.

"She's starry-eyed, Gerard. We may have another marine

biologist on our hands," Rodger says to Dad.

I shrug, but it's surprising. I didn't just study the specs or marvel at the engineering of the vessel this time. I'm amazed by the scientific discoveries uncovered by scientists *because* of the *Alvin*.

We pick up the boxes in the foyer and head to Dad's office on the second floor. Last year, I wanted every little spec of the *Alvin* upgrade. I was obsessed with the construction of the titanium alloy and how many ports would be installed. This year, I couldn't care less about the specs. I almost tell Dad that but don't.

I almost explain that this year, I want to be the one to go inside and explore.

"Happy Birthday to you . . . Happy Birthday to you . . . Happy Birthday, dear Beanie. Happy Birthday to you!" Scarlett and Mom sing to me at the dinner table Friday evening. Our meal was a small roast and a few cupcakes for dessert. Nancy had to go to a Cape Cod Arts Committee meeting and Dad ended up stuck at WHOI. I split my cupcake with Mom. Scarlett has been out every single night this week, and every single night I wonder if she sees Andrew.

"So, what did you do last night?" I ask when Mom brings our dishes into the kitchen. She refuses to allow the housekeepers to help us every single night.

"Bonfire party on the beach. It was kind of lame in the end," she says with a delicate scoop of her spoon to the top of her cupcake. She always just eats the frosting.

Lame? I would have given anything to go.

"Oh yeah?" I ask, really punctuating the ease in my voice. "How come?

Scarlett sighs and sips her coffee. She never spills. I always drink too fast and accidentally dribble down whatever I am wearing.

"Because all the tourist girls come and throw themselves at the lifeguards. It's pathetic. And because the tourists are *so* loud, the cops find out and we have to break the party up. If it hadn't been for Andrew, some of us could have gotten into trouble." I perk up at Andrew's name.

"What could you get in trouble for?" I ask.

"For underage drinking. Hello, most of us aren't twenty-one. And none of the desperate tourists are either."

"Aren't we considered tourists? We only come to Nancy's house in the summer."

"We have a history here. And I come out way more than just the summers. We know the locals. Or I do, anyway. The tourists don't know about the good spots so they latch on to us for the fun parties."

Us.

I don't have an "us" except for Ettie and the Pi Naries.

My suggestion to go to touristy Nauset Light seems so stupid now. I should have let Andrew pick the spot. Mom comes back in but brings her coffee to the couch, flipping through a *Projo*, as she usually does every single evening.

The rules that Andrew mentioned gnaw at me. I haven't had a chance to research because Mom has been job searching.

"So," I say slowly and concoct a believable story. "Ettie asked me how long she should wait to call a boy if he gives you his number." *Act casual.*

"Ha, a boy gave *Ettie* his number?" Scarlett scoffs and stands up.

Scarlett considers me. "Forget it," I say.

"You always make a boy wait two days. At least. Or he'll think you're desperate." She brings her plate to the sink. "I need to get ready for tonight," she says.

"I want to know exactly where you'll be, Scarlett," Mom calls.

Once Scarlett is gone, I slap my hand to my forehead.

Andrew must think I'm completely desperate.

What took you so long? he had said. I slap my forehead again.

Two days? I had waited eight hours to call.

TEN

"SO," I SAY TO MOM AND LEAN OVER THE SIDE OF the couch. "I'm going to go to the beach tonight. The comet is set to come through on July third. A field dress rehearsal is crucial so close to the execution of the actual experiment."

"Sure," Mom says. She scrolls through job listings on her laptop. "What beach will you be going to?"

"Nauset," I say quickly.

She nods and goes back to the Web searching. Lying to Mom is easier than I thought. Not the lying part, but that she would believe me so easily. I wait for it but she doesn't even push and ask me what time I'll be home.

I race up the stairs to wait for Scarlett to leave. Once she does,

I'll get dressed in my Scarlett-approved outfit.

After I put on a bathrobe, I survey my bedroom. The telescope is packed under my desk hidden behind my empty suitcase, just in case Mom pops in my room. The calendar for the scholarship is there, all filled in, and my application is in its blue folder.

Still, I feel like I'm forgetting something.

It's just paranoia from stealing clothes and lying to Mom. It's manifesting itself in guilt. With my hand on the doorknob, I can't shake the feeling. What the hell am I forgetting?

Shake it off. In sixteen years you've never lied to Mom—ever. You always do exactly what you are told.

I shut the door and stand in the stairwell waiting it out so I can go in Scarlett's room. I'll change into the second outfit of the Scarlett Experiment.

Scarlett chatters on the cell phone while walking down the stairs. Her Egyptian Musk perfume trails behind her. Once she turns the corner, I tiptoe down to the second floor, curl my fingers around the thick wood of her bedroom door, and sneak inside.

I check my watch: seven fifteen. I snatch a pair of shorts and a white tank top. I race to her bathroom, where I can be concealed behind a closed door. Something else is missing though. I need a *little* something else to really embody Scarlett. A small bottle of Scarlett's Egyptian Musk sits on the marble countertop. The oil is specially blended for Scarlett by a store in NYC. The bottle looks like a crystal jewel—I uncork it and roll the oil on my wrists and neck like I've seen her do countless times.

"Put it on the pressure points," she has said with a flip of her hair.

"Who are you going with?" Mom's voice echoes up the stairs as I lift a leg and lean it on the tub. With my razor in hand, I'm ready to snatch up any stray hairs that may be hiding out on my leg.

"God, Mom. I'm just going with some guys," Scarlett whines.

"No, Scarlett. Not just *some* guys. Who?"

"You never ask *Bean*."

"We don't worry about Bean."

"If you must know . . . Curtis. Remember him? His parents live in Sandwich? His friend Andrew is coming too and he's going to be a police officer. Is that safe enough for you? He's only the nicest guy alive. No wait, Andrew can't go. So it's Curtis, his *harmless* friend Tate, and my very innocent friend, Shelby. Is that okay? Do you want their phone numbers? Blood type?"

I smirk and when I catch my reflection in the mirror I cock my head. Andrew isn't going with them because he's going out with *me*. I can't place it, but I look . . . different. It must be the manicured toes or the outfit I'm wearing. The denim shorts only reach to the top of my thigh. Maybe it's the Egyptian Musk.

Mom makes Scarlett promise twice that she will check in on her way home. I wait until I hear the sound of the front door closing.

I check myself in the mirror one last time. I could pass for Scarlett with brown hair. Maybe.

When I walk into the living room, Mom has brought her laptop to the table and is eating straight from a vanilla fudge ice-cream container. I clutch a dark blue cardigan near my waist like this will magically prevent Mom from seeing that my shorts come up way too high.

"Where you headed?" she asks with a lick of the spoon. She doesn't even look at me.

"To Nauset Light," I say. "Remember?"

"Right, right. You bringing the telescope?" Mom asks.

"No, not tonight."

"Mmm," Mom says. "Okay." She's absorbed in the job listings. She clearly doesn't remember the story about the field rehearsal.

"So I'll see you . . . ," I say.

In the background, PBS is showing a Moody Blues concert.

"Nights in white satin . . . never reaching the end . . . ," the TV croons. Last summer I would have been sitting there, eating ice cream with her.

I hide my wrists underneath the cloth of the cardigan. I'm not sure if anyone else can smell it, but the Egyptian Musk is pouring over me.

"Give me a kiss good night," Mom says. "I'm going to bed after this."

I had made good headway to the door, but I double back. I kiss Mom quickly on the cheek. Her skin is always so soft.

"You smell like Scarlett," she says.

Oh boy.

"It looks like she spilled some in the bathroom. I cleaned it up and it kind of got all over me."

Mom hums along with the TV.

"Your sister is so careless. Isn't that oil expensive?"

"Don't tell her. Or she'll think I did it," I say.

Mom sways her ice-cream spoon through the air like a conductor. I back away.

"Mom? The perfume?"

I'm almost at the front door.

"I won't say anything. Have fun!" Mom says and lifts a hand from her seat. She waves and when I close the door, she's still singing.

I have to make sure that wherever Andrew and I go, Scarlett is not going to be there. I cannot find myself in that position. She would never understand why I lied to Andrew about my age and would tell him the truth immediately.

As I walk toward Main Street, I keep reminding myself: I go to MIT. I'm going to study astronomy. It's not really a *bad* lie if I don't mention it again.

A line of people curls around the Bird's Nest Diner. Tourists will wait for clam chowder for *hours*. June on Main Street means the smell of fried fish and French fries wafting down the block. It's full-on fried food aroma. I hold my sweater over my forearm. Some people add their names on a waiting list and join the line. Couples hold hands, some clutch bags of purchases, and people turn their heads to ogle items behind glass windows. At the Seahorse that necklace is still calling my name but it will have to wait a bit longer. According to my cell it's 7:26.

7:28.

7:29.

No red pickup truck. Maybe he won't come?

I peer down the street, lift my chin, and even rise up on my tiptoes.

"Come on, Star Girl, I'm hungry."

My head whips straight ahead to Andrew, looking at me from behind the wheel of the red pickup. Wow, how could I miss his car? He's rolled the window down and is leaning his arm on the passenger seat.

I slide in next to him. My knee jumps up and down and I worry that Andrew will notice.

"You like seafood?" he asks. He has strong hands—I can tell from the sculpt of his forearms as he grips the steering wheel.

"Definitely," I say. I like fish and chips and Nancy's lobster bakes. I only brought twenty bucks; I hope wherever he's taking me has a cheap eats section.

"Ever had grilled scallops?" he asks.

Dad grills at home all the time. Every time we barbecue, he wears his MEAT IS MY LIFE apron. Tucker always showed up at our cookouts. Sometimes Trish came too. It was a *thing*. We would grill, Tucker would come over. I guess he won't now. Not anymore.

"I love scallops!" I say, but it's a lie. I've never had them before.

"Great. I have an idea."

"What?"

Andrew pulls out into Main Street traffic and we're barely on the road for two minutes before he's pulling off into a parking lot that abuts the fishing docks. I've been here a thousand times; is there some secret restaurant that I don't know about?

I get out of the car, and right next to the docks and marina office is a big sign that reads: HATCHMAN'S FISH MARKET.

"This is a restaurant?" I ask.

"No, just a market. You can buy fish straight off the Orleans boats."

The sun hovers above the ocean and it'll be sunset in a couple hours. Little pops of light glimmer across the water and onto the parking lot making everyone walking to and from the market look like they should be in a Monet painting. I guess anyone can look beautiful if they're in the right light. Ahead of me, sparkles of sunlight roll over the harbor and golden shimmers lick the boat docks. I hesitate, walking slower. I still feel like there's something I'm forgetting to do.

"What's up?" Andrew asks.

"You know that feeling? Like you forgot something, but you can't remember what it is?"

"Yeah . . ."

"I can't remember what it is!"

Andrew laughs and I do too. "Maybe dinner will help jog your memory," he offers.

Andrew extends his arm. His palm is open to me; I place my hand in his and let him lead me inside. The sour smell of fish and salt water overwhelms me and I can't imagine how I thought this was like a painting. This is how it smells in the cafeteria when they make fish sticks, but worse. I bring my wrist to my nose and breathe in the Egyptian Musk. I note that Andrew hasn't mentioned the foul odor in here. I guess he's used to it, working on a lobster boat.

"Andrew!" It's Scarlett's Curtis. I immediately survey the market for my sister. The only other people in here are an elderly couple. Curtis looks me up and down, a smile creeps over his face.

"American flag string bikini," he says with a slow drawl.

What the hell does Scarlett see in this guy?

"Scallops, I need, like, a dozen," Andrew says to the guy behind the counter.

"You going to beachcomber tonight?" Curtis asks, shooting another glance my way. "I get off in, like, ten minutes. I'm meeting Scarlett at Shelby's house."

I let out a breath I didn't know I was holding.

"Nah," Andrew says and lets go of my hand to take out his wallet. Andrew pays before I even get a chance to reach into my pocket. "I can't go out every night like you."

"Have fun . . . ," Curtis says, though the word is drawn out and it's clear "fun" is code for something else. He winks at me. The bells on the door jingle and we're outside in the Monet painting again.

I reach into my pocket for the money to help pay for dinner. It's the right thing to do, even if Scarlett would never offer to pay. I am reminded of the first day on the beach when she expected that the boys would drive her home the minute she asked.

"I should split this with you," I say.

Andrew's eyes light up.

"You don't have to pay; I asked you out," he says.

"But you should take it; it's . . . fair."

I want to show Andrew that I don't believe he is required to pay for me. I want things to start out equal between us.

Andrew takes the twenty and slides it into my jean pocket.

"I want to treat you," he says. "That's the nice thing to do."

His fingers press against my hip bone and I take a breath. His index and middle finger linger against me. Something erupts in my stomach, maybe lower. I need to take in some air, but it catches a little in my throat.

"Thank—I mean, thank you."

"Come on, Star Girl," he says with a wink. "Let's go; we should get there way before sunset."

"That reminds me," I say, stepping into the car. "I have to be back by around ten or so." Mom has never given me a curfew, but she always checks for Scarlett around ten. "I have to help my mom early in the morning," I say, thinking fast.

"With what?" Andrew asks, and we turn out of the fish pier, back onto Main Street.

"My sister's going-away party," I say. "It's this *big deal* to my aunt Nancy."

Oh crap. What if he knows Scarlett has an aunt Nancy? Okay, don't panic. I can improvise.

"Wow, sounds annoying," he says.

"You have *no* idea," I say with a deep exhale. I hope he can't sense my relief.

I cozy into my seat, but we don't turn toward Nauset Light; we keep driving in the direction of Aunt Nancy's house.

"We're going to Nauset Beach? Not Nauset Light?"

"Yep."

In a few blocks we'll pass Aunt Nancy's street. Laurel Street,

Squire Court, and there it is: Shore Road. I peer down the lane only to see shadows cast by the long colonial street lamps flanking the sandy street. I wonder why people do that when they pass someone's street that they know, look down it like that person might be standing there. I want to see if Andrew has ever felt the same way, but I decide that it's probably better not to say every thought that goes through my mind.

But I do want to say that today I am sixteen years old. I want to share this with Andrew because I know he would be excited. It's on the edge of my lips, but I know I can't. Then I would have to admit I lied. Whatever, it's not like we are going to start a relationship. It's one date. It's the Scarlett Experiment.

We drive past the beach guard booth, where they charge the tourists twenty bucks to get on the sand, but we don't stop in the parking lot. We drive to a lane at the far end of the parking lot, designated for the outer beach, a part of Nauset you can go to only if you have a car with four-wheel drive.

"We're going four wheeling?" I ask. I know Mom and Dad wouldn't approve, but Scarlett definitely would.

We pull up to the guard booth for the outer beach campsites. "Campsite twelve is open," the guard says. Andrew pulls ahead. "Is that okay?" he asks with a hint of worry in his voice.

The sand road lines the coast for miles. I must be making a funny face because Andrew pulls to the side of the lane. "I should have asked you, right? I'm so bad at this."

"Bad at what?"

"You barely know me and I'm taking you to the outer beach. I could be a psycho."

I scoot over in my seat, grip the door handle, and press myself against the window. I pretend I am screaming and trying to escape. Andrew laughs. It's true, I wouldn't normally do something like this. But that's the point.

Besides, Scarlett vetted him.

"I'll take the risk," I say. I can't explain why I feel so comfortable already. I have my cell phone and Nancy always makes me put Mace in my purse just in case.

"I'll get you back by ten," he says. His eyes seem so blue in this light.

The wind whips through the pickup and blows my hair about my face. Andrew turns up the radio even louder so the song playing oozes through my hair, the seats, and the salt water misting my cheeks. The singer croons: *Hello, I love you, won't you tell me your name?* I've never heard the song before, but I like it.

As we drive toward the outer beach, the ocean flies by us. Well, scientifically that would be impossible, but it *feels* like that even though we're only going around ten miles an hour. There are lots of other people down by the shore, grilling, swimming, and flying kites.

Andrew holds the steering wheel with one lazy hand and the other rests on my seat back. He seems happy. Maybe he just likes the outer beach? After all, it is a beautiful night, though unseasonably humid for June.

The roar of Andrew's truck quiets to a growl as we approach an empty campsite. We pull into a small spot with a number 12 on a sign. We're only a hundred feet or so away from some people at the camp next to us. The ocean stretches away as far as I can see.

"Is this our spot?" I ask.

"Yup, until I have to get you home for curfew," he says, turning the music down.

"Curfew, huh? You've mentioned that a couple times," I say. "You know, repetition is the essence of all experimentation. I mean, to ensure that the scientific hypothesis is solid, observations must repeat themselves." Andrew beams at me, but I literally want to throw my hands over my mouth. "But sometimes in social situations it can show you're nervous," I grumble quickly.

"Wow, I'll have to remember that," he says.

As I am about to get out, I hesitate. At my feet, resting on the mat, is a navy blue cloth arm sling.

"Did you hurt yourself?"

Andrew hesitates but keeps his fingers on the door handle.

"It's not mine," he says. "A year ago, my friends Mike and Curtis were in a car accident." He doesn't tell me which friend wore the sling.

He also doesn't elaborate or make eye contact. Various embarrassing experiences have taught me that when people don't want to talk about something or when I accidentally invade their personal space, they evade eye contact.

"So why are you repeating yourself?" I ask, moving the conversation away from the car accident. "About getting me home by ten."

"Just haven't had to worry about curfews in a while."

"My parents . . . ," I say and open the door. "They're kind of strict."

"But you're eighteen. Can't you do what you want?"

"To an extent," I say, hoping this is a sufficient response. I make sure to meet his eyes when I say, "I'm doing what I want right now."

"I can respect that," he says.

Couldn't have said it any better myself.

ELEVEN

ANDREW UNEARTHS A GRILL FROM BENEATH SOME blankets in the back of his pickup. He folds down the back hatch of the truck so I can sit. I sneak a peek at my cell phone, praying that Mom and Dad haven't called. Nope. It's only eight fifteen.

While Andrew lights the charcoals on a small grill, I survey the coastline. It changes every year with the storms. The Chatham break is a split in the beach where the bay and ocean meet. A small lagoon separates our beach, and in the distance, large swells crash against a sandbar.

Andrew salts the scallops and grabs some butter from a small cooler.

"So where is your sister going?" Andrew asks. "You said your parents are having a going-away party."

Think fast. "Um, she's studying abroad for the fall, so my aunt, who we stay with during the summers, is throwing this huge party."

"You don't sound happy about it."

"It's not that," I say, jumping to the ground and kneeling down in front of the smoking grill. It sizzles each time Andrew adds a scallop.

"So if you're happy about the going-away party, why the scowl?"

"Am I scowling?"

"A little."

"I don't know why we have to make such a big deal about her leaving," I say. "Good-bye parties in general confuse me. I mean, why make a big deal about saying good-bye?" I'm surprised it's easy to say all of this to him.

Andrew shrugs. "Sometimes just saying good-bye isn't enough. Like if you make an event out of it, it'll be easier."

I wish Andrew could be my date at the party. If Tucker did show, he would see me with Andrew and kick himself. He'd wonder how he could possibly give up a girl like me.

Just thinking about Tucker makes me want to go home and recheck my coordinates. Andrew keeps cooking the scallops and I can't help but compare his frame to Tucker's. Andrew is so much more built. Tucker is scrawny compared to him.

"Wanna try one?" Andrew asks.

"What?" I jump. "I mean. Okay."

He laughs a little. "You were deep in thought." He holds a

succulent scallop out to me on a silver fork. I blow on it and take a bite; the butter slithers over my tongue.

"Wow, good," I say and swallow. He nods once to himself, like it's an achievement.

The waves crash on the shore. It's headed toward low tide. It's still light out and the smoke from Andrew's grill makes the sky a lavender gray. The stars are just starting to pop through the sky, but we have some time yet.

Maybe I should mention my projection for Comet Jolie? Or would that sound too much like Bean?

I hand Andrew the fork and sit down on the sand a few feet away from the water. I lie down so my hair falls beneath me and the chill of the sand cools the back of my head. I try to seem elegant and relaxed.

The smoke from the grill swirls up to the sky.

"They're almost done." Andrew lies down next to me. The sides of our bodies barely touch and I am very aware of the hair on my arms prickling. "What do you see?" he asks quietly.

"I can *barely* make out Cassiopeia. She's on her side, watching us from her tipped-over throne."

"Is that right, Star Girl? Can you tell my future from those stars?"

He shatters my Scarlett confidence with his glance. He draws me to him, like a lighthouse calling the ships home. My heart is pounding. Is this when people kiss for the first time?

I kissed Tucker so many times, but it wasn't like this, with him staring into my eyes, with the beach and the waves. It was in a bio lab or in my backyard. I want to kiss Andrew so much that my chest aches. I never wanted Tucker like this, with my whole body.

There's a quick sizzle from the grill behind us and Andrew jumps up before we can kiss and before I can explain that numerology and star charts are complete hogwash.

Andrew uses a plastic spoon to divvy up the scallops. We have some chips, and if I were being myself and not Scarlett, I would have licked the oil from my fingertips. Instead, I wipe them delicately on a paper napkin and take small buttery bites. I tell myself to eat slowly instead of gulping everything down like I usually do.

After we eat, I enjoy the view. I expect Andrew to join me, but he stands at the open driver's-side door of his truck. He crosses his arms at the wrist. His fingers grasp the bottom of his T-shirt and he slides it off. I have to do a double take.

There's something scrawled on the underside of his arm, but I can't make it out because he moves too fast. Is it a tattoo?

It's almost fully sunset and the horizon burns an orange pink. I close my eyes, inhaling the salty air. I really do love Cape Cod. Andrew's feet crunch quietly over the sand. There's a click as he turns on the headlights. He stands in front of me at the shore, looking out at the ocean.

Andrew glances back at me. Standing there, smiling like that, his swim trunks barely clinging to his waist, he's a movie star. The captain of the swim team at home. He's the quarterback. He is the antithesis of Tucker. He is someone I could never get by being Bean. I want to say something witty. I want to be fascinating.

"Come on," he says and extends a hand to me just like he did at the fish market.

"We really should wait twenty minutes to avoid cramping," I say. It slipped out. I cringe and have to look away.

Andrew places his hand on his stomach and laughs so hard that his face turns red. He comes over and pulls me up so my eyes are at his chin. He searches my face.

"You're funny," he says. He shakes his head. "How about I promise you I won't let you get a cramp." He laughs when he says this and his whole face reddens again. It's a good thing he thinks I'm trying to be funny. I don't know if I could be funny intentionally.

"I didn't bring my suit," I say, gesturing to Scarlett's short shorts.

He takes a step back so his heels touch the water, he looks me up and down.

"Afraid to get wet?"

This question makes me shudder.

"No . . . ," I say, but my voice wobbles.

I'm trembling and I have no idea why. Shudders run through me again and again like I'm freezing. Can I make this stop?

When I think Andrew is going to take a step to join me on the sand, he pivots on his heel, runs into the water, and dives. The bottom of his feet slip into the sea.

I can't really be nervous about cramping, I have to ignore the statistical data. I'm pretty sure Andrew wants me to follow him into the water.

"You coming!?" he calls.

"Isn't it freezing?" I call back.

I stand and shift my weight from my right foot to my left and back. Andrew bobs out there in the shallow water, the mix of the rising moon and the falling sun makes the ocean a stormy blue. Scarlett would go. Scarlett would jump in.

"It's not bathwater. But the lagoon here is a lot warmer than beyond the sandbar. Come on in, Star Girl!"

These short shorts are kind of like a bathing suit but I take them off anyway. I slip off my sweater and it pools onto the sand. I kick my shoes off next. Soon, I'm standing in my bra and underwear. I can't believe I chose tonight of all nights to wear my pink polka-dot underwear. Never in a million years did I think someone might see them. The people down the beach can't tell I'm not wearing a bathing suit.

Guess it's now or never. I hold my breath and take a step into the surf.

Pinpricks of frigid cold water stab my feet.

"Holy crap!" I cry out. "You think this is warm?"

"It's good once you get in!"

Scarlett wouldn't complain. Scarlett would be brave. *Keep going. Be Scarlett.*

I slosh through the shallow water. *Be Scarlett.* Cold. Rippling over my thighs. Frozen. *Be Scarlett.*

"Go under! It will help!"

I take a deep breath and dive, arms in a point.

Paralyzing. Freezing. The icy water presses over my cheeks and my hair. I shoot up and gasp for air. Andrew's lean arms cut through the water toward me.

I scream a little, I can't help it. Andrew laughs again and we both smile at each other under that lavender sky.

"Oh my God, Andrew," I say. I stretch my legs out, but I'm still unable to touch the bottom. I start treading water. Andrew is tall enough that he's standing solidly on the ground. "I think the people on the *Titanic* were this cold."

"You're sick," he says with a laugh, but his jaw quivers, his teeth chattering.

He pulls me toward him and I wrap my legs around his waist. Andrew supports me by sliding his hands around my lower back. I hold on to his body and it's surprising how well we fit. I didn't even think about how I should maneuver my body. The sun's last rays make the water lavender, just like the sky. A mix of sun and moon.

"You're crazy to make me do this," I say through chattering teeth.

"Certifiable." He looks in my eyes and down at my probably blue lips. The tips of my fingers burn from the cold.

"I want to kiss you," he says quietly.

Tucker could never have held me like this. Andrew is so strong, it's effortless.

"Can I?" he asks. "Kiss you?"

"In a sec," I say. My teeth chatter.

I press a cold hand gently onto his chest.

"What are you waiting for?" he whispers. "Hypothermia?"

We laugh through chattering teeth. I want to hold on to this moment for as long as possible. Right now, we're in the in-between. We're hovering in the water, together, and I am in his arms, in someone's arms, in this incredible way for the first time in my entire life.

This isn't simply an experiment. This is very different.

"It's just . . . ," I say with a small shake of my head. "This moment right now, we can never get it back. If we kiss we'll never be two people who haven't kissed before. It will be . . . the after."

He has stubble on his chin. One of Andrew's hands rests under my thigh and the other runs to the back of my head. "I never thought of it like that before," he says. We hover there; he examines my mouth.

"Screw it," he says.

Andrew hoists me to him and our lips meet.

He opens his lips, and I open mine, too.

Please let me be doing this right. With a turn of his head, Andrew kisses me deeper.

Please let me do this right.

His lips part from mine and Andrew's eyes are kind, warm. He smiles at me but only by lifting one half of his mouth. Scarlett says she loves guys with crooked smiles—this must be what she means. My whole body shivers again, but I can't tell if it's the temperature of the water or Andrew.

His hand rests on my hip and I can feel the rhythm of Andrew's legs as he walks us toward the shore. The movement is one I've never experienced before. When we get a few feet from the sand, my legs slide down his, and I'm standing in knee-high water, looking up at him and the constellations just starting to shimmer in the sky.

"Let's go; you're freezing," he says. He grabs my hands and

once we get back to the truck, I immediately slip back on my shorts and wrap my arms around my body, trying to keep in any body heat. I wring out some of the salt water from my hair, and lines of icy water drip down my back.

"You know," I say, squeezing the ends so drops make little divots in the dry sand below me. "Hypothermia is possible in water at a temperature less than eighty degrees."

"Hey, that's *one* fact I know," he says from the back of the truck and pulls out two huge beach towels. He shakes them free of sand and wraps one around me while I'm still wringing the water out of my hair. I was going to grab my sweater but this is better. He wraps the other towel around himself, and pulls the grill closer so some of the still smoking embers warm us up. "Want to show me more constellations?" he asks, pulling me up next to him on the hood of the truck. We huddle together.

Before I start explaining, I wonder about the car accident he mentioned earlier and if it had to do with that team jersey he wrapped around the tree trunk.

"Can I ask you something?" I say.

"You bet."

"What were you doing on the street the night we met?"

Andrew turns on his side to me. I mimic his movement.

He rests a hand on my hip. I try to act like someone has touched me on my hip before. I love his warmth.

"My friend Mike died," he admits.

I wish I hadn't asked. "I'm sorry," I say quietly.

"Curtis? The guy you met at the beach? He was driving Mike's car and . . ." He hesitates, but I can see where this is going.

"He was drunk. Curtis was all amped up. Mike didn't have a seat belt on and—"

"He hit the tree," I say, barely above a whisper.

"He hit the tree."

Andrew isn't looking at me as he utters the words. I never thought sad eyes could sparkle, but his do. It's not a happy shine, but it's not tears, either. We're quiet a moment but of course, I can't help the logical part of my mind. Curtis was driving the Jeep.

"How does Curtis drive?" I ask. "If you kill someone don't they confiscate your license forever?"

"He was in jail for nine months. When he got out he had court-ordered outpatient rehab. He literally got his license back four days ago. It's considered a restricted license."

Curtis was *in jail*? Why is Scarlett hanging out with him?

"It's not only Curtis," Andrew continues. "*I* should have been there that night. I could have stopped that accident from happening. I go over and over it in my head. Every night I have a new scenario. A new way I could have prevented that accident."

It's not his fault. He didn't make Curtis drink and drive.

"It's a logical fact," I say and sit up straight.

"What is?"

Andrew follows my lead and sits up too.

"You can't control anyone. Experiments, sure. You can change the variables, establish the controls, and record endless results. But humans? Even humans used in experiments are, at best, unreliable. And . . . I'm rambling," I add quickly.

I play with the frays on my jean shorts.

"No, you're not. Keep going."

"I'm just saying. You can't make someone do something they don't want to do." I shrug. "People aren't puppets. You could have done a variety of things differently, but you couldn't have controlled the outcome."

"I know," Andrew says, but it's defeated, like he doesn't believe me or doesn't want to talk about this anymore. "Mike's mom tells me all the time that I shouldn't blame myself. She's just being nice. I'm sorry but I know that if I had been there that night, it never would have happened."

"Well, that's insane."

I lean back on my hands, but they're slippery from the water that's still dripping from my hair. I slip and bang my elbow. "Ow," I say.

Andrew doubles over, holding his belly.

"Oh my God, Star Girl. You make me laugh."

My cheeks are so warm. That was *not* a Scarlett thing to do. Her gazelle-like leaps across the studio at Aunt Nancy's run through my mind.

"Hey!" Andrew nudges me. "Tell me about that Cassie lady."

"Cassiopeia?" It takes me a second to catch up with the change of subject.

I tell Andrew all about Queen Cassiopeia, her vanity and her toppled throne. I show him Polaris, the North Star, too.

"How do you know so much about this? I wouldn't be able to remember it all," he says.

"It's my whole life. The moon was full at the beginning of the month," I explain. "So it'll be a New Moon in about week.

That's pretty much the best 'seeing' conditions I could ask for. You know, when I track the comet next week."

Comet.

Waterman Scholarship.

Registration.

Birthday.

My stomach drops out. I can't scramble fast enough.

Registration is June 26th. *Today* is June 26th. I hop off the car.

"Holy crap, Andrew!" I cry.

"What? What?" He slides off the truck.

"I gotta go. I gotta go! I have to register for my scholarship. *That's* what I forgot to do tonight!"

"What scholarship?" Andrew's tone matches my panic.

Oh crap. I snatch up our towels and plates. Andrew follows suit and fishes his keys out from his pockets.

"I don't have time to explain. I have to send in a registration tonight and it needs to be in exactly by eleven. What time is it?"

"Damn! I said I'd get you home by ten. It's ten-thirty."

"Screw the curfew. It's due in thirty minutes!" I screech.

"Well, then let's get the fuck out of here," Andrew says. He gets everything in the truck in about ten seconds. I hesitate at the passenger door, stopping for one second.

"Thank you," I say.

"Don't just stand there," he demands in a joking way. "Get in the car!"

"Affirmative!" I cry and then hate myself. I say this to the Pi Naries, not to hot guys like Andrew. With the grill packed and our stuff in the back, we peel out of the camp. We race down the sandy road. Ahead of us is a big dune. Andrew revs the engine.

"Um, Andrew . . ."

He goes even faster. Up and up we go. This is not twenty miles an hour on Overlook Drive in Tucker's ancient Volvo.

"Big hill . . . big hill!" I cry.

Andrew guns the engine and we're airborne for a second. With a slam we're on the ground.

Andrew cries out, "Woo-hoo! You should forget a deadline all the time, Star Girl."

"I've never missed a deadline before," I cry. I have to yell over the wind rushing through the windows.

10:34.

I knew the registration email was due today, on my birthday. I knew it. It was on the calendar. It was on the *checklist* and I completely missed it. I had been so worried about the Scarlett Experiment that I didn't even spell-check it once. Forget the spell check. I could miss it altogether.

"We'll get you there," Andrew says.

We have to slow down past the guard or Andrew could get ticketed for speeding. Either way, I am sure they'll hear something from all the people we zoomed by at fifty miles an hour.

10:41.

Once we turn back onto the main street that leads out of Nauset, Andrew goes about seventy miles per hour.

"Turn at Shore Road," I cry and point down Aunt Nancy's street. It's possible that Andrew knows this house or that he's picked up Scarlett here before. It can't matter. I cannot walk home and make it in time. I will have to think of an excuse later.

The Waterman Scholarship has to come first.

"What happens if you don't make it?" Andrew asks. We're nearly there.

10:43.

"I can't even think about it," I say.

"Which one is your house?"

"The last one on the right."

He slows to a stop and I grab my bag from the floor. Any second I am expecting Andrew to mention something about the house and Scarlett, but he doesn't.

My hair is wavy from the salty water and I probably look like death. I can't care about it even though I desperately want to. I get out of the car.

I do have a second to say good-bye.

I lean a hand in his window. "I'm sorry about this," I say.

10:44.

"You're beautiful," he says without missing a beat.

"Oh, so you like girls who look like rabid, stressed-out animals?" I ask, picking up a string of wet hair and letting it slap onto my chest.

"Can I call you tomorrow?" he asks.

"I'd like that," I say. I have to go and before I back away again he lays his arm over the passenger seat and I can finally see what his tattoo says: *swim to the moon.*

"Hey, I have an idea," he says through the open window. "You like parties?"

I'm not exactly sure. Party invites don't exactly fall in my lap every day.

"Want to come to some too-fancy party at a restaurant tomorrow night? It's not black tie or anything, but it's dressier than normal."

I almost say yes immediately.

But I can't. It's my birthday dinner at the Lobster Pot and I'll be with Mom, Dad, Scarlett, and Aunt Nancy. It would be amazing for me to be at a party with Andrew.

"I can't," I say. "I have a family thing. But I wish I could." I back away slowly.

"Okay," he says with a glance to the clock. "Shit it's ten fifty. You gotta go."

"Bye!" I cry and haul ass up the front steps. I pause once I have the key in the door. Andrew's taillights already swoop around the corner. I want to dance! I want to sing!

I want to complete my damn registration.

I turn the key very slowly. I bite down on my lip as the door clicks and unlocks.

It's 10:52. I have eight minutes to boot up the computer, sign in, and attach the documents.

Aunt Nancy's house opens up to a foyer that leads directly into the kitchen. I expect Mom to be sitting there. She's bound to be in the lounge, in front of the TV. But the den is black, silent.

Forget that I'm late for registration, I'm late getting home. I've never even come home a minute after ten. Hell, I've never come within an hour of it. Tucker and I always went directly home when we were supposed to. I'll have to find a way to explain this to Mom and Dad.

I grab Mom's computer and hug it close to me. Courtesy of many lessons from Scarlett, I hold the house keys closed in my fist so they won't jingle. The sand on the bottom of my feet makes little crunching noises as I glide through the house. I will definitely leave a trail. I freeze. I'll clean it after I finish registering. I run up the staircase to the second floor and stop outside Mom and Dad's bedroom. I rise onto the balls of my feet. . . .

They are both completely passed out.

No one waited up to see if I came home.

No one knows.

With a dash, I run past Scarlett's room next and only glance in, but she is a lump under the covers. Her blonde hair cascades from under the sheet. Even Scarlett is back early.

I came home after Scarlett! She probably thought I was on the beach looking through my telescope. She would never imagine that I could possibly be in my underwear, in the ocean, with Andrew Davis.

I scurry up to my bedroom, shut the door behind me, and turn on the computer. As it boots up, I tap my foot. I hope Tucker was wrong about the site rejecting registrations at 11:01 p.m. He probably said it to tease me. He knows how gullible I am.

10:59.

The desktop boots up.

Sign into my email. Attach the documents. Loading . . . loading . . .

The clock switches to 11:00.

I've missed the deadline. I collapse into the desk chair. I have no other choice. I have to register late, without spell-checking and without making sure my drafted cover letter makes any sense. I don't know if they will accept these documents; I'll find out immediately if I receive a bounced-back email. Great.

I click it and it sends.

Bounce backs are usually within a few seconds. I stare at my email and refresh about fifteen times. When the clock strikes 11:03 I jump up and do a little dance in the middle of the room.

Tucker was wrong! Jerk. I almost reach for my phone to call him but stop, lowering my hand. I can't call him. What would I say? What is there to say between us?

Andrew totally came through. And the bonus? He doesn't know Scarlett well enough to know this house. I refresh the page of my email one more time, just to be safe. There's a *ding* and an email from the Waterman Scholarship highlights in my inbox. I gasp at first but read the subject line: REGISTRATION CONFIRMED.

I exhale and shut the lid of the computer. I walk toward my closet to get changed for bed.

I stop before the mirror on the back of the door.

You're beautiful.

I want to see what Andrew sees. Whatever it is, it's something no one has before. Not even me.

I take a step closer to the door, investigating myself through the sheen of the tank top. I take one last glance at my damp outfit, my hair flowing in wavy layers down to my ribs. Andrew's eyes, his infectious laugh—all of it comes to my mind. The tattoo on his arm, *swim to the moon.*

I peel off my clothes and jump into bed.

I can't wait to see Andrew again. I jump a little and giggle but have to throw my hand over my mouth. The Scarlett Experiment is promising.

Actually, that's a complete understatement.

So far, the Scarlett Experiment is a complete success.

TWELVE

"SIXTEEN. I STILL CAN'T BELIEVE IT," MOM SAYS the next afternoon. "I'm sorry again that we have to shop on your special day, Beanie."

"Mom, stop apologizing. My birthday was yesterday," I say. I don't want Mom to feel bad.

"But today is your big celebration!"

"It's okay. Really."

"Maeve, Bean knows this was the only day we could get the whole fitting room booked before Scarlett leaves," Aunt Nancy butts in.

We're in Viola's Dress Shop in Orleans. Why they need such a fancy shop here on the Cape seems unnecessary, but here we are, buying Scarlett a cocktail dress for her party.

They chose the theme of Titanic Dreams. *Titanic . . . Dreams.* Thousands of people died and we're throwing a good-bye party. Aunt Nancy has somehow convinced herself that anything with an ocean liner is classy. I suppose the fact that I am even noticing the layers of irony would make my English teacher proud.

I sit in a cushy seat while Scarlett steps out from behind the curtain of the dressing room.

"Lovely," Aunt Nancy coos.

Scarlett wears a black cocktail dress with thin spaghetti straps. Her boobs kind of hide under the material. My heart jumps. I hope Scarlett gets it. That would be a perfect dress to wear with Andrew. I immediately imagine Andrew and me at Pleasant Inn, the formal ocean-side restaurant in town.

Mom steps behind Scarlett and they face a full-length mirror. Mom raises the bust line up so it covers Scarlett's breasts completely. Dancing has made Scarlett's boobs a lot smaller than mine. Even though she's skinny, I'm tall, so we happen to wear a similar size. No ballerina worth her legs has more than B cups, Scarlett says.

"You'll just have to wear a strapless, padded bra," Mom says, dropping the fabric. "Do you like it?"

Scarlett cocks her head so her blonde curls fall in long ringlets down past her shoulders. Our hair is almost the same length. I don't know why but for some reason I feel like I've won because I realize my hair is longer. "It's okay," she says with a shrug.

Swim to the moon . . . what an interesting phrase. I wonder

what it's from? Why did he want it tattooed on his arm? Did it hurt?

"What's not to like about it?" Aunt Nancy squawks. I snap up in my seat. Scarlett knows she needs to be excited about everything to do with the party. If she doesn't swoon over the dress, Aunt Nancy will moan about Mom not having a job, Dad's measly salary, and how if only Dad had taken that office job when Scarlett was born, she wouldn't have to support all of us. Before I jump to save her butt, Scarlett breaks into a big toothy grin.

"It's perfect, Mom. Elegant."

"Oooh *lovely*," Aunt Nancy says, but she isn't replying to Scarlett. A salesgirl slides over a rack of thick, pastel dresses. Wow, Nancy is going to look reeeeeally pink.

"Okay, Beanie," Mom says and gestures to the pastel puke-fest on the rack.

"Okay, what?" I say.

"These dresses are for you."

I gasp—it's quiet but loud enough that Nancy mistakes it for happiness.

It's exactly as Gran predicted. I want to rip the dresses off the rack and smother Aunt Nancy with the lace. I can't say no; I don't have another dress for the party that would be appropriate in any way.

I push the curtain aside and slip off my T-shirt and shorts. Everything I am wearing today is mine, of course. I could never wear Scarlett's clothes in front of her. I cannot wait until she leaves tomorrow.

I try not to listen to the slip of the satin and the metal of the hanger as Scarlett changes out of the elegant black dress in the little room next to mine.

"Oh, I like this," Aunt Nancy says. Mom hands me a pink dress over the door. The ruffles on the bottom are scratchy. It's got thick straps and a straight neckline that cuts right over the bust. How the hell does it even go on? Headfirst? Feetfirst?

I pull it over my ankles and up my legs. The material is so thick.

Baby pink. Barbie pink. Cotton candy pink. Three layers of heinous frill and tulle.

I look like a tiered cupcake.

"I *don't* want to wear this," I say to the mirror inside the dressing room. The reflection is completely different than what I saw in the mirror last night. There is no way Andrew would call me insanely beautiful if he saw me in this.

"Well, come on out, let's see it," Mom says. She's got that surprise in her voice, the one that never expects me to disagree.

I slide the curtain aside and do come out. My bare feet are cold from the shop floor. Scarlett studies a notebook to avoid laughing directly to my face. She is so red-cheeked I want to chuck her stupid notebook out onto Main Street. On a page are notes handwritten in pencil of a dance she is meant to memorize before Juilliard orientation.

I try not to look at myself because I'll cry. The poufy fabric is shocking even in my peripheral vision.

"Beanie, you look wonderful," Aunt Nancy says and places her plump hand to her chest. "*That* is the dress. That's perfect."

"Maybe I could try a couple of others?" I ask. The rest of the dresses on the rack seem no better.

Aunt Nancy drops her hand from her chest and it plops into her lap.

"Beanie, this is Aunt Nancy's party," Mom tries to explain.

"I thought it was Scarlett's party," I say.

"Both," Nancy clarifies.

"What do you want to wear?" Mom asks.

I shrug and say, "Something else." The tulle presses the dress out so I can't even see my knees.

"Something black? With spaghetti straps?" Scarlett says and rolls her eyes. There's a burn in my chest and I look away. I hate that she knows what I want. I hate that when I need her on my side, she makes it worse. Can't she pick my side and stay on it like the other night and the teen dance debacle?

You gotta get a stronger backbone or people will walk all over you.

"Statistically speaking, I'll never wear this dress again," I say and try to channel Scarlett. "It's just that . . . it's not . . . it's not . . ."

"It's not what?" Mom asks.

"You always wear your science club T-shirts and old hand-me-downs. This is going to feel different," Aunt Nancy adds. "More mature."

"Much more mature," Mom parrots.

I want to say that this dress isn't me *at all*. I could find something else. My shoulders are sun kissed and my nose is bronzed. Even my hair has streaks of blonde highlights. I know it's only a few days into the Scarlett Experiment, but I feel different already.

"It's just a dress, Beanie," Mom says. "You don't care about these kinds of things."

I do now. I do.

Both Mom and Aunt Nancy look like all their happiness rides on me wearing this stupid dress.

All the dresses on the rack look like I should be a flower girl in a wedding. I don't know what to ask for, but it's not this dress with the scratchy fabric and the padding in the skirt.

What I would ask for, Scarlett is already getting, and I don't want her to know how much I wish I had her style.

"Maybe there's another color?" I ask.

"This is tasteful," Aunt Nancy says. "This one is perfect for you, you just can't see it."

I can see it. I can. Scarlett has never worn anything like this.

"You know Bean doesn't usually wear dresses," Mom says. "She's naturally a lab coat kind of girl."

I don't want to be a lab coat kind of girl anymore.

"They don't make dresses out of white lab coats," Scarlett says. She and Aunt Nancy laugh. Together. Like two small canaries sitting on a branch after a quick swim in a birdbath.

"Scarlett . . . ," Mom says gently, but her mouth curves upward. *Scarlett, come on. Help me out.* Scarlett sighs and leans forward in her chair to touch the hem of the dress.

"She could wear something more fitted, or without"—she rubs the fabric between her thumb and index finger—"all this lace."

"Lace is proper," Nancy says. "You're older, Scarlett. You can wear a formfitting dress. You're a dancer."

I can't see the top of my toes.

It's a tutu.

It's this dress or I make a scene. And there is no way I am complaining. Not while Scarlett is here watching me. It's clear I am not going to win this.

"You know," I say, my voice on the verge of breaking, "it's actually a very *sturdy* material. Long lasting," I say to the floor. "Probably water resistant."

"Great. It's settled. We will have to get her a better bra. I think that one's too small," Nancy says.

My cleavage is all Nancy can talk about. I'm not a little kid. I'm not a doll for them to dress up.

"So," Mom says once I'm back in the dressing room. "Scarlett, some wedges would be great with that dress. If you wear heels you'll sink into Nancy's lawn."

I would love tall wedges.

"Bean will probably need flats," Mom says.

"Ballet flats! Perfect," Nancy suggests.

Heat sears through me and I'm reminded of when I was five and Scarlett had a Barbie party. I was forced to wear so much lace padding under my dress, I could have floated away. I didn't mind it then. I didn't mind it when Mom would go shopping for me and leave a stack of sweaters on my bed with a note: *Try these! I'll return what doesn't fit!* She never asked me what I wanted before she went. Never has she said: It's your choice. What is important to you?

I cannot wear this dress in front of Tucker.

In the car ride on the way back to Nancy's house, I stare at my hands. Mom, Dad, Nancy, and even Scarlett need me to be predictable and reliable. When I'm studying the stars then they know who they are, they know what their roles should be.

Last night, these fingers ran along Andrew's jaw. He brought his lips to mine and whispered that I was beautiful.

Swim to the moon.

I love the way the phrase sounds in my head.

I loved his lips on mine.

I loved who I was last night.

THIRTEEN

"IT'S NOT LIKE THEY HAVE TO HIDE IT. LIKE THEY'RE celebrities or whatever," Ettie says that evening on the phone. I am out on the patio sitting in an Adirondack chair. The sunset falls over Pleasant Bay and skirts the tops of the trees.

The cupcake dress is wrapped in plastic in my bedroom closet and hopefully soon will be the victim of a horrible spontaneous closet fire.

Mom is blow-drying her hair up in her room, and Dad is tinkering with WHOI paperwork in the living room. Next to him are Mom's résumé and about fifty cover letters.

"I haven't seen them since Hilltop," Ettie says.

In my head I am kissing Andrew in the ocean.

"Let him come," I say and shake my hair back over my shoulders. "I'm tired of being upset about Tucker."

"This new optimism wouldn't have anything to do, per se, with a guy named Andrew, would it?"

She's finally getting to what I know she has been dying to talk about. "How is he, anyway?"

Ettie thinks Andrew is seventeen. I shaved off two years when she asked. Whatever. I'm sixteen (okay, barely); he's nineteen. It's not a *huge* deal. He's still a teenager, technically.

A small voice, deep down, asks, *then why are you lying about it?*

That small voice replies: *And what's worse? He doesn't know the truth.*

Scarlett joins Dad at the table. They examine a subway map of New York City. I ignore Ettie's question and switch subjects.

"The dress they bought me for Scarlett's party looks like a frosting factory exploded on some pink fabric."

I glance to see if anyone is checking up on me. I'm far enough away at the end of the patio, but I whisper anyway.

"And next time I see Andrew, I'll wear the dress Scarlett got. It's short and black."

Ettie's silent.

"I have to tell my mom I need to stay out until midnight. I've never had to worry about a curfew before. I don't know how many times I can convince Andrew I have to 'do something in the morning.'" I make air quotes even though Ettie can't see them.

I know what it means when she's so quiet. "What?" I ask.

"Nothing," she says, though I can tell it's something.

"Spill it, Ettie."

"Seems like a lot of stuff to be manipulating just to see a guy."

"He's not *just* a guy, and I'm not manipulating him."

"Do you know what will happen if Scarlett finds you in her clothes again? She'll kill you and you'll never see Andrew again. You got away with the bikini, but how are you going to pull off a fancy dress?"

I thought about showing up to that party at the restaurant in the cupcake dress. I wouldn't even look sixteen. I'd look twelve. If I wore the black sandals I have and Scarlett's dress, that would look perfect. I'd look older. More sophisticated. And I could continue the Scarlett Experiment.

"Bean?" Ettie says.

"Yeah," I say, coming back to the moment.

"Did you hear anything I said for the last two minutes?" I'm quiet, and Ettie sighs.

"If you do wear it, steam clean it in the bathroom when you get home," she says. "Hang it up and run the shower. It'll get rid of any smells or wrinkles after you wear it."

"Since when are you a stealth mode expert?"

"Movies. TV. Summerhill girl's bathroom."

"Excellent."

When we hang up, my plan is set.

I can't stop what is going on with Andrew, I don't even know how it started.

And either way, I don't want to.

I head upstairs to get dressed before we go to the Lobster Pot for dinner. I'm zipping up my jeans when Scarlett steps into the doorway.

"Ahem . . ." She dangles by her fingertips a small brown bag with lime green paper handles.

"Yes?" I say and cross my arms over my chest. I still hate her for not defending me at the dress shop.

She comes in and sits on the bed. She lifts the brown bag.

"Happy Birthday," she says.

I sit down too and face her directly.

"You got me something?"

"Don't I always?"

Well, yeah, now that I think about it, she does.

I scoot next to her and take the small bag. I reach in and wrap my fingers around a slim glass bottle.

"Wow. I should get you stuff more often. Look at that smile," Scarlett says.

The crystal bottle of Egyptian Musk lies in the palm of my hand.

"Your perfume," I say, my cheeks warm. Mom must have told her about the other night. "I only wore it that one time."

"What time?"

Oops.

"The other day," I admit.

She sighs. "Ask me when you borrow my things, please."

"How did you know I liked it?" I ask.

"You smelled it at home, like, ninety times. And I do live with you, dork."

I didn't know she saw me do that. I didn't think she noticed me very much at all.

"I ordered it online and had it sent to me. I didn't think it would come in time."

The perfume bottle glints from the track lighting above.

"Thank you," I say and curl my fingers around the little vial instead of hugging my sister. I think she might embrace me, right then. But she doesn't. She gets up instead, leaving the scent of Egyptian Musk trailing behind her—it smells better on her, more exotic.

"Don't worry about that dress," she says, stopping at the door. "The one for the party."

"Easy for you to say."

"It's mostly going to be my friends, anyway. You won't even know most of the people there."

"Tucker will be there. Maybe he can take a picture and send it to Becky for a laugh."

"Stop it," she says, still lingering at the doorway. "Who cares what he thinks?"

She leaves and her soft footsteps descend the stairs toward dinner.

"Me," I whisper when she's out of earshot.

I set the perfume on my night table and hurry down the stairs after my sister.

Lobster carcasses sit on each of our plates—well, all except Scarlett's, who only ordered a garden salad with grilled chicken. Silver tongs and discarded tails litter the table. Butter stains my paper napkin. Scarlett's bowl of salad is empty with only dregs of vinegar left behind. If it were me, I would dip pieces of bread into the salad dressing. Scarlett doesn't do that . . . ever.

I love the sweet smell of the hand wipes after a great seafood meal. It means dessert is coming. Lobster Pot chocolate cake is on its way. The frosting is about ten inches thick. Mom and Dad lift a blue box from under the table—it's as big as a cereal box but way wider. How did I not notice it? Dad must have gone back to the car when I was ripping my lobster to shreds. They send it down the table to me.

"Scarlett!" Dad calls.

She hangs on the bar talking to a bartender but saunters back to the table.

The blue present makes its way to my seat. Attached by a piece of tape on top of the blue box is a white envelope and another box, but this one is magenta and much smaller. I definitely know who the pink box is from—Nancy.

I tear open the white envelope. I expect a card, but there is only a ticket. A *plane* ticket.

"San Francisco!" I cry. "I'm seeing Gran?"

"She sent it earlier this week," Mom says with a huge smile.

There is a folded note inside that says, *See you Labor Day weekend, XO, Gran and Gracie.* There's a P.S. in Gran's sturdy handwriting: *We'll let you drive Gracie's Jetta.* In Gracie's slim writing beneath that it reads: *But you might not ever want to drive again!*

Scarlett sits down and I pass her the note from Gran.

"Wow, lucky," she says.

I can't help but notice that Nancy has one lone eyebrow raised.

"Right before school starts?" she asks.

"Okay!" Dad chimes in quickly. "Open ours."

I pull off the thick blue paper and find there are a few items in the box. A set of sticky stars for my ceiling.

"These ones are accurate to the New England sky in March," Dad says, because he knows me too well. Beneath that package is a small box and another envelope. Inside the small box is a set of silver studs in the shape of stars. I place them in my ears right away.

"She should clean the—"

"Too late, Nancy," Dad says.

Inside the other card envelope is two hundred dollars cash.

"Dad . . . ," I say. The envelope sits in the palm of my hand. "This is too much."

"That's to see Gran," Mom says. "And to have fun."

Nancy squirms in her seat and I know she wants to say hundreds of things.

She purses her lips as the chocolate cake is brought out. Little candles flicker on top of the cake and Nancy stops her tantrum to sing.

"Happy Birthday to you . . . ," our table sings, and soon other people in the dining area sing too.

Scarlett's tiny voice chirps over the crowd. She texts on her phone while she sings along. The waiter lowers the cake to the table in front of me. Mom, Dad, Nancy, and Scarlett all smile as their rousing rendition comes to a close.

"Make a wish, Beanie," Mom says.

As the little flames flicker, I do wish:

I wish I could be who I am when I'm with Andrew—but all the time.

I blow out the candles, and as the swirls of smoke curl to the ceiling, I pray that birthday wishes come true.

Slices of cake are passed out as I open Nancy's box.

A set of keys sits inside on a bed of pink tissue paper.

Car keys.

No way. My jaw drops. "These are . . ."

"Don't get too excited. It's my car. The Volvo, which means it won't be brand-new."

"Are you kidding me?" I cry. Nancy has never done anything like this, ever. She never got Scarlett a car! I'm ready to jump up and hug—

"You can really expand your horizons with this car. Get some new hobbies. You could even come down here on some off days from school."

Visit?

Scarlett keeps texting, but her lack of response tells me she's surprised. Her all-too-casual reaction is a clear giveaway.

"This will be very helpful for you to do things outside science. Scarlett loves to dance, but she also loves movies, art, and all kinds of things. You could do that too."

"Can I go?" Scarlett asks without a glance up from her phone. I close the lid on the box with the car keys.

"Mom." Scarlett finally looks up from her phone. "I need to go home and change. I can't go to the party in this."

"Hold on, Scarlett."

"I *leave* tomorrow, shouldn't I get to do what I want to?"

Scarlett says, though this time it's a whine. "I stayed the whole dinner."

Gee, thanks. Feeling the love here.

"Oh, go, Scarlett." Mom turns back to Nancy. "This car is too much."

"I have to get a new one anyway!" Nancy says. "And it's too late, I already signed over the title."

It's 7:48. Andrew texted earlier and said he was going to the party around 9:30. I want to be with Andrew. I want to be with someone who sees what I wish everyone else would see.

Scarlett tucks in her chair. "See you guys," she says.

"Where are you going?" Mom asks.

"To a party with Curtis and Tate."

She motions to the bartender. Except now, he's not in his red Lobster Pot shirt. He's waiting for her in a T-shirt and jeans. Now that I look, I think I recognize him from town the other night. I make sure to keep my head turned away in case I see him out with Andrew sometime. I don't want him to recognize me.

My stomach sinks. If Scarlett is meeting Curtis, I can't go to the party to meet Andrew. Scarlett will probably be there. I won't get a chance to see what she's wearing, but knowing Scarlett, it's tight and short.

"Happy Birthday, Bean," Scarlett adds before leaving.

Dad gets the check and Mom cleans up all the wrapping paper. Her cheeks are red.

Nancy is still squawking away about how good the car will be for me and all the interests I should and shouldn't have. I want to be anywhere else but here. For the first time in sixteen years I actually wish I could go do something else instead of our mini-golf tournament.

"Ready to beat your old man?" Dad asks. He leans a hand on the back of my chair. I smile because I would never disappoint Dad. He could never guess that I would rather be meeting an older boy at a party than playing mini-golf.

"As always!" I say and follow my family out the door.

FOURTEEN

I WIN BECAUSE DAD ALWAYS THROWS THE MINI-
golf game on my birthday. Within fifteen minutes of getting
home, Dad is snoring on the couch and Mom is reading in their
bedroom. Nancy is in her room getting ready for bed.

I knew what I was going to do the second I hit the eighteenth
hole at the windmill. Even though Scarlett is potentially going
to be there, I want to go to the party. I'll peek in and see if she's
there. If she is, I'll go home, and no one will know. If by some
shred of a miracle, she isn't there, I can text Andrew and pretend
I got out of my "family obligation" early. Andrew said it was kind
of formal, so it's the perfect occasion to wear the black dress.
First, I have to make sure Scarlett isn't wearing it.

Asking for a later curfew is a risk, but I'm trying it anyway. I need to think of an excuse to go out tonight, and no one can see what I am wearing. I don't feel so bad lying about this. I'm doing what Nancy wants me to do—I'm pursuing other interests. It's just not on her terms. This is on my terms and they wouldn't understand.

"Mom," I say gently as I stand in the doorway of her bedroom. I make sure to dress in jeans and a T-shirt to avoid suspicion.

"Yes?" she says, turning a page.

"I have some star charting to do and, well, I was kind of hoping to head down to the beach. I know it's late, but it could be an important night."

Mom shrugs. "Sure," she says.

Seriously? That's it?

"Great!" I say. "And I was sort of wondering if I could come back a little later. You know? Like, eleven?"

I check the clock: 9:40. Scarlett's barely been at the party an hour.

Mom is quiet, her eyes focused on the page. She's considering this so I talk fast.

"Because the darker it is, the better the view of the night sky. And I'll bring my cell phone and—"

"Bean, make sure to put your presents up in your room?" Mom asks, her hand on the next page of her book. She still hasn't looked up at me for more than a few seconds. I blink a couple times. She isn't considering my curfew—not at all. "I don't want to hear it from Nancy," she adds.

The moonlight shines through the panoramic windows and

all I see is the harbor in the distance. I don't want to look at Mom because I don't want to see her *not* looking at me.

"I think it's fine if you research tonight," she says.

"I'll make sure to be here at eleven. On the dot."

"See you then," Mom says, nose still in the book. She isn't coming up for air, she and Dad have that in common when they are engrossed in something they like.

I decide to run with this good fortune. I snatch the dress and sneak up the stairs. As I pass Scarlett's bedroom and make my way to the third floor, an uneasiness nibbles at me. As I close the door to my bedroom and tuck the tag into the inside of the dress, that *feeling* I had at Viola's dress shop prickles over me again. The one when Nancy and Mom decided on ballet flats without even checking to see what kind of shoes I would want for the party. The uneasiness lingers as I zip up the dress and pull my hair back into a low ponytail. Only when I call out, "See you guys in a bit! I have my cell!" does it float away. I hate when I can't pinpoint my emotional reactions.

I have a Scarlett Levin plan in place: I stash pajamas in a bag under an Adirondack chair. At midnight, I'll walk around the back of the house, grab my PJs, change in the darkness of the patio, and come inside. I grab a little black sweater from the front closet. I think it might even be Mom's. I send Andrew a text.

ME: Where did you say this party was?

ANDREW: Are you coming!?

ME: Maybe. Trying to get out of family stuff.

ANDREW: Break Away Café. Want me to get you?

I can't tell him to leave and get me yet. Scarlett could be there and I have to try to scope it out first. Break Away is the bistro that overlooks the runway at the tiny Orleans airport. It's literally about four blocks away. It's definitely walkable.

Crap. I forgot the actual restaurant is on the second floor. I won't be able to scope it out first to see if Scarlett is there. Whatever. I'll improvise.

I tiptoe over the gravel in Nancy's driveway. It crunches beneath the flat bottoms of my sandals.

I move as fast as I can in this tight dress.

I turn onto Mooring Street, where the Break Away is located. I pass by a group of girls sitting on top of a picnic table outside of the country store. I know those girls. I recognize the one with the long black hair. These were the girls in the Seahorse. They wave at me, so I stop. I could go over—they're smiling.

I pull my sweater over my shoulders and the click of my sandals on the pavement stops at the edge of the sidewalk.

"I like your dress," one of the girls says. She is small with a shock of short platinum hair.

"Did you ever get that necklace?" the girl with the black hair asks. I'm surprised that she remembers me.

"Thanks. It's my sister's. And no, not yet. I want that necklace, though; it's amazing, right?"

"Definitely."

"What are you up to?" I ask.

"Meeting up with some guys we talked to on Nauset Beach."

I could see myself hanging out with them.

"Nice," I say. The girl with the black hair seems like she can talk to boys on the beach without needing to wear her sister's

American flag string bikini. She probably has her own.

"I'm meeting a friend at a party," I say. "Well, I guess he's more than a friend."

The girls ooh and ah. "Have fun. . . ," they say nearly in stereo.

I would love more than anything to invite them. I want to be that girl, one time, the one who has an invite to an awesome party, the one who has all the backstage access.

"I'd invite you, but it's not my party . . . ," I say.

"That's okay," the girl with the black hair says. I start to turn away.

"You should come out with us this weekend." I turn back. She gestures to the other girls at the table.

"Really?"

"Yeah," she says, and stands up. "Give me your phone."

"Great!" Too enthusiastic. Calm down. "I mean, that would be cool."

She types in her number. "I'm Claudia."

"Sarah," I reply and give her my cell phone number.

"I don't leave until August, so I'm, like, begging them to stay." She nods to her friends.

"Me too!" I say. "I mean, I'm here until August."

"Perfect. Maybe I'll have one friend who's here for the *whole* summer." She smiles at me and it hits me that *I* am potentially this friend.

I glance at the time—10:06.

"Crap. I have to go."

"Have fun!" they all call. I wave and head off toward the Break Away.

I have to do these tiny running steps all the way to the restaurant parking lot. I get there by 10:10 and scan for Curtis's Jeep, but I don't see it. I don't know what kind of car the bartender from the Lobster Pot drives, so I have no idea if Scarlett is inside. Some people are idling out front smoking cigarettes and I approach a girl with long dreads. I don't have a choice. I can't go up there and risk it *in* Scarlett's dress. I walk up to her and throw my shoulders back—another Scarlett trademark.

"Have you guys seen Scarlett? Blonde? Ballerina." Pain in the ass, I want to add.

The girl with the dreads turns to one of the guys next to her, who I didn't recognize at first. It's Tate from the Lobster Pot.

"She left with Curtis, I think," he says. I immediately take a step back. Maybe he won't recognize me all dressed up. My hair was down at dinner.

"Like five minutes ago," the girl with the dreads adds. "Do you have her number?"

"Oh yeah. Definitely. Thanks," I say casually and keep checking to see if Tate tries to place me. "I'll text her. You know. On the phone." I back away before I keep rambling on nervously, but they don't seem to care because they're back in a conversation and don't look up at me again.

Freedom! I can go into the party and I don't have to worry. Happy Birthday to me!

I head up the stairs. I wish I could tell Andrew all the good news about my birthday, that I am going to see Gran *and* that I got a car. But I can't, so I will have to settle for telling him the next best thing: that in five days the comet will be mine. I take another step and on cue, Andrew walks out onto the darkened stairs. The light from inside the restaurant highlights his frame. He is wearing jeans and a blue button-down shirt that really brings out his tan, and has a jacket slung over one arm. He looks incredible.

He hurries down the stairs but stops abruptly, looking me up and down. He shakes his head a little. "Are you trying to give me a heart attack?" he asks.

Andrew extends his hand to me in his now familiar way. When I take it, he draws me to him and kisses me gently. As we head upstairs, the music swirls out the second-story windows and across the tiny airport.

"What's the point of watching people take off in airplanes to go somewhere that you're not? Seems like a tease," I say.

I want to fly. Get in a plane, feel the engines rumble beneath my seat, and take off and see the world. Explore all the places I want to go.

Upstairs in the restaurant, there's a huge buffet in the corner and the smell of barbecue, dressings, and corn on the cob fills the room. People are everywhere: eating, dancing, and ordering drinks. A live band plays in the corner; the music is so loud it makes the floor shake.

I wonder if anyone can tell I'm officially sixteen. My hair is coiffed up in a clip. Ettie seemed to think it would make me seem older.

Andrew hangs his jacket over a chair once we get inside. This is his boss's fortieth birthday party and banners surround the room. YOU'RE OVER THE HILL, TERRY! I wish that it could say HAPPY BIRTHDAY, SARAH!

"It's open bar for wine or beer," Andrew says.

Crap. What's open bar?

"Whatever you're having," I say.

"I'm having a Coke because I'm driving. I hear the wine is pretty good," he says.

I wonder how many other decisions he makes every day because of the accident. I immediately wonder how many decisions I have made because other people have pressured me in my life. I don't like it, but I think people are more influential on me than I'd care to admit.

"You okay?" Andrew asks.

"What?" I say, and Andrew places a couple of dollars in the tip jar.

"You're frowning."

"No, I'm totally fine," I say and shake myself out of it. On a positive note I figured out that "open bar" means *free*.

I take the glass of wine and sniff the contents. I've never had alcohol before and hopefully Andrew can't tell.

What would Scarlett do? Scarlett would have some wine and relax. She wouldn't immediately be able to recount the police officer's statistics when he came to school to discuss drug and alcohol abuse. Even though that is exactly what is humming through my mind.

I sip.

"Ugh," I say and pull away. "The ethanol alcohol ratio is really very high. At least eight percent. Like sour grape juice. Why do people drink this crap?"

Oops.

He breaks into that same big teddy bear laugh that I heard on the phone the other night.

I clear my throat and toss my hair back. "I mean it's a bit more bitter than I realized. I'm a beer girl myself." Not that I ever had beer either.

"Wow," he says. "That is exactly why I like you."

"What? What is?"

"You, Star Girl." He pauses then adds, "You."

Andrew's hand links around my waist and we enter into the fray of the party.

He asks me to dance and we do. I keep trying to sneak a peek at his tattoo, but his shirt is covering it. Our bodies fit and Andrew can definitely move to the beat. He doesn't make me feel like I should worry what I look like when the dance floor is packed with people. But, either way, after forty-five minutes or so of dancing, I should check out my hair and makeup.

"I'll be right back," I say to Andrew. A line of sweat rolls down my back as I walk down the hallway to the ladies' room. The satin of the dress moves softly against my body, and my hair is coming out of its updo in long tendrils that curl on my shoulders. I catch a glimpse of myself in a wall mirror. For the first time in a long time, maybe ever, I feel *gorgeous*. This is exactly what I needed after the debacle at Viola's.

I come out of the stall a couple minutes later and check my makeup. There's a girl at the mirror already. She's got a black bob and bright blue eyes. Her sundress is a pretty, deep green. She didn't do it up for tonight, like me.

"I like your dress," I say and open my little bag.

She puckers her mouth and applies a lip gloss.

"Thanks," she says with a quick glance at me. "Don't I know you?" she asks.

Oh no.

"Yeah, you work at the Lobster Pot, don't you? I heard tips suck there this summer," the girl says.

"No. I don't work there. I—"

She blots her lips together and clicks her purse closed.

"Not like last summer," she says, talking over me. "We were raking it in at the Blue Oyster. Still early, though." She reaches into her bra and hikes up her boobs to show more cleavage. "See ya," she says and blows past me.

"See ya," I say, and once she leaves I lift my boobs up just like she did. Yikes, I don't think they need to be pushed up any more. I push them back down and leave the bathroom to join Andrew. When I sit down at the table of Andrew's friends, he immediately takes my hand. One of his coworkers, Susie, leans across the table toward me.

"Sarah, is it? Our friend Andrew here is the best secret keeper on all of Cape Cod. He won't tell us anything about you."

He wipes his brow with a napkin; we're both sweaty from dancing. "She's going to MIT in the fall," Andrew says. "There—I told you something."

My gut tightens to hear the lie from Andrew's mouth. I wish we could pretend I never said anything and that somehow it could be spontaneously erased from Andrew's mind. I forget sometimes that I even lied about my age. We haven't really talked about it since that first day at Nauset.

I wonder immediately if Susie knows Scarlett. I am thankful yet again as I look across the table at Susie that Scarlett is going to be gone for a month. Somehow whenever anyone but Andrew asks about my "future" I get tongue-tied. Looking into the eyes of someone you are so blatantly lying to *feels* wrong.

Except when I lie to Andrew.

He likes me dressed in Scarlett's clothes. He wants me to be going to MIT in the fall. I explain to Susie that astronomy is my passion and perhaps I'll go on to work at NASA or SETI one day. Susie leans her chin on her hand.

"So interesting," she says.

"There's a meteor shower next month," I say, happy I can actually keep talking about something that is patently true. "Perseid," I explain. Susie's skin is weathered. Even though her eyes tell me she's younger, I see what hours upon hours in the sun have done to her skin. She asks me questions about the comet and my experiment. I glance at my cell—it's 11:30 p.m.—the girl from the bathroom approaches the table.

"Hey, Suse," the girl in the green dress says, but she's looking directly at Andrew.

"Maggie!" Susie's voice almost squeaks. She sounds like Mom whenever someone buys her a gift she really hates. "Sarah was telling us about a meteor shower next month."

Andrew sips on his Coke and leaves his hand around my chair.

"Oh really?" Maggie looks me up and down. "We met in the bathroom. Did you buy that dress at Viola's?" she asks me.

"I brought it from home." Another lie, but it just flies out.

"Oh, you're a *tourist*," she says and crosses her arms. "Classy, Andrew."

Her eyes narrow and I'm reminded of the popular girls at school, Becky Winthrop's friends. Mean girls are apparently not included in the category of people influenced by the Scarlett Experiment.

"What was the name of the meteor shower again?" Susie asks me.

"Perseid," I say, but it is hollow.

". . . Fascinating," Maggie drones. "Did you guys come from an event before this?" Maggie asks.

"No," I say. *Something* is going on. Who is this girl?

My hands lie in my lap and Andrew's fingers intertwine with my own. Maggie's shoes are flip-flops with little blue gems.

Maggie is also in a summer dress.

So is Susie.

My cheeks warm. No one else is dressed like me. Oh my God. Scarlett says being overdressed is more embarrassing than having toilet paper stuck to your shoe. And I'm *completely* over-dressed for this party.

Maggie smirking at me with her eyebrow raised.

A rush of heat throttles me.

Images rush through my mind:

Becky Winthrop.

Tucker.

The comet and that cupcake dress and a *car* for my birthday.

She needs more interests.

Change. Become someone else.

You gotta get a stronger backbone or people will walk all over you.

"Is this what girls do?" I blurt out. "To each other?" My words are short.

Maggie's smile falls. I stand up and snatch my purse. Andrew stands up too. I almost take a step away, but I stop and ask Maggie, "I'm curious. Do you guys have some kind of online forum? Or newsletter that you send out? Because you're good. You're all the same. You know exactly how to make someone feel like complete shit. You're like every single girl in my high school."

Susie snickers and nudges the woman next to her.

"Excuse me," I say and walk away.

"You're a bitch, Mags," Andrew says.

There's the scrape of his chair and Susie says, "Andrew, give her a second."

My whole body rattles. I'm vibrating head to toe as I march from the table and out of the Break Away.

I pull the sweater a bit tighter over my shoulders, but it's not enough to stop the chills. Once I get to the parking lot, I catch a reflection of myself in a car window and roll my eyes. I lift my purse up to cover my cleavage.

I want to call Mom and Dad. It'll make them feel better when I've asked to stay out so late. Maybe if I call them it will make *me* feel better to hear their voices.

"I told you I didn't want to see or hear from you, Maggie," I hear Andrew say from the top of the stairs. His anger makes his words sharp.

"Whatever, Andrew. That girl is a *tourist*. Who dresses like that for a summer birthday party?"

I step farther into the parking lot and take out my cell. The phone rings a couple of times on the other end.

"Hello?" Mom says.

"Hey, it's me, Bean." I exhale away from the mouthpiece of the phone so she can't hear my voice shaking.

"Beanie?!" She's either surprised or angry, I can't tell which one. Oh boy—here it is, I should have brought the damned telescope. She somehow knows I lied.

"Just wanted to remind you I'll be out late tonight. You said I could stay out a little later? For my birthday? Remember? Like eleven? Eleven thirty?" Making excuses seems safe. I wish I hadn't called.

Mom yawns.

"I thought you were home already," she says.

"But—" The rest of my words stop at my teeth.

"Be careful," she says.

Mom always says, "Be careful." She says it to everyone, even when they go to the grocery store. She hangs up.

She thought I was home?

I immediately dial Tucker's number without thinking but click end at the first ring. Ugh. That means he'll see the missed call. A tiny voice wonders if he'll call back. I don't want to answer it either way. I can't tell him about my humiliation tonight at dinner or here at the Break Away in a dress that's too fancy for the occasion. Tucker's not mine to call anymore. He's not the same. We're not the same.

I can't call Ettie, either. She's at an overnight for band camp.

"Sarah?" Andrew calls my name from the middle of the stairs.

I thought you were home already.

I won't go back to the party. I never want to go in there again. *Who dresses like that for a birthday party?*

It's actually really hard to think someone is home when they aren't. People make noise—even in a big house.

"Sarah?"

"Yeah?" I call, but my voice squeaks.

Andrew's footsteps move to the asphalt.

She thought I was home?

Radium, potassium, neon. My bottom lip trembles. Crap. *Constellations. Name the constellations. Cassiopeia. Ursa Major.*

"Sarah!" Andrew's voice echoes behind me.

That uneasiness is back. That same uneasiness I felt before I left to meet Andrew. Like there is a hole in the center of my belly.

Andrew meets me at the edge of the parking lot. He steps in front of me and searches my eyes.

"Maggie's crazy. She's my ex. We dated last summer. And she wasn't supposed to be here tonight." He takes a step toward me and cups my face with his hands. The calluses on his palms rub at the apples of my cheeks.

"I thought this was a fancy party," I say.

"It *is.*"

"I didn't know I was overdressed. I thought, I thought . . ." I can't finish.

"You could wear a prom dress to the fish market and I wouldn't give a shit," Andrew says.

The intensity in his eyes lifts my spirits a little.

"Really? A prom dress?"

He drops his hands. "Yes. And I'm sure you'll tell me—"

"That would be highly impractical. The satin or the sequins could get caught on any number of shelves or—" He stops me with a kiss. Whenever he looks at me like that, I can't be Scarlett. I slip up. How does he have this effect on me?

When Andrew pulls away he kisses my nose, too. "Let's get out of here. Wanna go somewhere? How about the beach?"

"Okay," I say. The embarrassment still churns my stomach even though it seems like my factual outburst was kind of . . . good?

Once we get back to his pickup, I lean my back against the truck.

"You certainly told her off," he says and raises his eyebrows.

"I've never done that in my entire life."

"You can hold your own. I like that."

Andrew presses against me.

His touch just makes me want to do something crazy. Before meeting me, Andrew had never met a girl who tracked a comet. What about a girl who could show him the deepest parts of the ocean?

"No," I say. "No beach tonight. I know what I want. I want to take *you* somewhere you've never been."

Andrew raises an eyebrow. "Where is that?"

I want to show him something real.

The real me.

FIFTEEN

"WHERE WE'RE GOING IS A SURPRISE," I SAY. "WE have to stop at my house. But no one can see us," I say.

"A covert operation? Excellent!"

I laugh from the bottom of my gut. A real laugh. My laugh. "Let's go," I say.

We get into the truck and I slide the window down, I want the wind to whip through my hair. Maybe I want it to sting my cheeks. Andrew's hand slides onto my kneecap.

"I should have told you about Maggie," he says.

"It's okay," I say and mean it. "My ex is coming to my sister's going-away party. No matter how badly I don't want him to."

Andrew squeezes my knee again.

"You should wear that dress all the time. Grocery shopping, taking out the garbage . . . ," he says. "I mean it. We can go clamming. I'll wear a tux and you wear that dress, it'll be perfect."

I laugh and playfully slap his arm. As we pull out of the parking lot, I say, "This is very serious. My family thinks I'm twelve. They want to keep me on the shortest leash they can. If they see you, there will be a lot of . . . questions."

"Sounds fun," Andrew says, and we turn down Shore Road. Once we get to Seaside Stomachache, I slide out of the car and Andrew kills the motor.

"You stay on the street," I whisper. He salutes me.

To the left side of the house is a long driveway canopied by trees. Dad's car is first in line. His WHOI security pass is in the inner console. Dad's key is a sensory key—it's electronic and when I get to a WHOI building, all I have to do is hold it up to the keypad and the door unlocks.

We'll have access to the shop where the *Alvin* is being repaired.

My heels crunch over Nancy's shelled driveway. My heart is thudding away. I tiptoe to Dad's car and try to keep low until I get to the driver's-side door.

This is kind of awesome. A shaft of light moves above and a shadow takes over the dashboard of the car.

I jump down and hide below the driver's-side door. The kitchen window overlooks the driveway. I peek up. Dad is washing something in the kitchen sink. His big head takes up almost the whole window. He could look down at any moment. He wouldn't see me in the dark, but he would see the inner light on in his car if he catches me with the door open.

I glance back at Andrew, but all I see is his darkened profile.

I need to do this by myself. I'm not at home, sitting on the curb outside the house, waiting for Tucker to show up. I'm not sitting around only thinking about science. I'm living my life. Nancy would be so proud.

I pull on the door handle, lay my belly flat on the seat, barely lift the middle console, and snatch the key. I close the door and I'm off.

I tip tap over the shells as fast as I can, and once I'm on the asphalt, I slide into the seat next to Andrew.

"Let's go, let's go!"

We use the side entrance to building 40.

"You realize this is trespassing," Andrew says. "At Woods Hole."

"Only kind of," I reply with a giggle. "I sort of live here in the summer. Well, I usually do, but I haven't been as much this year."

We step into the darkened foyer. Only a couple floodlights illuminate the hallway toward the mechanic's shop.

I take Andrew's hand.

"I've never been here," he says. "Even in the day."

He stops and pulls me back.

"Wow," he says. He looks through an enormous window and a soft blue light illuminates his face.

Through the window are four enormous tanks. Inside them are dozens of starfish: small, silver, black, big—all different kinds. They creep slowly through the water in that periwinkle light.

"Did you know?" I say. "Starfish have eyes on the ends of their arms. They're microscopic. So if they lose an arm they lose an eye, too. Kind of sad."

Andrew cups my cheek like he did in the parking lot and exhales.

"What?" I say.

His eyes glitter from the watery light filtering through the glass.

"Where have you *been*?" he asks with a shake of his head.

"What do you mean? I've been—"

"Where have you been?" he says and holds his hand behind my head. Only this time when he asks, it's not a question.

"East Greenwich, Rhode Island?" I offer.

He laughs but keeps it quiet.

"Come on," I say, and pull him down the hall toward the *Alvin*.

When we reach the shop, I listen but don't hear anything beyond the door but the hum of the HVAC. We step into the room and the *Alvin* sits beneath one spotlight. There it is. The viewports are gone and the cameras, too. The personnel hatch where scientists enter the *Alvin* is open. I bet by this time next week, it'll be completely disassembled.

It's usually six feet long, but the *Alvin* seems smaller somehow, without all its parts.

"Okay, Star Girl. What is *that*?" Andrew asks.

"It's a deep-sea submersible. It's been to the *Titanic*. A couple times, actually."

Andrew runs his fingers along the side of the titanium shell of the *Alvin*. It makes everything in me warm to see him caress the machine I love so much. I bend over. At first I'm not even sure why I'm compelled to do this, but I slip off my shoes. I do it slowly like I've seen girls do on TV.

"The day I knew that the stars would be my life, my dad took me to the planetarium in Boston," I say.

"Never been," Andrew says. He leans his hand against the *Alvin*. I catch him checking out my legs, and his eyes move up over the rest of my body until they reach my eyes.

"I sat in the darkness and my whole future changed. It was the first time I ever realized that space could potentially go on infinitely. Can you imagine that? Stretching outward? Forever?"

Andrew takes a step closer to me and drops his hand from the submersible. I reach up to the clip holding my hair and let it go. My hair tumbles out and flutters onto my shoulders. I'd seen some of the girls do that in the hallways at school. I'd seen it in movies and TV, too, but never had the opportunity to try it myself. Never understood its impact—until now.

"From that night on, I studied all the constellations. I knew what I loved and who I had to be."

"I respect that," Andrew says quietly.

"But maybe it's changing. Have you ever had a moment like that? When who you thought you were shifted?"

Andrew nods. "The day Curtis first took me to Brewster. He volunteered at the juvie camp before I did and got me into it." He takes another step and stops inches from me. I love the hum of the body heat between us. "It meant a lot to me to help. Still does."

"Why doesn't Curtis work there anymore?"

"Once you're charged with involuntary manslaughter, you can't exactly volunteer at a juvenile detention center after that."

"Did he love it as much as you do?"

"More, I think. I think that's why he—" He pauses. "—is how he is these days."

"So, why are you lobstering if you love Brewster so much? Can't you work full-time at the camp?"

He backs away, putting distance between us, and leans on the *Alvin* again.

"Sometimes you have to do what's right, even if it's not what you love, for a bunch of different reasons. Mike's entire family lobsters. His brothers run the whole line of boats now. They really needed someone to manage it, help finance, run the offices . . ."

"So you lobster to help them?"

"I have to."

"But it's *not* your fault that Mike died."

"I know you don't agree but, I have to," he says and runs his fingers along the side of the *Alvin* again. "I do it for Mike."

He keeps his eyes on the sub when he says, "Thanks for taking me here. This is amazing." He has changed the subject again like he's done nearly every time I mention the accident. Again, I let him. We didn't come here tonight to work out our innermost problems. I want to kiss Andrew's pain away. I want to comfort him. I lean in first and our lips meet.

He shows me the way. My mouth follows his movements and it's better than when we were in the water. Because we're here.

"Where have you been?" I whisper when we pull apart.

He runs a hand over my head and says, "Brewster, Mass."

We share a laugh.

"So tell me. Why the deep-sea sub?" he asks and keeps us so close our chests touch. I want to keep him this close to me forever.

"Scientists believe that the deep ocean is what life would be like on other planets. Deep-sea life can survive without light and without oxygen. It's completely plausible that life at the bottom of the sea would be similar to life billions of light-years away. The *Alvin* is the closest thing I've got to a spaceship."

"You make everything I see . . . better. More interesting," Andrew says.

First he kisses the nape of my neck and slowly comes back up to my lips. I want him to do more than kiss me. I am surprised by what I want. Andrew leans his back against the *Alvin*. He pulls me with him so we lean together against the sub. We keep kissing.

He runs his hands over my body again and again until my knees buckle.

"I've never broken into a government facility before," Andrew says as we idle in front of Nancy's house.

"I've taken up your whole week," I say. "And you just met me."

He cups my cheek in his warm hand.

"I like it," he says.

A soft breeze blows through the window and against my skin. I'd almost forgotten the debacle with the dress until the wind cools my shoulders. I made a fool of myself and the memory cracks the polished veneer of the night and the *Alvin*.

Andrew has been watching me. He shakes his head.

"Trouble. You are going to be trouble."

"How so?"

"I like you," he says. "And that's trouble for me."

My shoulder and chest are cold when he moves away. I shiver, wanting to understand what he means but loving the mystery a little.

"I can show you the comet next Friday, if you want. It's the one I've been tracking all summer. It finally reaches its perihelion."

"Whatever it is you said sounds great. Perry-redion."

"Perihelion."

"Exactly," Andrew replies.

He's not running from me. He's not scared of my science talk or the facts I know. He's not even confused about a massive submersible that inches across the ocean floor. Sure, the Scarlett clothes are convincing and I wouldn't have gotten very far without acting like my sister. I can share all of this with him—and it's okay. At least it's okay so far.

I want more from Andrew, more than the information he's giving me about the accident, more about who he is on the inside. I want to spend so much more time in his arms, delving into all of the details. I've never felt like this. It makes my breath shudder.

"You sure you won't be sick of me?" I ask and clear my throat. I unlatch the car door.

"You?" he says with a smile. "Never."

SIXTEEN

THE NEXT MORNING, I WALK DOWNSTAIRS AND text Claudia back. She sent me a message when I was out with Andrew last night, inviting me out with her and her friends for July 4th. I tell her definitely.

I slip my phone in my pocket when I get to the living room. Scarlett's three bags are piled in the foyer. The black dress is on a hanger in the closet and I'll make sure to steam clean it this afternoon when no one is around.

I eat cereal on the lounger, which, usually, is expressly forbidden, but Aunt Nancy is at a Daughters of the American Revolution meeting. "Beanie, go get your sister. Tell her we have to go," Mom says from the kitchen.

I place my bowl down and head upstairs.

"So," I say, stepping in Scarlett's doorway, "you'll just have to achieve MTP in New York City." MTP is Scarlett's acronym for "maximum tanning potential." Nancy finds it horrifying and drones on and on about SPFs and skin cancer.

I glance around her room, trying to see what clothes Scarlett's chosen to leave behind. Scarlett can't take *everything* to New York . . . can she? After all, she said she doesn't see the point in bringing her swimsuits to the city. Some of her drawers are open behind her and she's left dozens of T-shirts and shorts.

"What did you do to your *face*? You look like a raccoon," she says. She scrunches her nose like something smells disgusting.

"What?"

My sister is seated at her vanity and dabs moisturizer on her forehead. I bend to see my reflection. Dark smears of mascara blacken under my eyes.

"I guess I didn't wash my makeup off," I say and use a tissue to wipe my skin.

"Wash that off every night. It'll clog your pores," she says and dabs a different cream on her chin.

My skin is a little raw from rubbing too hard.

I sit down on the end of the bed next to a red summer dress. It's very short and would probably show the bottom of my butt cheeks if I ever wore it.

"That's nice," I say about the dress. "Kinda skimpy."

"Yeah, well, Curtis seems to think I should be wearing nothing all the time. He basically had this off of me in fifteen minutes last night."

"Curtis?" I say, playing dumb. Scarlett admires her reflection and pulls at her tanned skin.

"Yeah, he works down at the fish market." She shrugs. "We're seeing where it goes this summer. I'm not into the dark hair, dark eyes look. But I do love his body."

"Ugh," I say, thinking of Curtis looking me up and down at the fish market.

Scarlett rolls her eyes. "You know, Bean, someday you're going to have sex and you're going to like it."

She doesn't get it. It's not Curtis's body that I think is disgusting, it's Curtis's entire existence. I wonder if she knows about the accident and that he was in jail for nine months. He doesn't strike me as the most forthcoming guy. But it also strikes me as something that all of his friends talk about and if Scarlett is here during the off-season—she has to know. Either way, I don't mention how much I know.

"Do you think he's a . . ." I choose my words while trying to seem normal. ". . . a good person?"

"What do you mean, 'good'?"

Nope, she's not going to give anything away.

"A good guy," I repeat.

"Yeah, why not? I mean he has feelings and is courteous or whatever. People aren't either just good or bad, Beanie. They're complex. Layered."

I circle back to her last comment about having sex and liking it. I can absolutely imagine taking my clothes off with Andrew. I've never considered having sex with anyone. Not until now. I'm not about to run off and do it tomorrow but

Andrew is different—special.

"I'm not afraid of kissing or sex," I say.

Scarlett whips around in her chair. Her jaw drops.

"Did you seriously just say that? Have you even kissed anyone besides Tucker?"

"He was my first boyfriend!" I say. She gets up and closes a drawer filled with bikinis. "Give me a break," I add.

"Any new boys on the horizon?" she asks.

"Are you really asking me this?"

"Yeah, why not?" she says.

I narrow my eyes. "No," I say. "No boys. But maybe you could bring one back for me from New York!"

She flips off the light but the rainy daylight blankets the room. We walk back downstairs. Scarlett doesn't say anything else. I kind of wish we could keep talking but she joins Mom in the foyer. I don't remember us ever talking about boys before.

She hikes her bag over her shoulder and readies her things for the bus ride from Hyannis to New York City. I finish my cereal on the couch.

Maybe she'll come give me a hug. I check out my reflection in the window. Black eyeliner still burrows in the corners of my eyes. I wipe them again with my napkin.

"See you soon!" Scarlett calls, and it singsongs through the hall. I guess that's a no on the hug good-bye. She's not big on public displays of affection, especially with me.

The rain hits the panoramic windows and skylights above in a steady, increasing rhythm. I place my cereal bowl down. I cannot stop replaying last night at the *Alvin* in my mind.

Rain comes down even harder and smacks the windows. The metal of the patio furniture clangs in the wind.

The phrase *swim to the moon* has been running through my mind for days. I haven't asked Andrew what it means, and Mom took her computer with her to go to a coffee shop after dropping off Scarlett, so I can't look it up.

Out the living room window, the rain comes down sideways.

No star gazing tonight. I glance over at the desk in the living room with Dad's copy of the Waterman Scholarship folder sitting on it like dead weight—the blue of its glossy cover mocks me. After I steam clean the dress, I'll go to the library and get started on how to format my essay in proper MLA format. Thank goodness for Sunday summer hours. Maybe I'll even figure out what Andrew's tattoo means while I am there.

I snatch the dress to start the steam clean routine and head upstairs.

The rain splashes around my ankles and the bottom of my flip-flops, making my feet slip and slide. I run up the cement steps of the Orleans library and when I grab for the silver handle, my slicked hand slips as another hand reaches for the door.

Curtis.

"American flag string bikini," he says. Is that what he's going to say every time he sees me?

We step into the darkened foyer and I wring out my hair; long strands stick to my back and I shiver when icy raindrops trickle down my spine. I'm standing in the library with someone who definitely knows Scarlett. I cross my arms over my chest.

The light above us flickers and makes a blinking sound. There's a line of windows at the back wall of the library. The sky has darkened even more.

Cumulonimbus clouds, I think. *We're about to have some—*

CRASH!

Thunder.

"You been having fun with Andrew?" Curtis asks.

"Yeah, he's nice," I say and shake my head again, sending droplets flying into the air. The white scar on Curtis's collarbone crisscrosses up to his neck. I need to deflect the direction of this conversation and of my eyes. I don't want him to know that I know about the accident.

"So . . . ," I say, thinking about Andrew's tattoo and that this is quite possibly the most expeditious thing I can do to change the subject. "Swim to the—"

Curtis leans a hand on the wall and crosses one ankle over the other.

"You're a nice girl," he says and draws out the word "nice" so it's a hiss. "A good girl. Too good for me."

I take a step out of the foyer and into the library.

A nice girl. Why does that sound dirty to me? Sexual?

The lights flicker again over the wooden tables and a sign on a desk reads REFERENCE LIBRARIAN. Curtis's eyes linger on mine and his tongue sticks out the side of his mouth a little bit. But he's smiling.

I inch backward toward the librarian's desk and my flip-flops squeak against the floor.

"See ya, Nice Girl," Curtis says and meanders down the aisle toward a computer table at the far end of the library. Great. The Orleans library has only two computers. That means I have to sit next to him at the computer if I want to access the card catalog.

Another huge crash of thunder outside makes the lights above the computers shake. There is a line three-deep for one reference librarian. It's summer! What the hell does everyone need the library for? I need to look up the MLA reference books for my Waterman essay, aka the most boring thing I have ever had the misfortune of being assigned. Andrew's tattoo floats through my mind too. I am not letting Curtis get in my way.

I sit down next to him and pull up the Orleans library database.

"Keeping me company?" he asks.

He can't know I'm searching the phrase of Andrew's tattoo. I start with the location of the writing reference books.

"If you must know I'm completing an essay, so I'm researching."

He keeps his eyes on his screen and I sneak a peek. Meeting locations: Alcoholics Anonymous of Cape Cod.

Oh.

I type a few things but exhale through my nose. My shoulders hunch a little and the muscles in my back release.

"People are damaged sometimes," Gran always says. "But you can't let their damage walk all over you. You gotta be there for them. Help them pick themselves up and brush off the dirt but you've got to protect yourself, too."

I keep my head pointed toward my own screen and decide that Curtis is disgusting, but he is trying. He seems like he's brushing off the dirt. Maybe he's just a guy who made a really bad choice.

"Andrew has an interesting tattoo on his arm," I offer. I try to sound very casual. I write down the call number of the MLA books on a small piece of paper, which also allows me to turn my head even farther from Curtis's computer screen.

"Oh, The Doors lyric? You a fan?"

"Of Andrew?" I ask. Curtis looks at me funny.

"Of The Doors," he clarifies.

"Oh. Yeah. Completely. Thought you might be too."

What the hell am I even saying?

"Nah. He's the sensitive one." Curtis clicks out of the browser and stands up. "See you later, Miss America."

"See ya," I say quietly, even though he is out of earshot. He leaves without explaining anything to me, not that he needs to or that it's my place to know.

Still, as Curtis walks away, I have an overwhelming urge to call out to him. To tell him that Andrew misses Mike too and won't have a drink because of what happened even though he wasn't even in that car. I want to tell Curtis that he's not alone in his grief. I want to tell him I'm sorry and that we all have to live with the ripple effects of our choices. Even me—a girl who lived in her sister's shadow way too long.

I'm sorry for both Andrew and Curtis.

Sorry for their loss.

The Doors. I think I've heard of them or something. Within ten minutes, I'm sitting in the back of the library with three books in front of me and all of them are about the 1960s. One is open to a picture of a band. In the center is a guy in the tightest pair of leather pants I've seen since Mom took me to a Broadway play in New York City.

He's hot, too. If you like that longhaired, tight pants, amazing mouth thing. Tucker does not have any of that. Actually, neither does Andrew. Well, except for the amazing mouth.

"Jim Morrison!" Mom says later that evening. She sits next to Dad and her tea steams next to a book on résumés. "I was too young, but Gran *loved* him."

"Gran?" Granny Levin likes dried herbs hanging upside down in her kitchen and tie-dye T-shirts.

"Yeah, Gran went to a bunch of their concerts."

It is necessary I speak to Gran about "swim to the moon." I think she'll like that phrase. I can tell her a little about Andrew. Just like I did with Ettie, I'll leave out the part about his age.

I am supposed to call her and Gracie once a week. But because she's been at her silent meditation retreat, I haven't been able to. The fact that she's spent seven days not speaking to Gracie seems impossible to me.

As I walk to the telephone to call Gran anyway, Mom's phone chimes.

I am dialing on Nancy's portable house phone when Mom says, "Looks like Tucker isn't coming to the party. You'll get your wish after all."

I freeze and draw a quick breath. I grip the phone hard. My index finger hovers over the last few digits of Gran's number.

So that's it. Tucker really isn't changing his mind about us breaking up. I hate that in some sick way, I thought he would and I was, even for a second, excited about it. It's like Tucker's decision not to come to the party is another jab to hurt me. Coward. He doesn't want to see me and have to own up to what he did behind my back. He probably thinks I'm still crying. He's probably pitying me right now.

"Beanie? Did you hear about Tucker?" Mom says.

"It's completely fine," I say and clear my throat. "Totally and completely fine."

I dial the last of Gran's number with a slam of the keys.

"Fine, huh?" Mom says with a slight smile.

I head out to the patio and close the door so she can't hear me.

Even though Gran has a couple days left on her retreat, when she gets home, she'll listen to her messages and call me and we can talk about Andrew. I want to hear her voice even if it's on a message machine.

It rings three times and I hear Gran's familiar honey tone.

"This is Jean and Gracie. I hate these things."

"We hate, dear. We," Gracie's voice says.

"We hate these things, so make it quick. If you're selling something, our answer is no."

"Gran," I say into the receiver. "It's Bean. When you can speak again we gotta talk Jim Morrison. I have discovered him and his leather pants. Call your granddaughter."

I don't say anything about Andrew on the message because if Gran hears me mention a *new* guy, that might mess up her silence. I don't want to tempt her back into the world of noise.

I head up to my room for Comet Jolie position charts. My

math must be exact to impress the scholarship committee—each epoch marks a moment that the comet has traveled. Consistency is key. I will punch in the coordinates and the telescope will slew to that spot in the sky. If it doesn't match the exact location I determined—even if it's a mere degree higher than what I calculated—all of my observations will be for nothing.

Everything I've been working for will be on the line out on Nauset Light Beach, the night of the perihelion.

This scholarship is my ticket out of Nancy's vice grip. My ticket to show Tucker that he can't win.

Maybe this is actually my ticket to a real future at MIT. Maybe one day, my lie will be my real life.

That night, after downloading a Doors album, I lie down in the darkness and listen to "Moonlight Drive." I rub some of Mom's lotion over my legs. My bed is comfy, the rain taps the skylights, and I stare up at the thousands of drops running down the glass. Scarlett has perfect skin. She's always putting on some lotion or cream, so they must do something.

Let's swim to the moon . . .

Beep. I think I hear something over the music in my headphones. *Beep.* Oh! It's my cell phone.

ANDREW: Breaking into any more buildings?

Must be strategic. What would Scarlett do? She would make a joke, be cool.

ME: All the time.

ANDREW: You like all this rain?

ME: I do, but my comet trajectory does not.

ANDREW: Friday night?

The Stargazer points out the bay window fogged up with rain. The weatherman said it would clear Friday night but I will make Dad drive me to clear sky if I have to. After all the work I've done, I. Will. Not. Miss. The. Comet. Jolie!

During the day tomorrow, I'll have to work on the final research and the comet trajectory and double check a few more mechanical things on my school laptop. A borrowed, sad laptop that can only sign on to the school science website and record my telescope data. Over the next few days, I have to make up for the time I've been spending with Andrew. I text back.

ME: Yep. Friday. Nauset Light Beach.

ANDREW: Okay. BTW Saturday night there's a Fourth of July party on Town Beach. Huge bonfire.

I visualize Scarlett's bus pulling into the terminal at Penn Station.

She's gone. No one will recognize me.

I can go wherever I want! No one has to know that we're related or that I'm only sixteen. I may have to juggle this with my plans with Claudia. Andrew believes I'm eighteen but I don't know if he would believe Claudia is too. I can't ask her to lie for me.

I'll work it out.

ME: Wouldn't miss it.

I put the phone down and press play on my music player. I let Jim Morrison take me away to sleep.

A few days later, it's Dad, Mom, and me inside the house. Nancy is somewhere out in the backyard with the party planner. Mom's in the kitchen packing up to go home for the day because she has a job seminar.

Outside, the sun blasts the white patio furniture. It's sunny, but the morning thunderstorms mean the sand will be wet until tomorrow.

Dad goes over my calculations at the table.

"I'm impressed, Beanie. You have a very small margin of error, which is inherent to the instability of comets."

"Oh, thanks," I reply. I smile and nod at the binder, but I'm thinking about Andrew.

I read last night that Jim Morrison died when he was really young, at twenty-seven years old. Maybe that's why Andrew feels so connected to him.

I run a hand over the plastic cover of my binder as Dad talks.

"What do you have left to do?" he asks. Dad stands and gathers his briefcase. I refocus my thoughts and sit up straighter in my seat.

"I've got to clean the optics on the Stargazer, and I have to organize my bag for the viewing."

"Excellent," Dad says. "Call me if you need anything," he adds as Mom's cell phone rings.

"Gerard, wait. It's Scarlett. Hi, honey," Mom says to the phone. Dad pauses with one foot out the door.

With the exception of the kitchen staff, it's almost like normal. Mom leans her elbows on the kitchen counter and rocks on the balls of her feet as she listens to Scarlett go on and on.

"Scarlett won a competition at school!" she cries to Dad. "Oh wow, honey," Mom coos into the phone. "Tell your father about the photographer."

Dad comes back in and places his briefcase down.

"Congrats, honey," Dad calls toward the phone.

Mom and Dad stand at the island, cell phone poised between their ears.

"Do you want to talk to your sister?" Mom asks me. "She won an award."

"Caught it the first time!" I say while walking backward toward the stairs.

Mom shakes the phone at me. She's trying to tell me that Scarlett is saying hello, but I can't remember a time Scarlett has ever asked to talk to me on the phone. Maybe part of me feels guilty, I don't know. All I know is she's the last person I want to talk to.

I can't say for sure what Scarlett would say to me or what she might want to know about my life. I only know about her life because I've been wearing her shoes. I could ask questions now, but until this summer I couldn't relate.

I guess I don't really know her and she doesn't really know me.

JULY SCHEDULE

IMPORTANT DATES:
July 3rd Comet Jolie reaches perihelion! Track
    comet. Kick ass. (Wear cute outfit. A is
    coming.)

LOOKING AHEAD:
Organize for Waterman Scholarship: due date
    August 8th.
- ☐ Application (16 pages, must be handwritten
  and snail mailed into scholarship board)
- ☐ Compile data, finish organization of
  calculations.
- ☑ Online registration—due June 26th
  (Birthday!)
- ☑ Comet Data, compiled in duplicate.
- ☑ Letter of Recommendation from the East
  Greenwich Observatory
- ☐ Personal Essay UGHHHHHHHHHHHH

VARIOUS:
- ☐ Cute clothes for various dates with A?
  Maybe some earrings from town?
- ☑ Find out about Tuck and his RSVP to the
  party.
- ☐ Ettie b-day gift?

SEVENTEEN

STARGAZER? CHECK. LED FLASHLIGHT? CHECK.
Approximately 524 bubble gum jelly beans? Check. And a cell
phone. I am supposed to use the cell, according to Nancy, if I
witness any "drunk townies" down on the beach. Mom and Dad
laugh and laugh like this is a preposterous scenario.

As I get to the foyer, Mom and Dad are in the kitchen watching a show about barnacles on the Discovery Channel. Dad sits
up straight in his chair and points at the monitor.

"They're going to reference me!" Dad says. "Wait for it . . ."

I've seen that episode about four times.

Scarlett brought that red sundress with her to New York, but
she left a short blue one with little white polka dots. I admit,

this isn't the most practical outfit for comet gazing on a chilly beach, but I've envisioned it: Andrew and me at night, comet high above, and wind playing in my hair.

"Want me to drive you?" Dad asks.

"No," I say, "it's okay. I should do this without any help."

"Good luck!" He waves from the lounger and tiny hairs sway in the central air. It's good I caught him before a new episode of Deep-Sea Creatures on PBS at ten thirty.

Once I leave, I'm halfway down Shore Road, eating my fifth jellybean, when a red pickup pulls up next to me.

Andrew rests his arm in the window. Is he wearing a blazer? I rise on my tiptoes to peer into the car. Is that a bow tie? Wait a minute . . . he's pushed up the sleeves of a *tuxedo*!

I gasp a little, the cracks in the pavement look like they're winking.

"Nice outfit," I say.

Andrew is almost giddy he's so proud of himself.

"Where's your ball gown?" he asks.

Scarlett would have thought to play up the joke. Scarlett would have worn a gown to make up for any indiscretions the other night. So instead I say, "It wouldn't match the telescope."

"You know, you could drive to the beach instead of lugging all your crap."

How do I explain this one? Confidence. *Scarlett* confidence.

"I'm a slave, remember?" I put my hand on my hip like I've seen Scarlett do countless times. "My parents have control of the car this summer," I say, which is halfway the truth and halfway lying. "And this could be considered stalking," I say, trying to channel my sister.

"You never said where to pick you up. I was going to be a gentleman and knock."

I get into Andrew's pickup and hold the Stargazer bag in my lap.

"I'm ready to see some comets," he says, and we drive toward the beach. When we pull into the parking lot, Andrew takes the telescope bag from my lap and his hands graze my thigh.

"Wait," I say as he moves to get out of the car.

"This is a very serious scientific experiment. I have to get everything right or there could be catastrophic consequences."

Andrew is smiling, but he stops and furrows his eyebrows.

"Yes, ma'am."

"You are here as an assistant."

He salutes me in his tuxedo and my heart nearly explodes he's so cute.

"Let's go," I say.

I adjust the backpack, and we head to the steep stairs leading down to the beach.

"So why the comet?" he asks as we pass under a street lamp. Andrew has paired his tuxedo dress pants with flip-flops. "Why the obsession?"

I almost say it's for school. For *high* school. I want to tell him every last detail about the scholarship. Instead, I gulp the truth away and choose my words very carefully.

"It's good to have a specialization when you're studying at MIT. You know, to come into school with a research project."

I have no idea if this is true, but it sounds right.

"Nice," Andrew says.

You're a nice girl.

"Nice . . . ," I say, lingering on the word as we step deeper onto the sand and closer to the shore. "I hate that word."

The farther we walk down the beach and away from the parking lot, the darker it gets, which is exactly what I need. Some people fish at the shoreline. A couple watches the ocean and the waves crash lightly onto the sand.

I stop down the beach at approximately a thousand feet from the parking lot and I look up. Andrew carries the Stargazer and I'm able to get situated much faster. Expected conditions, low-grade light pollution. There's the constellation I need, Orion. I place my backpack on the sand and take the telescope from Andrew.

"What's wrong with nice?" Andrew asks.

"Nice is what you say when you get an A on a science exam," I say as I set up. "It's what I say to my mom when she asks what I think of her outfit. *Nice.*"

Andrew takes one end of a blanket and spreads it out. I unfold four smooth stones from Nancy's backyard.

"You brought your own *stones*?"

I cock my head and let my expression tell Andrew to shut up.

"Okay . . . ma'am. What next?" he says.

I take out my red LED flashlight, which allows me to see my equipment without affecting the night vision. I grab my star chart, unzip the bag, and set up the Stargazer. I unfold the plastic base that comes with the telescope. It ensures that no matter where I am, I have a flat surface. I unearth my level. By the lamplight, I make sure everything is even.

I get ready to start the exposure on the telescope. I check my watch. Eleven thirty. Twelve minutes.

"If my calculations are correct," I explain, "the coordinates of this comet will be directly to the left of that star up there. Tonight's the first night you can see it with the naked eye."

Andrew looks up to the sky. "I don't know what I'm looking for."

"I'll show you."

No, this eyepiece won't do. I switch them out. Yes, that's better.

I type the coordinates into my ancient Summerhill laptop, hit enter, and the coordinates locate the comet based on my previous calculations.

"Why do you have your old high school computer?" Andrew asks.

Oh hell.

The sticker across the top says: SUMMERHILLSCIENCE-LOANER2.

"I bought it from them," I say quickly. "They sold it to us cheap senior year. I only use it to collect data. I need a newer one for the fall."

I don't want to lie, but I can't focus on that right now. I have to make sure everything is lining up accurately.

"Wow. You look really professional," Andrew says.

"Please be right," I whisper as the Stargazer focuses on my right ascension and declination. "Please be right."

Silence . . . silence.

Both Andrew and I stare at the laptop.

"I programmed it to beep if the coordinates are a match. So if it does, it means my calculations are exact."

"We need that beep," Andrew says. "It's going to," he adds. We both stare at the Stargazer. "Any second . . . it has to."

"You have no idea how any of this works, but thank you for the support," I whisper without moving my eyes from the damn telescope.

"Anytime, babe."

BEEP.

"Yes!" I cry.

"Thank God," Andrew says, and he, too, exhales heavily. Without the telescope, I point out the white, fuzzy ball creeping across the sky. It's funny to see it up there while I stand down here with Andrew. It's just been the Comet Jolie and me for eleven months.

I record the right ascension and declination. I know it's accurate, but I keep checking my coordinates and the position of the telescope.

I did it. I'm radiating.

"Look at you, Star Girl. I haven't seen you smile like this before."

"I didn't need those damn computerized predictions, Andrew. I worked it out myself. Month after month! My science teachers said it was silly. Because look at that!" I point at the telescope. "It's perfect."

Andrew cracks his knuckles and kicks off his flip-flops.

"All right, step aside, little lady. I gotta see this comet."

I can't help smiling even more.

Andrew leans forward, presses his eye to the lens, and squints the other. He doesn't say anything, just puts his hands in his pockets and looks through my Stargazer up at my comet.

I hold my hands in front of my waist and grip them tight. I don't know what Scarlett would say right now. I don't know how to be her right now because she would never be in this position. She soars across a stage; people watch her; they clap. She was born for the stage. I wasn't born for that kind of life. This, right now, sharing this with Andrew is the real me. Even though I am not eighteen and I'm not going to MIT, he's really seeing me. I know it for sure now: I don't have to be scared to show myself to Andrew. The Scarlett Experiment may have caught his attention, but he likes *me*.

Andrew pulls back from the telescope and points at my Stargazer.

"That," he says, "is fucking cool."

A warmth radiates down my chest to my stomach. "Cool isn't exactly the most scientific word, but it is really extraordinary and *rare*," I say. Andrew links his arm around my waist.

"What does the Perry Hation mean?"

I don't correct him because the mispronunciation is really cute.

"When the comet is closest to our sun, it breaks up and melts away. The Comet Jolie is the brightest comet in a century. I've tracked it since the University of Hawaii discovered it eleven months ago. Back then it was seventy million miles away."

"I won't even ask how they found it," he says and kisses the nape of my neck. I draw in a little breath from the softness of his lips. He pulls away, but I want him to do it again. "Thanks for inviting me."

Andrew lies down on the sand and holds his hands behind his head. My summer dress barely falls to my knees, and I conclude this is not the most convenient ensemble to have worn. Andrew squints up at the constellations above and the comet streaking across the sky. I squat down to record other observations: the tail, the brightness, and environmental factors.

"Want to know how it works?" I ask.

"Sure," he says, but it's polite, distracted. The sudden detachment in his tone makes me nervous and of course, I start stuttering.

"The telescope will take a series of pictures of the comet. When I'm done, I'll go home, upload them to my computer, analyze all the other nights I tracked its coordinates. If I was right—well, I don't know," I finish lamely. "It could help with grants, scholarships."

I put down the pen, snap off the red light, and let the stars do the rest of the talking. I lie down on the cool sand next to Andrew.

"Are you okay?" I ask after a couple of silent moments. "You're suddenly kind of quiet."

Andrew's eyes still look up to the sky. Soon his warm hand is on top of mine. "I've never seen a comet before," he says.

"Cape Cod has some of the best viewing conditions on the East Coast."

"I feel like I have to tell you something."

He is on his side looking at me again just like on our first date.

"Does it involve tutoring a girl named Becky or any girl for that matter?"

"No . . . ?"

"Continue."

He raises one eyebrow but shakes his head seemingly to refocus.

"I—" He hesitates and pinches some sand between his thumb and index finger. He lets it drizzle back to the ground. "I—took a leave from school."

"From BC?"

He nods. "I've been living here all winter. I'm supposed to start back up in the fall. So I sort of . . . lied to you about being in school right now."

"Why?"

"What I told you the other night at the *Alvin*. I need to work for Mike's family. Lobstering. With him gone, they need someone."

"But that's not what you want. You said so."

"I owe it to them."

I shake my head. Like Andrew's guilt about the accident, this decision also seems illogical to me.

"You're frowning," Andrew says.

"No. No, I'm not." I shake my head quickly.

"You can't see your face. Wow! Now look!" He laughs and I cover my face with my hands.

"Stop," I cry, and despite the serious moment I laugh at my palms.

"Sorry. I know we haven't known one another that long. But I thought I should be honest with you about the fall. I'll be here on the Cape, it's only an hour away."

"Did they ask you to do that?" I ask. "Work for them?"

"Who? Mike's family?"

"Yeah."

"Not exactly."

I sit back on my elbows. "Are you asking me my advice?" No one except Tucker has ever asked for my advice. "I'm probably not very good at giving it," I add.

"Yeah, I guess I am."

"I proceed at my own risk."

I could be Scarlett. I could be aloof, throw my head back, and tell him not to worry. But that's not what *I* want. He showed me tonight when he looked through that telescope that he gets me. The supreme, logical, hyper detailed me.

"Let's talk about probability. Let's pretend you were at the party, but you didn't get in the car that night. Let's also pretend that you told Curtis and Mike to go, but you didn't want to drive with someone intoxicated." He shifts. I know that changing positions or deflecting your gaze to an object instead of someone's eyes are all signs of being uncomfortable. "Forget it."

"No. Keep going."

I exhale. "Look, I don't need to get into a deep discussion of Bayesian probability or quantum mechanics."

"Please don't."

I chuckle again and continue, "Probability is all about how likely something is to happen. If you frame every situation in your life in terms of a probability, think about this: how many times did Curtis drive drunk and how many times did Mike get into that car before even though he knew Curtis was drunk?"

"A lot."

"Exactly. Now, probability says that every time they drank and every time they were together, the same likelihood existed that they would get into the car. The same probability existed that they would get in an accident."

"That's not very uplifting. Wouldn't the probability be higher because of the times we drank? We drink often."

"No. The ratio is the same. There are more variables, I guess, and I would have to do some real math here to find an exact probability, but think about it this way. Forget equations. You are a human being with free will. I don't believe our decisions were programmed into the universe during the Big Bang or that they're written into the fabric of time. You didn't push Mike into the car. You didn't tie him down. He made a decision. Why do you need to make the events of that night your responsibility?" I have to catch my breath. "Wow," I add quietly. "I might be a teensy overinvested in this."

Andrew is quiet and I give him the moment to check on the laptop and Stargazer. It hums along nicely and Jolie is there in the sky above.

"You're not mad? That I didn't tell you?" he asks when I sit back down.

I am in no position to hold a grudge against him, especially with the intricate stories I'm weaving. Yet, my sense of injustice nibbles at me.

"I'm not mad. It just seems strange to give up what you want."

We're quiet for a while and Andrew finally says, "My family isn't even on the Cape this year."

"Why not?" I ask. I can't fathom being here without Nancy, Mom, Scarlett, and Dad. I imagine the stores, the roads, and the house, empty with only me inside. It wouldn't be the Cape, it would be some kind of weird hologram.

"My little brother is only twelve and my stepmom is having a baby. It just didn't work out this summer."

This is the perfect moment to tell him about my own lies; to tell him that I am Scarlett's sister, and how old I really am. But I can't bring myself to do it. I have to be Sarah, going to MIT. I can't be *that* part of me. The part where I am in high school or where I'm Scarlett's sister. He is getting to know the real me, I am getting to know the real Andrew. These minor logistical details aren't what make *us* special. They aren't what is keeping us together right now.

"She's twenty-nine. My stepmom," he says quietly. "She was my dad's dental hygienist; he's a dentist."

My head whips to him.

"That would make her ten years older than you."

"You got it, Star Girl. It's creepy."

I clear my throat. Age is not something I'd like to be discussing right now.

"You know the Stargazer is modeled after some of the deep-space telescopes they have in the middle of the desert? The ones that look for life way out in the universe?"

Andrew rubs my back a little as if to say it's okay I changed the subject this time. I look through the viewfinder again and at the comet blazing through our solar system. "It'll be strange for the night sky to be without the comet," I say. "It's almost like a friend to me now. I know that's cheesy."

"No, it's not."

On a night like tonight, I could jump up and touch the moon.

"When did you turn eighteen?" Andrew asks.

Or not.

"Oh, um. In May," I say.

"Good thing I met you in June, eh, jailbait?"

"Yeah," I chuckle but it's sour. "Jailbait . . ."

"Have you ever . . . ?" he starts to ask, his eyes still on the stars.

"What?"

He leans on his hip.

"Have you ever . . . ," he starts again.

The exhilaration of the comet still courses through me. He doesn't finish the thought. In a flash, he sits up and his eyes focus ahead on the shore.

He looks up at the moon above and says, "It might work."

"What might work?" I ask, sitting up too.

He stands up and holds out his hand to me. The waves swell and crash against the shore. The water slides up to meet the seaweed and shells scattered against the beach.

"I've got something to show you," Andrew says. He pulls me toward the shore.

"But the Stargazer!"

"That comet isn't going anywhere," he says.

"That's not true. It's actually going approximately three hundred miles a second!"

In between laughs he says, "We're only going down to the shore."

I try to keep up, but my flip-flops slide off.

"My sandals!"

"Keep running!" he says.

So I do, I keep running and running after this gorgeous boy and my bra strap keeps falling off my shoulder and I don't care. I don't care. I don't care.

Andrew grabs me around my waist and spins me around. When he places me down, my feet touch the top of something crunchy—seaweed.

His hands are strong behind the small of my back. Andrew pulls me toward him, my mouth meets his and I again pretend that I know what I am doing when he kisses me with his mouth open. He switches the position of his head and I do too. He grips me even tighter.

When he pulls away, he smiles like he has a secret lodged deep inside.

Far up the beach, the beam of the lighthouse revolves around and around, sending rhythmic swirls of light up the distant sand. Where we are is dark except for the moon shining down.

"You have to stand where I am for it to work," he says.

"For what to work?"

"Wow, do I know something my genius astronomer does not?"

My *genius astronomer.*

He bends over and moves the seaweed aside. The moon's rays make the sand beneath bright white.

With his index finger, he draws an *S* shape in the sand, an *A*, and so on. Soon, my name is spelled out on the beach and it . . .

I gasp . . . it is *glowing*. I look from the moon to the sand, to Andrew's smiling face.

"It's the phosphorescence that makes it glow in the dark," he says.

"It's—" I throw my arms around him. "It's wonderful!"

When he kisses me, his hands run up and down my sides and a tingle shoots through my whole body. He tastes sweet, like peppermint.

"Thank you!" I say and hug him again. His hand remains around my waist as we walk back to the telescope and our little spot on the beach. Once I make sure everything is still recording accurately, I lie back down next to Andrew.

"What were you going to ask before?" I say.

He runs a hand through his hair and looks up at the sky.

"Have you ever . . . ?" he leads but stops again.

"Have I what? Just say it!"

"Had sex with a guy before?"

"Oh," I say with a hard swallow and switch the flashlight on and off.

"I'll take that as a no," he says.

I sit up with my legs stretched out in front of me. "I want to. I just haven't had the chance. School. Classes. And the whole right guy thing."

Tucker and I kissed and he felt my breasts over my shirt. Our relationship was so cerebral. I could anticipate what he would say. I knew everything about him. I thought I felt it with my body, but I didn't, not really. Not like this.

Andrew rises onto his elbow. "I know it's been like two weeks or something so this might be too much. What I'm about to say."

"Say anything."

"When I'm with you it's bearable. For the first time since Mike died, I'm really happy." He puts his hand on my knee.

"Wow," I say. The highlight of his knuckles glows under the soft light of the moon. "I don't know what to say to that. It feels . . . important."

"I want to make you feel good," he says. "As good as you make me feel."

"You do," I say, and his hand moves farther up my knee to my thigh. "You're one of the most sincere people I've ever met."

"No, Sarah. That's not what I mean . . ."

With his other hand, he presses on my stomach and I lie back on the sand. He kisses my kneecap. He replaces his palm with his mouth. I shiver.

"What are you—" I ask, but it catches as his lips trail over my skin. "Doing?"

The moon and the darkness make shadows on Andrew's face. All I can see are the curve of his lips and the slight stubble on his chin. How is this boy mine?

"Is this okay?" he asks and rests his cheek against my knee-cap. His face moves slowly toward the middle of my thigh. "I don't want to do anything if it's not okay," he whispers, and his breath on my skin makes me jump.

I like it. And it is okay. The shivers running up and down my spine are making me shudder again. The sound of the waves, the soft graze of his lips on my knee, my thigh. His hands press against both my thighs, opening them up, his nose and mouth graze my inner thigh . . . what was I supposed to be doing? I take in a sharp breath. I've never felt that before.

Breathe. Breathe. Try to catch your breath, Bean. Look at the stars. Can't see the stars; his hands grip my thighs. Cassiopeia, soft, up, down. Comets. Comets, comets, comets,

shooting

stars.

EIGHTEEN

"BEAN!"

Let's swim to the moon . . .

"Bean!"

I blink and Mom's blue eyes stare down at me. Her right eyebrow cricks up. I rip out my earphones. I fell asleep with "Moonlight Drive" on repeat.

"I've been calling you. Your father needs your help at work today." She pulls back to look at me more clearly. "You fell asleep in your dress?" Mom says and glances from me to the Stargazer wrapped tightly in its case. "Is that Scarlett's dress?"

"She gave it to me. I was up late last night because of the comet."

I'm amazed Mom noticed I'm in Scarlett's dress. Or maybe it's more that she noticed I'm not in my pajamas.

"I want to hear about it at breakfast," Mom says. "So come on. Dad says you offered to help with some cataloging."

"But it's Saturday and a holiday."

"Did that ever stop your father?"

"Good point." After my birthday dinner, I think I was apt to say anything so I could get out of there and to Andrew at the party.

Mom walks away but pops her head back in the room.

"And don't forget, we're hosting Nancy's Daughters of the American Revolution Fourth of July barbecue tonight."

I'm supposed to see Claudia and then go with Andrew to a bonfire. Mom leaves the room before I can tell her I have plans, but this involves . . . *telling her I have plans.* I could say I'm going with Claudia to Main Street, which is partially true.

Once Mom is gone, I lie back on the bed. I run a hand over my stomach, fearful to touch anywhere below the belt. I'd heard of oral sex, sure, but no one ever told me. No one ever explains that you can barely breathe, that it feels, that it feels . . . I sigh, I can't imagine what sex must be like. Oh my God, I'll have to do it to him. I'll have to give him a *blow job.* I throw my face in my hands.

I kind of want to, but I have no idea how to do anything like that. I can't ask Ettie, she's only been on one date. I *really* can't ask Scarlett, even though she would totally know what to do. I could ask Claudia if we got to know each other better.

I could ask Gran. What the hell am I talking about? There

is probably no worse question in the world for me to ask Gran. I can barely keep these lies together at this point, and once I get Gran on the phone, it will be like I took a truth serum. She has that effect on me.

"Beanie!" Dad calls from downstairs. I don't want to take off this dress. I don't want to forget last night, the phosphorescence in the sand, my name glowing in the dark, and the feel of his lips. Everything down there is—different. Alive.

"Beanie! I have to be at work early today!" Dad calls.

I jump into my routine, wash my face, brush my teeth, and wear the dress to help Dad at work.

"Well?" Dad says when we get in the car. "Coordinates?"

"Perfect. One hundred percent accurate."

"Conditions?"

"Low light pollution. Seeing conditions could *not* have been better."

"Was there anyone else on the beach?"

"Oh. Um. You know, kids. People fishing or whatever."

"I mean astronomers."

"No. No. Me. Just me. You know, me."

Am I all right? Does having oral sex make you babble? Is that a side effect? I try to ground myself in facts. The square root of pi is 1.7721, approximately. One of the brightest constellations you can see in the sky during the winter in Rhode Island is Orion.

"You okay?" Dad asks.

"I'm tired," I reply. "I didn't get all packed up until midnight."

I recite the Comet Jolie's right ascension and declination.

Andrew's warm touch. His fingers push up the hem of my dress. His strong grip on my hips. Is this what people mean when they say they're falling in love? When they feel it with their body and their heart? I realize the heart is an organ, but this has got to be what they mean.

I cannot think of oral sex while sitting in the car next to my father. Think of Jim. Jim Morrison facts. First song, "Moonlight Drive." Zodiac sign? Sagittarius.

"So are you ready?" Dad asks, and my head whips to him.

"For what?"

"Waterman Scholarship? Think you have a shot at defeating Tucker?"

"Definitely," I say, and the moment I see Tucker in my mind, I am sure. "Oh yeah. I have a shot."

My stomach drops.

I should have been prepared. I knew this would happen. But it still sucks.

I come to a complete stop in the maintenance shop doorway. The *Alvin*. My *Alvin* has been completely disassembled. Strewn into hundreds of specific piles, the *Alvin* is categorized throughout the room in black and white lettering. Dozens of marine biologists in white lab coats walk through the maintenance shop talking to one another and making notations on their clipboards. So much for a holiday.

A side panel lies on the floor; it's a piece of the *Alvin*, which makes up the body of the machine. In my mind, Andrew runs his fingers along the titanium.

Rodger seemingly comes out of nowhere and joins me at my side.

"It'll take all summer," we say almost in perfect unison.

I want to walk around the room, pick up all the metal parts, and hold the *Alvin*'s guts to me. The top of my toes almost touch the pile of viewports, the twelve-inch portals the scientists look through into the underwater world. I squat down and as my fingers graze the acrylic plastic, Dad says my name.

We head toward his lab on the second floor and I wave good-bye to Rodger before disappearing behind the double doors.

"You know you don't absolutely have to help me catalog today. You could celebrate. Go to town. I think I saw some people your age hanging around in the café."

"I don't know them, though. And I don't think they'd want to hang out with me," I say as I follow behind Dad up the stairs to his office.

"Why would you automatically assume that they don't want to hang out with you? That you have done something wrong?"

I don't assume that.

Do I? Do I assume people don't want to spend time with me before actually checking to see if they do? I've never actually sat with Becky Winthrop or any of her friends. With Andrew I have been pretending to be like Scarlett because I assumed he wouldn't want to hang out with me. It's true. He liked me at least initially because of the Scarlett Experiment. People purposefully spend their time with my sister. I have one best friend and one former boyfriend. That's it.

"I don't assume that people don't like me," I say under my breath.

I follow Dad into the air-conditioned office. I sit down at the desk and Dad plops a binder before me. I was surprised Claudia wanted to talk to me. Maybe other people have invited me to do things and I've said no before giving it a chance. Maybe all of this is my fault, just not in the way I thought.

You watch the world, Bean.

Tucker's right. I do watch the world. I do assume.

I do all of those things—alone.

NINETEEN

ME: Happy Fourth of July!

During our Fourth of July barbecue, I send a text to Claudia. It's weird, I've never been nervous to send a message to a girl who could become one of my friends. Girls like Claudia, the ones who always know what to wear and what to say to guys, don't usually want to talk to a science girl like me.

My phone chimes.

CLAUDIA: We're in town already. Text me when you get here.

I text below the table so Nancy can't see. She's been making small comments lately whenever my phone beeps or chimes.

"I love this barbecue sauce," Mom says and licks the tips of her fingers. She hums a little as she eats, stopping only to pop another piece of chicken in her mouth. The wind breezes through Nancy's small barbecue party. We're outside in the backyard. I'm in a short skirt and black tank top. The skirt is mine, which means it's fifty thousand years old and too short. The tank top is Scarlett's. Nothing I own has spaghetti straps.

We sit at the edge of the property at a table that Nancy imported from some company in Maine. Apparently, they used to make picnic tables for the Kennedys. There are four picnic tables, each lined with white candles and linen tablecloths. Waiters walk about offering more drinks or napkins. I recognize some of the crew from the catering company Nancy hires every year.

The backyard is lit up special just for us and I wonder where Nancy finds the people to do all her bidding. At some of the tables next to ours, Nancy's Daughters of the American Revolution pals discuss the lobster forks and Nancy's choice in salted butter. Even though they are each in a different dress they seem the same to me.

"What are you doing tonight?" Nancy asks, drawing my eyes to hers. Her summer dress is too big. The straps keep falling off her shoulders and the hem lies along the grass like a long tongue.

"I'm going to meet some girls in town," I say. I don't mention that I'm only meeting them briefly before meeting up with Andrew. I wipe my mouth with a linen napkin. Nancy raises her eyebrows high and resumes a conversation with one of her friends, most likely about me.

We finish up dessert and I head out to Main Street. I text

Andrew to pick me up, not at the house but in front of the Bird's Nest Diner instead.

When I approach the line of shops, restaurants, and busy foot traffic, I text Claudia.

ME: Here!

CLAUDIA: We're at Plymouth Rocks, penny candy.

Nice. That place happens to be one of my favorite stores on Main Street. When I was a kid, I loved their dollar notebooks. I finally get within sight of the store. Claudia is there but with only one of her blonde friends. They sit on a bench waiting for me. Two guys come out of Plymouth Rocks and join them at the bench. They look like they're our age, but I can't be sure. They have on the typical outfit that all the guys at Summerhill wear—preppy shorts, flip-flops, messy hair.

When Claudia sees me, she tips her chin up and waves.

Be Scarlett. These girls don't know about my past or my life in the bio lab. *Be Scarlett the first night you watched her on Main Street.*

"Hey," I say and keep my hands in my skirt pockets. I've seen Scarlett do this about a million times. I shake my head so my hair falls down my back. Chelsea, Claudia's blonde friend, sits down in one of the boy's laps. Gabe is his name, from New Jersey. He leaves Saturday like most tourists do: Saturday to Saturday.

"I love that top," Claudia says to me.

"Thanks," I say with a shrug. "It's old," I add, remembering one of my Scarlett rules. *Stay uninterested, then they will be more interested in you.*

Claudia introduces the other guy as Will and kisses his cheek.

Okay, so they've clearly coupled up already. Claudia and Chelsea stand up and we start walking toward the gazebo. I still keep my hands in my pockets.

We head to the legit sweet shop on Main Street, the Candy Manor. We want to grab bags of fudge and candy before the band starts. I've never been to the Candy Manor without Scarlett or Mom. It's pathetic. I know this as Claudia and Chelsea trade candies.

As I pick out a red lollipop shaped like a lobster, Claudia peers in my bag.

"Oooh!" she says. "Sarah has a ring pop."

"It's the last one!" Chelsea cries.

I slip the ring out of the bag and dangle it on my index finger. We're standing in the middle of the crowded shop. "It is mine but I am willing to part with it on a negotiation basis only. . . ." I make my voice singsong like Scarlett does with her friends and hold the ring pop high above my head.

Both Gabe and Will ready on their toes to grab it.

"I'm a gymnast. I can jump," Chelsea says, and her tongue sticks out the side of her mouth a bit. The eyes of these four people are on me. I would have just given the ring to Claudia, no questions asked, but this is what Scarlett does. She makes a spectacle.

A rush flows through me and I drop the ring pop.

After Gabe and Will both nearly slip out of their flip-flops from wrestling in the middle of the store, a Candy Manor employee pushes through the crowd.

"Pay and go. It's too crowded in here tonight for that business!" The woman has a finger pointed directly at me.

Claudia throws her arm over my shoulder and laughs so the woman can't see and we escape back out to the street. Hundreds of beach chairs litter the green. Red balloons hover and sway from the pillars of the gazebo and it smells like cotton candy and popcorn. Little carts are scattered about the field and the same lady who has sold the neon, glow-in-the-dark bracelets for years is still here, selling them for fifty cents.

People have been saving their seats since breakfast, so we walk through a maze of beach chairs and picnic blankets. We head back toward Main Street where we finally find a vacant bit of grass by the stone wall. The wall separates the field from the main road. I sit closest to the wall but lean back on my hands. Claudia and Chelsea sit across from me in the boys' laps.

"What's Rhode Island like?" Gabe asks. "Never been, only drive through every year."

"It's exactly like Connecticut," Claudia says before I can answer. "I'm from Old Lyme," she adds.

"That's, like, ten minutes from me," I say. We share a smile and I immediately hope we can hang out in the fall.

"Do you come every summer?" Will asks me.

I'm not sure what to say exactly, I don't want it to seem like I don't have friends here. I want them to think I have tons of options for tonight. But at the same time I want them to hang out with me.

"Yeah, it's fun," I say "but there are *no* parties so I'm bored a lot." As I am talking, I feel ridiculous. This isn't me, but they are captivated. I throw my hair back again and it's so long it touches the grass.

"God. I couldn't care less about parties," Claudia says.

"At home it's just the basketball players barfing in the field near the 7-11," Chelsea adds. "Claud and I don't even go."

She doesn't go?

Claudia tells us about her theater company in Old Lyme and her role as both Dorothy last winter in *The Wizard of Oz* and the lead in *Cabaret* in the spring. We move from the grass up to the stone wall because we can't see the band and a woman nearby changes her baby's diaper. The whole field is swarming with people.

My cell reads eight thirty. I glance down Main Street toward the Goosehead Tavern. No red pickup.

"So I guess I'll audition for *Our Town* this year, but I really love musical theater," Claudia explains. I'm still surprised that she's not a Becky Winthrop type, a cheerleader or party girl.

I would never have approached these girls, never would have believed we could have had a thing in common.

Dad is totally right. I do assume. I thought I had Claudia figured out but I never gave her a chance.

I make a point to listen.

"What about you? Where's your boyfriend?" Claudia asks. "You were pretty dressed up the other night to see him at that party."

"Oh, him. What do I need a boyfriend for?" I say and shrug. "Guys take up too much of my time."

Claudia and Chelsea laugh. Chelsea nudges Will in the ribs. "She's smart. I should lose you."

"I make them *think* I like them," I say. "I'm sort of seeing this guy and I guess we're 'seeing where it goes.'" I make air quotes. "I'm not into the blond hair, blue eyes look," I say, remembering the talk with Scarlett. "But I do love his body. So, he'll do for right now, I guess." I add a shrug.

The group snickers and holds their hands over their mouths. Claudia and Chelsea focus on something behind me and Gabe gestures for me to turn around.

But I know. I immediately know because this is too much like a movie. No, it's not a movie, it's Murphy's Law. My gut clenches.

Andrew is frowning but flinches, shaking himself out of the moment.

I hop down from the stone wall onto Main Street.

"Andrew," I say, because more complex sentences seem hard right now. "This is Claudia, Chelsea, Will, and Gabe." I'm all breathy and high-pitched.

Andrew simply nods and gives a polite smile.

"We're going to watch the fireworks on Nauset Light," I squeak. "I'll call you tomorrow, Claudia."

Claudia and her group say good-bye and stifle their own laughter. Andrew and I walk together, but he's silent. I want to say I'm sorry immediately. Actually, I want to curl in on myself, into a little ball. I could be daring and take his hand, but he keeps his in his pockets.

Under the light of the street lamps, his expression is dark, brooding.

"Where are we walking?" I dare to ask.

He stops and runs one hand over his hair. "I don't know. Do you want to go anywhere with me?"

"You know I do," I say, and the frown is still set on Andrew's face.

"No," he says and shoves his hand in his pocket again. "I don't."

"Can we please talk? I want to explain," I say. "I know it sounded horrible."

We walk in silence away from Main Street. Just as I turn my back, the brass band warms up. With a glance down the long suburban street, the glitter of the red, white, and blue tinsel that circles the gazebo winks under the streetlight. I want to run backward, erasing everything that just happened, but I know, the *universe* knows, that time travel is not possible.

Andrew keeps walking and the conductor starts the festivities. In their red uniforms and blue caps, they are dots at the end of the street now. I am dying for the music to start so it fills the silence.

"Hip hip!" the band announcer cries.

"Hidey-ho!" the crowd returns. They do this three times and as I turn the corner, Lighthouse Beach comes into view. The band begins, but the brass is muffled by the waves and wind.

Andrew keeps his distance. Good. It'll be easier to take when he breaks up with me. I got through Tucker, and I can get through this.

Except, this is my fault and I need Andrew in a way I didn't need Tucker. We share something deeper, real.

Once we get to the beach parking lot, he leans his hands on

a wall that separates the asphalt from the dunes. About fifty or sixty feet below, the waves crash again and again. Andrew looks out at the ocean. The sunset is behind us because this beach faces east. The sky is a twilight blue, almost lavender, like on our first date.

I want to spit or slap myself. Either one will do.

The waves swell and crash and the moon is low on the horizon. It's been almost three weeks since Tucker broke up with me so the moon is nearly waxing crescent again. It's amazing how much and how fast things change. I would do anything to make the boy next to me even look in my direction.

"I didn't mean what I said," I explain, but my voice is very quiet.

"It didn't even sound like you," Andrew says. We both don't dare to raise our voices to a normal speaking level. Even though the band is a half mile back, the music swells through the opening ragtime number. "Is that you? I mean, the real you?" he asks.

"The real me?"

"A girl who would say that about me behind my back."

"I like you so much," I say. I clear my throat because I can hear the panic and desperation in my voice. "I wish I could express how much. And it's surprising me because I'm not usually in this situation."

He finally looks at me and the furrow between his eyebrows makes shame flare in my stomach. I've never hurt anyone. I can only imagine how Tucker felt when he came to break up with me. It took me *ages* to understand what he was trying to say.

"What do you mean? You're not usually in this situation?" he asks.

All of my excuses sound so ridiculous and childish. I want to kick something.

A couple of cars pull up to the line of spaces overlooking Lighthouse Beach. There are some couples far off at the other end, but when I see a family and two kids getting out of the car, I walk down the stairs to the sand.

"Sarah?"

I don't look back, but Andrew's familiar footsteps follow me onto the sand. I slip off my sandals and hold them in my hands. My toes crunch on seaweed when I finally make it to the shore.

The moon shines over the water even though the stars are just beginning to peek through the cobalt blue sky. Soon that blue will be gray, then black and all of the constellations will come out.

"It's easy for you," I say, dropping my gaze from the world above.

"What is?"

I cross my arms over my chest. Andrew's frown is gone and instead, there's interest in his eyes. This is the Andrew I know.

"Being you," I say. "Being who you are. You know what you want to be. I don't mean for a job, but on the inside. You know *who* you are. I don't. I see pieces of myself now and then."

"I find that hard to—"

"Believe it," I interrupt. "I know who to be when I track comets. When I talk about science. I guess . . ." I have to stop and gather my breath. My cheeks warm and I bring my fingertips to my face. I didn't think I would be so emotional. Not about Andrew being hurt, that makes sense, but because I am confessing something so deeply true and I've never said it out loud before. Maybe I didn't really know how to say it before today.

Scarlett, Tucker, and Dad were right about me.

"I just assume no one likes me," I say but can't bring myself to meet Andrew's eyes. "I just automatically assume it. It's easier than putting myself in a situation where someone . . ."

"Could reject you?"

"Bingo."

"Who are those girls? Who cares what they think?" Andrew says. He sounds like Scarlett.

Andrew reaches out for my hand and the warmth and tender grip of his skin nearly makes my knees buckle I'm so relieved.

"They're really nice, actually. Those girls? That was *all* me. They were coupled up and I felt stupid."

"You never did that with me, did you? Show off because you were nervous?"

I make another split-second decision. I tell another lie, simply adding and adding to the countless number I have told.

"No," I say. "I've never pretended to be someone else with you."

A wave of nausea flows over me. These words are sour so I have to couple it with something true.

"You always remind me how much I matter. The me on the inside. The one I'm piecing together," I say.

Andrew turns me toward him and bends his knees so our eyes meet.

"Can I just add that I have never felt so stupid in my entire life?" I say.

Andrew doesn't let go of my hand. He gestures to the sand and we sit down just as the first firework explodes in the sky. The blast vibrates deep in the center of my belly. The tiny glittering arcs fall slowly back to the Earth.

"I told you this already," he says with a shake of his head. "You are so different than anyone I've ever met."

"My strangeness is interesting. Great."

The second firework explodes above his head in a red burst and now tiny glitters of crimson lights rain down from the sky.

"Anyone who goes to a library to research my tattoo is a girl I want around."

I gasp. "What? I . . ."

"Curtis told me." Andrew is smiling now.

I bring my palm to my forehead with a smack. Andrew's laugh echoes in the street and the fireworks *pop, pop, pop* in a silver and gold finale and the whole beach lights up.

"I wanted to be able to talk to you about it," I say and rub at my forehead. "About something other than science."

A succession of gold and yellow fireworks explode above our heads.

Andrew reaches his arms around my waist. I let him. It's familiar here with his warm hands around my body.

"I'm really sorry," I say.

He nuzzles his mouth into the nape of my neck. I turn to face him completely and we kiss so deeply that I wonder why people don't kiss like this every chance they get. Andrew lays me down on the sand next to him.

"Andrew," I whisper, and he pulls away. He looks in my eyes and brings his palm to my cheek. "I can't catch my breath."

Andrew's warm breath tickles my ear. "Let's swim to the moon, uh-huh," he sings, but it's soft. "Let's climb through the tide . . ."

I giggle. "Okay so now that the secret's out, why that tattoo?"

"Mike loved Morrison's poetry," he replies, and he twists his arm so the tattoo faces me. "It just stuck with me once I started reading it."

"Swimming to the moon is scientifically impossible."

"But isn't that what makes life great? Something unexpected?" Andrew asks.

I search for an answer in his eyes.

"I don't know," I reply, and it's the truth. "Everything in my life has been perfectly planned. Meticulously organized." *Until you*, I want to say but don't. "You know Jim Morrison has been dead since 1971. That's over forty years," I say.

"Yep," he says and squeezes me. "He'd be in his seventies by now. Maybe I love their music so much because I can never see Jim live or read new poems. That's what makes someone so untouchable, you know? When you know you can't really have them."

I squeeze Andrew because I know he's talking about Mike, too.

It just comes through me; I don't even know why I say it. Maybe I say it because it's true and right now saying anything true roots me to the ground.

"I can't stop thinking about you," I say. "All the time."

He kisses me again and we only pull apart when a group of women laugh up near the stairs. Their voices echo over the beach.

I feel alone with Andrew even though there are people around. We decide not to bother with the bonfire party tonight with all of his friends. Who needs a beer keg and a drum circle when there's Andrew and me under the stars?

As the last of the Technicolor sparks rain back to Earth, we spend hours on the beach. I don't even know what time it is when the beach starts to empty out. All I know, all I *need* to know is this: Andrew, the constellations, and me.

TWENTY

"BEAN!" MOM SAYS THE NEXT MORNING AND OPENS
the door my bedroom. "Phone!"

I'm still in bed with one eye squinted open at my cell phone;
I missed a text from Claudia at 11 p.m.

CLAUDIA: Details on that guy? Beach soon?

She doesn't seem weirded out by last night's fiasco. I am about
to text her back when Mom calls me again, "Beanie! It's Gran!"

Gran! Thank God! I'm out of bed, down the stairs, and when
I hit the bottom all the glass chandeliers shake. Nancy's face
scrunches when she looks up from flipping through an address
book. On the table in front of her are RSVP cards. I bring the
phone outside to the patio and shut the door behind me. I sit

down on my favorite Adirondack farthest from the door.

"Finally! Someone with some sanity!" I cry.

"Break on through to the other side!" she sings through the phone.

And on cue, the truth serum is in effect.

"Gran. I think," I whisper, "I think I'm in love."

"It's a little too late, dear. Jim Morrison is dead," she whispers back.

"Har. Har. No, with a boy. He loves The Doors." I'm back to speaking at a normal decibel.

"And I just thought you missed your granny."

Nancy opens the patio door; I am sure she's trying to eavesdrop, but I don't think she can when I'm all the way down here. Even though she's Gran's sister, she doesn't understand our relationship.

"And now you do too?" Gran asks. "Love The Doors?"

"It's more than that. I want to talk to this guy, connect with him, you know what I mean?"

"Sure do."

Gran talks to me about the '60s, the Vietnam War, and space travel. She tells me about The Doors and other bands she liked during that time. I tell her all about the Comet Jolie. I don't tell her about Andrew and me on the beach. But I do ask this.

"Do you think . . ."

I have no one to ask. And let's face it, what we did on the beach has been on my mind since it happened and I want it to happen again. But I'm not sure what you're supposed to do or when you do it or how you ask for it again.

"Do you think . . . ," I try again.

"This is a sex question isn't it?" Gran asks. I open my mouth but nothing comes out. "You took too long to respond, dear," she says. I can imagine her at her house in San Diego, overlooking the water. "I guess we have come to that magical age. Spit it out," she says, and I wish I was there sitting with her and Gracie.

"Well, are you supposed to *want* to touch a boy? I mean, when you love him?"

"Hell, honey, you can want to touch him even if you think he's a complete ass!"

I laugh at this. It echoes out to the trees and bay in the distance. I haven't laughed in this house in a long time.

I take a breath of salty air to ask something else but can't find the courage to admit I would lie to someone about my age. I want Gran to tell me it's natural, that people lie all the time. I want her to invent some way that I can be with Andrew and continue to let him think I am going to MIT in the fall. I never thought the lie with Andrew would go this far. I never thought he would want to be with me.

"Have you ever—" I start.

"Oh, just ask," Gran says, laughter still on the edge of her tone.

"Have you ever told a lie?"

"Depends," she says. "What kind of lie?"

"One you couldn't get out of without admitting that you've lied?"

She's quiet. She and Gracie are probably sharing some kind of "knowing look" and Gracie has sat down from whatever task she is doing to hear the whole thing recounted when Gran gets off the phone.

"Yes," she says. "But I was a little younger than you."

"What happened?"

She sighs deeply before she talks again and it's the exasperated sigh I love. She's probably at the kitchen table with her hand resting on top of Gracie's. I scoot into the chair even more and the breeze slips by, bringing with it the aroma of another dinner that Nancy's chefs made for us.

"I wanted a classmate to like me," Gran says. "She was the most popular girl in school. What was her name?"

"Missy Thomson!" Gracie says in the background.

"Right! Missy Thompson. So I told her I was getting a dog, which of course, I wasn't."

"Why did you do that?"

"I wanted her to come to my house so the other kids would know just how fun it was to hang out with me. Anyway, one day during class, I bragged about getting this wonder dachshund named Mustard. I had a whole story. Where Mustard was from, his size, and what we would do with him when he got here."

"But there was no dog."

"Nope. No dog."

"So what happened?"

"She came over and nothing I could come up with made any sense. I thought I could say the dog was getting delivered in a couple weeks, but we had nothing to prepare for the dog's arrival. No crate. No food or toys."

"Wow. Did you feel terrible?"

"Within five minutes, Nancy told Missy I had lied. So I had to tell the truth. No one talked to me at school for a long time. It took people months to trust me again."

Gran's quiet and there's a clank of something in the background, which means Gracie's up from the table and probably fixing something to eat.

"Telling a lie is tricky business," Gran says.

I knew she would listen. Gran talks to me like I'm an adult and not like a kid who has her head stuck in every science experiment she's ever conducted.

"Want to tell me about it?" she asks. Her mouth must be close to the phone because it makes the speaker on my ear vibrate a little.

"Not yet," I whisper.

"Maybe some other time?" she says.

"Definitely. Some other time," I repeat.

"I'm really good at giving sage advice. Can I give you some super sage advice?"

"Sage me up."

"You should only give someone what you think they deserve," Gran says.

"What they deserve?" I ask.

"You are on the inside. Deep in your muscles. That's you. The body is the extension of you. Only give someone your fingers, your skin, and toes if they deserve to touch your soul."

"Wow, Gran," I reply. "You should be silent for a week all the time."

She laughs and it's so familiar, something I can completely

count on no matter what is happening in my life.

"And one more thing?" she says. "If you're lying to someone you love, well then they aren't getting the real you. They're getting a fraction of you."

A fraction of me. It feels exactly the opposite with Andrew. Because of the lie, he's seeing the real me in a way no one ever has before.

"I can't wait to come see you," I say.

I tell Gran I love her and when we hang up, I sit on that lounger looking out at the water for a long time.

Andrew isn't getting a fraction of me. The lie about MIT is just circumstantial. It was just a dumb thing I said to get him to keep talking to me on the beach to test the Scarlett Experiment.

I shuffle the peas on my dinner plate a couple of days later.

Who am I kidding? The lie about my age and MIT wasn't a big deal before, but now, it's bothering me. It's becoming a wedge that I have to make fit into so many of our conversations.

"Tomorrow's the best beach day of the season so far!" the newscaster's voice echoes from the TV.

"Coming to work with me tomorrow?" Dad asks. "You can finish your essay in my office. We've got about a month until it's due, right?"

"One month exactly," I say but don't know if I really want to go to WHOI.

"That reminds me!" Nancy says with a jump. She waddles to her desk in the corner of the kitchen. "I have to reserve the tent at least two weeks in advance."

This party is all she can talk about. I stab another pea. Scarlett comes home August 5th. One month until she comes back too. Less than that, actually.

This is all going by too fast.

I've been waiting for Andrew to text me with our plans for the night. It's been kinda quiet between us since the debacle on the Fourth.

"Ettie called," Mom says. That's one call from Claudia and two calls from Ettie that I have to return. I don't know what to say to Ettie. I feel like I can't talk to her if I don't tell her Andrew's real age. I don't want to lie anymore than I have to.

"Want me to proof your essay this weekend, Beanie? That'll give you time to revise," Dad asks.

I stab another pea. Stab. Stab.

"That would be great," I say, just wishing we could talk about something else. Anything else.

What this means is I actually have to start the essay. My phone beeps.

Yay!

"Haven't we gone over this?" Nancy asks.

"It'll just take a second," I say and slide it out of my pocket. I am about to read my message when Nancy snatches the phone and places it down next to her knife. I rub at the top of my stinging hand where her talon fingernails scraped my skin.

"Really, Bean. I don't know what's gotten into you. Bringing a phone to dinner. You can have it when we're done eating."

Dad's eyes narrow past me on the television in the other room.

227

"First, you whine about the gorgeous dress you have to wear to the party," Nancy says.

Actinium, aluminum, americium . . . antimony, argon . . . what's after argon?

"You didn't show any interest when we mentioned going to a cake tasting the other day. It's like you didn't even hear me."

I didn't.

"And *I* haven't seen you working on your scholarship."

"I work on it in my room. And when did you become an expert on my work habits? I thought you *wanted* me to social- ize?" Nancy only notices what she wants to see and that's every single detail that proves just how unlike Scarlett I am in every part of my life. I talk on my cell and hang out with my friends just like Scarlett, but to Nancy, it's not the right *kind* of social- ization.

Mom says nothing. Dad watches the TV.

Nancy's face is all geometric shapes, pursed lips, and squinted eyes.

"What's going on with you? Are you even listening to me?" Nancy says.

I slam my fork down on the table. Mom and Dad jump in their seats.

"Nothing's *going on* with me," I say.

"Oh, I understand perfectly well." Nancy points at me. My chest heaves, I'm so mad. Nancy turns to Mom. "This is all that boy Tucker's fault. You better get those two in a room to talk to each other at the party."

"He's not coming to the party," I yell. "You're like the dictator of extracurricular activities. Why can't you be more like Gran?"

"Scarlett! I mean, Sarah!" Mom scolds. She can't even be angry with the right person.

"Wait, what?" Dad says. He raises his eyebrows—he's trying to catch up.

"My sister is a burnt-out hippie!" Nancy says.

"You don't know Gran and you don't know me. And I don't want to wear that stupid cupcake dress either!"

"Beanie, calm down!" Mom yells.

"Cupcake?" Dad asks.

"It's a beautiful dress!" Mom says.

"You'll do what you're told," Nancy says, still pointing. "If you want any help from me, under my roof, you'll do what I say!"

"Do you even hear yourself? Do you even actually know anything about me?"

"Bean, calm down!" Mom says.

I get up so fast Nancy's bajillion-dollar chair hits the floor. I walk to Nancy and snatch the cell phone so quickly she flinches. I lean in close to her and fear prickles behind her eyes.

"I hate that dress." I say it quietly, but my voice shakes. "And I won't wear it!" I turn and my feet clip against the wooden floor.

"Where are you going?" Mom calls.

"For a walk," I say without looking back.

"You get back here! You will wear that dress!" Nancy yells after me. Just as I am about to pull the door closed, she squawks to Mom, "You need to control that girl!"

I slam the door and bring my hands to my mouth because the noise is really, really loud. I run my fingers over glass to feel for cracks. On the other side, Dad says, "What's a cupcake dress?"

They are all silent for a few seconds then everybody talks at once. Their muffled voices rise and fall within the house. I can't tell what they are saying. It doesn't matter. I could script it accurately.

I lean my forehead against the cold glass.

"See? I told you." Nancy's voice is *right* next to the door. I shoot up and back away to the next step in case she opens it up. "She has been cooped up in a science lab much too long!" Nancy says, but her voice retreats farther away back into the house.

I move down the front steps to the street.

The street lamp highlights my chipped toenail polish. I can't believe I talked to Nancy like that. I'm just so tired of swallowing my words all the time.

Also, Mom and Dad don't need to control me.

Something in the corner of my eye catches my attention. I look toward the street lamp at the end of the cul-de-sac.

Andrew sits on the hood of his pickup.

I almost forgot I got a text message. My cell phone is still clenched in my hand; I open it.

ANDREW: Am I a stalker if I'm on your street?

Relief flutters through me and even makes my cheeks tingle. For a second, I think he might be a hallucination because he's exactly who I need right now. The hazy blue light of his cell phone just barely shines on his beautiful features. With each step to him, my chest releases. I ache to be closer to him, to someone who doesn't classify me, who doesn't put me in neat, labeled boxes. Andrew looks up from his phone and scoots over to make room for me. By the time I make it to him, I can smile. He doesn't have to know about the fight with Nancy.

"Let out?" he asks.

"Escaped," I say.

I lean into his body and his arm scoops around me. I inhale. He smells like soap and suntan lotion. Comfort.

"Stalking is a felony in Massachusetts," I say.

"Up to five years in prison for a first time offender," he says with a proud lift of his chin. "I'd risk it for you."

It's enough to make me want to cry.

"I was about to come to the door. Surprise you," he adds.

Adrenaline pings in my chest. He would have heard the fight.

"Surprise me? With what?" I ask and simultaneously try to figure out a way to explain to him that he *really* can't come to the door—ever.

"Party," he says. "Curtis's house. Want to go? It's only like two minutes from here."

"Sure," I reply and glance back up at Seaside Stomachache. That house has never earned its name more in its existence.

TWENTY-ONE

CURTIS'S HOUSE IS ACTUALLY THE STAFF HOUSING for the Wequasset Inn. It's the other super fancy resort on the Cape and the employee housing sits on the bay with a massive water view.

"But Curtis doesn't work at the Wequasset," I say as we pull into the end of the driveway.

"His parents won't let him come home, so he stays here."

There's a tug on my gut. I couldn't imagine being ousted from my house forever. The accident can't be the only reason. I don't get a chance to ask anything else because we get out of the car. Bass music and loud voices echo from the windows. Andrew turns the knob and we walk inside.

Candles line the mantle above a defunct fireplace. Wax drops onto the ground near a couple of guys with long hair comparing scars on their knees. The music is pumping. Andrew, the boy who gets all the looks from the girls around us, leads *me* through the party. The music plays and the slide on the electric guitar goes up and down. I catch myself in the mirror. Here, as the music plays a hypnotic song, I am beautiful. My hair falls over my shoulders and as the guitar slides again and again, Andrew leads me through the tanned and blond people—lifeguards.

We find Curtis in the kitchen pumping beer into a cup from a silver thing on the floor. Ah. A keg. Scarlett is always saying people are getting "kegs of beer," but I never knew what it looked like until now.

"Hey!" Curtis says, waving us into the room. He's not that drunk yet or at least he seems sober. Andrew hands me a drink in a large red cup.

I take a sip.

"You like it?" Andrew asks. "They usually buy shit beer."

The froth is kind of bitter, but it's okay. I'm not about to go to the next rager at Summerhill, but I don't mind the taste.

"Did you know it takes five ounces of CO_2 to run a keg?" I ask.

Andrew laces his arms around my lower waist, drawing me to him. I try not to spill my beer when we kiss. Our mouths taste like the beer and in that moment it's just us. No Nancy, no cupcake dress. No Mom yelling at me across a kitchen table.

"That's why you're amazing," he says.

"Because I can remember nearly every scientific fact I have ever heard?"

"Yep."

"No, no, she's in New York!" Curtis says behind me, and this gets my attention. Andrew turns around and laughs.

"Give it up. Scarlett is done with you," Andrew says, and the sound of Scarlett's name from his mouth is a burst of adrenaline through my stomach. "Broadway ballerina and your fish market ass?" Andrew says, and laughter erupts around us.

"Scarlett?" I ask, trying to dig for information.

"Yeah. Curtis hooks up with her. Her family comes up to Orleans every year. I just like to give him shit. She's way out of his league."

So much for Scarlett thinking she's at local status.

We lean against the kitchen breakfast bar.

"She's a ballerina," Andrew says.

"Oh," I say, trying to sound like this is new information to me.

"But she's a major bitch. She's having this huge party at the end of the summer. We've never even been to her house, but we all have to go and get dressed up."

We. He said we. *Andrew is invited.*

Of course he's invited.

I want to cringe. Instead I grip on to Andrew even harder.

"What's the party for?" I ask. I want Andrew to talk so he can't tell my voice is weak.

He takes a sip of his beer. "Not sure. Her grandmother or someone is throwing it."

Scarlett would never leave Andrew out of the party plans; he's

Curtis's best friend. Andrew would have shown up at Scarlett's party even if we *never* met. If I don't say something before the party, he'll see me in that horrendous cupcake dress and put it all together. My cup nearly slips from my hand and some beer sloshes onto the floor.

"I got it," Andrew says, planting a kiss on my nose and crossing the kitchen to grab a paper towel. In the second he's gone, I lean hard against the kitchen counter.

He's been coming to Scarlett's house all summer, he just hasn't known it. He clearly hasn't paid very close attention to his invitation. He will know the instant he pulls onto Shore Road. He'll know the second he looks at the invitation.

When he comes back he wipes the spot on the floor and then the outside of my beer cup. He hands it back to me and it's drier but no easier to hold. My hands tremble. Andrew leans into me again and continues, "Anyway, Scarlett bosses her friends around, talks to people like they're idiots. And everyone lets her."

"Not your favorite person?" I ask with a shake in my voice. I say it in my head again and again. *Andrew is invited to Scarlett's going-away party. Of course he is. Why didn't I see it?*

I am supremely stupid. I am absolutely going to have to tell him I'm Scarlett's sister, there's no way out of that.

"Scarlett's okay," he continues. "She's just not my kind of person."

"Who is?" I ask.

"Not you," he says, but Andrew's uneven smile tells me he's playing. "Definitely not my type."

The tips of our noses are just inches apart. Andrew kisses my lips but just barely. When he touches me like this I don't think about the going-away party or the lies I told. His hands are so warm on my body and when he pulls away he keeps his eyes on my mouth. I don't know what he finds so fascinating about my lips.

"You're exactly what I want," he whispers. I exhale. No one has ever said anything like this to me. Not until now. "And you smell *so* good," Andrew says and inhales deeply. He kisses me again and his stubble pricks at my skin, but his lips are so soft. He runs his mouth over mine again and again. Goose bumps erupt over my arms.

Andrew's lips press against mine and our kiss deepens. I'm completely engulfed in his arms. If anyone will understand why I kept my identity as Scarlett's sister a secret, Andrew will. He'll get what my family thinks of me and who they think I am. I will figure this out no matter what. He already likes the real me. He knows me. We keep kissing, I don't even know for how long.

I just have to find the right time to tell him.

An hour or so later, Andrew is saying hello to some of his friends outside and I'm still leaning against the kitchen counter. I'm on my third beer and my chest is warm. How the hell am I going to even start to tell Andrew that Scarlett is my sister?

I am deep in my problem when Curtis comes into the kitchen and stops next to me.

"American flag string bikini," he says in a low voice.

Curtis stands across from me and leans a hand on the counter.

"It was an experiment," I say and take a large step away.

Curtis squints, confused at first, but he cocks his head. "Oh yeah, you're a science freak," he says.

I sip on my beer, trying to act casual.

"MIT or some shit, right?" he says and swigs from his cup.

His eyes are glassy. I remember our drug prevention lecture during health class. Glassy eyes. Slurred words. He is intoxicated. I am supposed to feel bad for him, for Mike's death and for losing a friend, but I can't find that place right now.

Behind me, through the kitchen doorway and down a crowded hallway, I search for a sign of Andrew's blond head.

"You think you know Andrew? You know, right? You know you're just temporary?" Some of his beer spills onto the tile floor. He doesn't notice. "Andrew doesn't even drink anymore. Can you believe that?"

Curtis gestures to me, his cup of beer tips and spills down my shirt. I jump back and a few people groan. It soaks through and trickles down my stomach to the waist of my shorts. Someone yells "Party foul!" from the back of the room. I turn my back to Curtis to find some napkins or a cloth.

"Did I get beer on you? Shit. I'm sorry."

I start patting my neck and chest with paper towels when Curtis pulls my shoulder to turn me around.

"I'll help," he slurs. "I'll help."

"I got it," I say. "It's okay, I have it under control."

One of Scarlett's friends, a girl with long dreads, steps into the kitchen. The sour smell of the beer is overwhelming. "You okay?" she asks, but I don't have time to respond. Curtis elbows his way next to me.

"Move, Shelby," he says to the girl. "Give me the paper towels. It's my fault, I should do it."

"Please stop!" I cry and step back from Curtis entirely. I'm about to leave the kitchen when he points his finger at me and yells, "You don't have to be a bitch about it." Curtis pulls at my hand and I drop the towels to the floor. "Hey, science bitch. I'm sorry. No. You're not a bitch. And I'm sorry about the beer. I'm *sorry*."

"Stop it!" I say loud and clear. I yank myself out of Curtis's tight grip but an immediate pain pins in the center of my wrist. "Let me go!"

I head for the hallway and cradle my aching wrist.

"I want to say 'I'm sorry' to your face," he yells. "I want to say it to you!"

Shelby steps into the kitchen even farther, as though she's shielding me from Curtis. I can't find Andrew in the crowd.

"Let it go, Curtis," Shelby says.

"I'm not talking to you. I'm talking to *her*! She's only my best friend's girlfriend."

There's a sharp tug on the neck of my shirt, choking me. I am yanked backward. Curtis is tugging me!

I catch myself on a side table and almost in the same instant I am pushed even farther. I grab on to the kitchen doorway to stand back up. Andrew has moved me out of the way of Curtis and rushed into the kitchen. His face is very red and his hands are clenched into tight fists.

"What the hell is wrong with you?" Andrew shoves Curtis so his back smacks against the refrigerator.

"Nothing! She's lying about me. I didn't do anything! She's lying!"

"I saw you. Don't you ever touch her like that again."

Curtis lunges at Andrew. Andrew stumbles back a few feet but throws his arms out to catch his balance. Andrew's back muscles tense under his T-shirt. He shoves Curtis away again so he falls into a kitchen table and chairs knocking them sideways. His sneakers squeak and slide on the linoleum.

"I didn't do anything!" Curtis screams. "She's lying about me."

What is he even talking about?

"What? Do you think you're too good for me now?" Curtis says and spit flies out of his mouth. His face screws up into uncomfortable grimaces when he talks. He tries to lunge at Andrew again, but Andrew is sober so it's easy for him to get out of the way or push back. Curtis tries to regain his balance but then swings a wide punch, missing Andrew entirely.

"Stop it, Curtis. Stop fighting me!" Andrew warns.

My wrist pulses in pain and I rub at it to dull the ache.

"You weren't there that night. You're never there," Curtis says, just on the edge of tears.

I can't pull my eyes away from the fight. My heart is pounding and I can't help but feeling that somehow this is all my fault.

"I was driving Mike to your house!" Curtis yells.

There's a huge crowd behind me now.

"You weren't there," Curtis slurs. More spit flies out of his mouth and into the air. "You think you're better than everyone. Better than me. With your slutty girlfriends like Maggie and that wannabe—"

"Don't say it," Andrew warns. "Don't do it."

Curtis gestures to me. "I don't need to say it." He pauses. "Slu—"

Andrew throws a punch and the hard smack of flesh against flesh echoes.

I push through the crowd to get out of that house.

"Sarah!" Shelby calls after me, but I maneuver through the bodies to the front door.

I escape to the front yard. Low tide and cigarettes permeate the air. I rub at my wrist; it's sore and I might even have a bruise in a couple of hours. I rub at it again—it really hurts.

I stand on the lawn imagining all the different ways I could have stopped the fight. Maybe I should have jumped on Curtis and brought him to the ground. I wanted to, but I didn't know I wanted to until this second. It makes sense to me now that his parents kicked him out. Maybe he is this violent and drunk all the time. What about AA?

"Sarah!"

I spin around.

Andrew hesitates in the doorway and runs outside. A red scrape swipes up his cheekbone. He opens his arms to me, wrapping me in his smell. His shirt is wet from sweat and his heartbeat slams against my head.

"Holy crap, I'm sorry," he says, and I can hear his voice vibrating through the tight hold of his body.

"What was that all about?" I ask.

"I don't know," he says, but his breath is still labored. "Mike. The accident, I think. Let's get out of here."

"I think—I think I want to walk," I say.

"I'll go with you," he offers. "It's my fault we're even here right now. I thought it would be a good time."

I need to think through what just happened in that house, what I saw, and why I've never seen anger and pain coupled with such violence before. Not in person, anyway, not with my own eyes.

I back toward the street. "I kind of want to be alone," I say.

"You're hurt," he says, and the concern in his tone makes me want to cry. He gestures to me. I'm still cradling my wrist but didn't realize.

"It's just bruised," I say.

"Do you want to get it looked at?"

"No," I say and back away again. Andrew stops walking to me. "It's not that bad."

Andrew stands by his car with his keys just hanging there in his hand. "I'm sorry. I didn't think. He doesn't act like that usually. Since the accident he's been . . ." Andrew hesitates. ". . . different."

"I know," I say, even though I don't. I haven't experienced grief and death in that way before. I hear about people dying all the time, but it's always stories on the news or someone's grandparents.

"Call me when you get home?" he asks.

I nod and head as fast as I can down the street.

I don't even bother to look at my phone. My wrist throbs in smaller intervals as I walk and when I get to Shore Road, I slow my steps. It smells like salty air and somehow, even though the beach is almost a mile away, sand scatters throughout the asphalt. Every street on the Cape somehow has sand on the road. I could search for a scientific reason, I could make sense of it in some factual way, but I don't want to, not right now. Logic isn't making me feel better right now.

I stop before Nancy's house and it's dark. No front porch light, no evidence that anyone inside is awake.

I go up the front steps, inside, past the kitchen table, and stop at the stairs. The crystal is in its place for breakfast—the silverware, too.

No one left me a note or anything. I slip my cell phone out of my pocket and make sure it's on silent.

Before I head up the stairs to my room, I stop at the long hallway that leads from the stairs to Nancy's wing of the house. I've only been down here a couple times. The hallway seems cast in silver from the snowy track lighting above.

Dozens of framed photos line the walls. I stop at the first one. It's oversized, like someone paid extra to make an old photo enormous. In the photo are Nancy and Uncle Raymond, her husband who died before I was born. They stand in their wedding attire before an archway of white flowers.

Dad doesn't talk very much about his uncle. Neither does Nancy, now that I think about it. I guess it's easy to leave out painful subjects from conversation.

I move from picture to picture. In one near the end, Nancy and Uncle Raymond sit on a sailboat. She wears a 1960s high-waisted swimsuit. She's older than she is in the photo with Gran, but I don't know how much older. She doesn't have the wrinkles on the sides of her mouth like she does now. She always looks like she's frowning even when she's not.

Or maybe she is. Maybe Nancy is frowning even when she's smiling because she's had to be alone in this house for twenty years.

You weren't there that night. You're never there.

How do we let go? I never understood that phrase. Let it go. Grief haunts. This summer I've seen it haunt Curtis, Nancy, and even Andrew, who wants to live his life for someone who's dead.

I walk away from the photos and stop at Mom and Dad's room. Through the partially open door, I peer inside. They sleep back to back. As usual, Dad snores like an idling motorboat. Mom is a small lump under the quilt.

When I get in bed, I pull the covers around me tight. Within a couple seconds, the phone vibrates and I jump, fumbling for it in the darkness.

ANDREW: I'm so sorry. Did I mention this?

ME: How is this your fault? I'm just freaked out.

ANDREW: Definitely talk tomorrow.

I keep seeing the angle of Andrew's elbow as he raises his arm and punches Curtis. I'm not even sure Curtis saw Andrew in that moment, or anything at all. As I lie there, I think for once in my life, I understand the power of grief. Like all scientists I have witnessed its power through empirical evidence. Grief scares me. For once, I wish I wasn't so adept at seeing things from the outside.

TWENTY-TWO

THE NEXT MORNING, THE CARPET BARELY SQUISHES under my feet as I step down the stairs. I figure the less noise I make, the better, after last night's fight with Nancy at dinner.

How can Andrew's best friend be someone like Curtis? Someone who accidentally kills his friend because he was drinking but then continues to drink. Why doesn't anyone say anything? *Do* anything?

I cross the living room to the kitchen. Nancy sips her coffee but doesn't acknowledge me.

"I don't know how we'll get everything done in just a few weeks," she says to Mom. They sit at the kitchen table together.

A few weeks? It's July 8th; I *have* to start the essay for the Waterman Scholarship.

I also *have* to tell Andrew I'm Scarlett's sister. I sit down at the kitchen table and rest my chin in my hand. Like I said, I just have to find the right moment. Last night at the party certainly wasn't a prime opportunity.

"Ahem . . . ," Nancy says.

I look up. Nancy has been watching me. Dad's reading the paper on the couch and Mom is flipping through an education magazine. God. I know I have to apologize though I'm not sorry—not at all. I want them to apologize to me. I want them to respect my feelings.

I get up to pour some cereal; my spoon clanks against the bowl. So many times when Scarlett was bitchy, Mom and Dad sat her down and made her talk it out. They're acting like everything is fine. Like I wasn't just screaming at our meal ticket.

When I sit back down Nancy asks, "Don't you have something to say to me, Beanie?"

Beanie. I wish I could sigh really dramatically.

I suck it up because I don't want to deal with this for the day and I'm not going to get what I want from Nancy. Not ever. I have no idea how to give her what she wants.

"I'm sorry," I say and attempt to sound convincing. "Just had a bad day yesterday."

Nancy nods once. She sits there in her nightgown, sipping on her coffee.

Mom winks at me when she thinks Nancy isn't looking,

but Dad keeps his eyes on the newspaper. A squeaking noise comes from behind me. A maid is using cleaner on the massive windows.

Nancy scoops another bite of eggs.

"It's a beautiful day. What's your schedule?" she asks me.

"Work on my essay for a while then maybe go to the beach," I say. Yes, let's pretend we're having a normal conversation.

"You could go with me to the salon if you'd like."

Oh boy. This could be Nancy's weird way of trying to make peace. It could also be a hint. I smooth my hair and wince from the soreness in my wrist. I almost forgot.

"What's wrong?" Nancy asks and frowns.

"I fell last night. It's just bruised."

She takes another bite and I conveniently pretend to watch the news on the TV so I don't have to tell Nancy that going to a salon is my own personal version of hell.

"I'm happy to see you're not going to WHOI every single day," she says.

"I love WHOI," I say immediately. "I just haven't had the time to go as much as I'd like."

I don't want Dad to be hurt. I dare to look at him but don't think he heard me.

"And I told you at the barbecue, I met a friend," I offer, and as the words are coming out of my mouth, I immediately regret it. "The girl I hung out with on the Fourth? Her name is Claudia," I add.

"That's right," Nancy says. "I thought that was just a story to shut me up."

"I didn't lie," I say, but my cheeks burn.

"You could invite her to the party if you want."

Then Claudia would have to see me in the cupcake dress and I'd have to look like a complete loser on multiple levels.

"I think that's great," Nancy adds and eats her eggs with her pinkie finger up. I had no idea that people could actually eat this way successfully. "It's good you're getting your head out of the clouds."

"She's on top of it, Nance. Give her a break today?" Dad says gently and puts down the paper. He grabs his WHOI briefcase and kisses me on the head as he heads for the door. Thank goodness I showered before coming to breakfast. My sheets still smell like beer.

"Did you ever find out if that boy Tucker is coming to the party?" Nancy asks Mom.

I am suddenly not very hungry.

"Well, he said he wasn't coming, but I think Carly is insisting, which really isn't necessary."

Mom avoids my eyes when she says this, but if I were Tucker I wouldn't want to go either.

Am I Andrew's girlfriend? Curtis said I was, but Andrew and I haven't exactly discussed it. It's been less than a month; I'm not sure if that's the right time to ask. I'm not usually in this position. If Tucker does show up, I don't want to explain that Andrew is my "sort of" boyfriend.

"They need to behave like adults," Nancy stresses, and I leave the conversation to go up to my room.

Is it wrong that I want to make it official? Is it wrong that I want Andrew to say I am his *girlfriend*? I put on a Scarlett bathing suit, a black one-piece with a very low plunge in the neckline. I almost wish Nancy and Mom would see me in it, just to make them notice me. My phone beeps.

ANDREW: Dune riding at sunset. You in?

Do these people ever work? I text back as much.

ANDREW: Yes, Star Girl. But the key word there was sunset.

Once I pack up my beach bag for the day, I text Claudia to see if she and Chelsea want to meet me at Nauset. Turns out she's solo again because her friend had to go home.

She agrees to meet me at Nauset and once we're on the beach, I know I have to explain about the Fourth of July. Within minutes of getting onto the sweltering sand, we're rubbing in sunscreen.

"Gabe left yesterday too. But we'll stay in touch . . . I think," she says with a shrug and slides on dark circular sunglasses. I'm wearing a cheap pair of aviators I got in town at the local pharmacy. I've seen Scarlett wear that style before.

"I bet you will hear from him," I say. "He seemed really into you."

"Every summer I meet a guy and I think we'll stay in touch, but we never do." She slides down her chair, crosses one leg over the other, and brings a hand to her chest. She says in a very heavy Southern accent, "As the leaves change color and fade away, so does summer love."

I laugh. "Hey! That was pretty good!"

She sits back up. "*What* the hell happened when you left the other night? Did you break it to that guy that you're not into him?"

I can hide my eyes behind my sunglasses, but my nose scrunches up when I say, "I kind of . . ." I roll my eyes at myself even though Claudia can't see it. "I just said all of that stuff in front of you guys . . ." I groan and hide my face in my hands. "I didn't mean it. I was nervous or something. It was so stupid."

"Nervous about what?" she asks.

"That you wouldn't like me or something. So I just showed off. I am actually *completely* into this guy."

"He's hot," she says. "Who wouldn't be?"

The sound of families talking and kids yelling from the shore fills the uncomfortable silence.

"Why didn't you think we would like you?" Claudia asks.

I chuckle but shake my head at myself. "I'm not—I'm not the most popular girl in school," I finally say. "I have friends and everything, I just don't have anything to say to *those* girls."

The name Becky is on the tip of my tongue.

"You thought I was one of *those* girls?"

Dad's words about me assuming people don't like me swirls through my head again. I don't want Claudia to be offended.

"No. No. I don't mean a snob or anything. I just thought you seemed—cool. And I wouldn't know how to hang out with you."

"Girlfriend!" she says and leans forward to me. "I *am* cool." We share a laugh.

"You don't think I'm lame?" I ask.

"No," she says. "I never know what to say to people. I just act all dramatic, quote plays and movies, and try to be funny so I don't have to try to think of original things to say."

It seems amazing to me that Claudia would be worried about how to fit in with other people. She seems so confident. I like that we both have no idea who to be all the time.

"So . . . ," she says and sips on a water. "Tell me what the hell happened! What's his name? What's he like?"

"Well," I say. "His name is Andrew . . ."

I tell Claudia the whole story but purposefully leave out the lie about MIT and my age. Just like I did for Ettie, I shave off two years so she doesn't know Andrew's real age. As I talk, she leans in, laughs, and asks me to tell her how he kisses. This is like having Ettie here, but different because Claudia has already dated a few guys. I wouldn't trade Ettie for anything but Claudia is great too.

We finally get to the part about Curtis and last night.

"How's your wrist now?" she asks.

"Okay, it's just a little sore."

"If I were there I would have kicked his ass for you."

We laugh again and split some homemade sandwiches.

"Are you going to be okay?" she says.

"Yea, I just need to think it through more."

"I would too," Claudia says.

As I bite into my ham and cheese, I think maybe, just maybe for real this time, I've made a new friend.

TWENTY-THREE

THAT EVENING, RIGHT AROUND THE TIME THE traffic leaving the beach is over a mile long, I slide into the passenger seat next to Andrew.

"Am I your girlfriend?" I ask plainly.

Andrew nearly spits out his soda. He swallows and looks over at me, laughing.

"I don't know; do you want to be?"

"You beat up your friend. You punched him because of me. One would logically deduce that I am your girlfriend."

The smile is gone instantaneously.

"I punched him because no one in their right mind should ever grab another person the way he did. No one should talk to you the way he did."

Oh.

"And because you're my girlfriend. I mean, if you want to be?"

"You know I do."

He leans in and kisses me, and I can taste the Coke. His lips are cold from the icy soda can.

"So," I ask, "where are we going dune riding?"

"Curtis has a bunch of buggies from his grandparent's place. There's about ten of us, and five buggies, so you can ride with me."

Curtis? Seriously? How can he *want* to spend time with Curtis? Especially after last night? And to be honest, how could he expect me to want to spend time with Curtis?

"How's your wrist?"

"A little sore, but it's better."

I can't put this together.

"You're quiet," he says.

"I was just thinking that some of the dunes are on conservation land and no one is allowed to ride on that sand," I lie.

"Don't worry, Miss Scientist, we're heading to Provincetown beach. It's not conservation land there."

We drive and the music plays. It's The Doors again, but I don't know the song. I don't ask, either, I just try to figure out what I am going to say to Curtis when I see him today. If we're going to ride dune buggies with him then he and Andrew must have made up. A couple small cuts run across the knuckles on Andrew's right hand. The scrape on his cheek is a faint red line.

We pull into the parking lot of Sandy Neck Beach and

Andrew kills the motor. "I'm such an idiot! You don't want to be around Curtis after last night. I'm used to him, but you're not."

My shoulders relax and I nod.

"I've been sitting here trying to figure out why you're being so quiet. I'm a dumbass. Let's go somewhere else. Anywhere," he offers.

I shake my head and look out at the parking lot. It's emptying out, but there are a few families packing their chairs and umbrellas in their cars. Mom, Dad, Scarlett, and I used to go to this beach. Dad liked to swim and I would hold on to his back. We haven't done that in a long time. Years, actually.

"Why doesn't anyone stop Curtis from drinking?" I ask.

"He's got to make his own choices."

We get out and stand by the side of Andrew's truck.

"Let's go," he says. "Screw the buggies. Anywhere you want."

"I'm not afraid of Curtis. I'm sad for him," I explain.

"He probably won't remember most of it today. The fight with me he will, but not what led up to it. He never mentioned you this morning."

I would never be able to be best friends with someone who could just forget the violent events of the night before. Not to mention that he got into a fistfight with his best friend. Ettie would never give someone a dirty look let alone hit a person. Tucker wouldn't either. I have to ask. The question is going to drive me insane until I get it out.

"How can you be *best* friends with someone who would treat people like that?" I ask.

Andrew hugs a backpack. He considers his answer and his

shoulders slump. He focuses on the group in the distance. Someone yells, "Andrew," and it's like the prince has arrived. That's how it always feels to me, anyway.

"Because he's been my best friend since we were nine. Mike was like our brother."

"But he's an alcoholic," I say. "I'm not saying get rid of him because he drinks too much. But whoever he was before, he's not now. He's dangerous."

There's a kind of sadness in Andrew's gaze I can't quite figure out. He seems to stare at nothing.

"Yes," Andrew finally says. "Yes, he's dangerous now."

My cheeks warm from the drop in Andrew's voice.

"I didn't mean to upset you," I say, unable to meet his eyes. "I can be too pushy sometimes."

"Nah," he interrupts me with a quick shake of his head. "You just said what I haven't been able to."

Across the asphalt are five neon-colored dune buggies, which really look like matchbox cars with huge wheels. Imminent death should be their name. Not dune buggies—deathmobiles.

We walk toward the group and I wonder if everyone will be talking about last night. I avoid Curtis's eyes and he seems to be doing the same. Whenever I check, his back is to me.

Andrew slaps the hands of his friends and they do a kind of handshake I've seen them do before. I want to know this handshake too. I watch, and Tate, the bartender from the Lobster Pot, catches me. I look away and when I do, Shelby, the girl with the dreadlocks, smiles at me. Smile = good sign. No need to break that down and test it.

"Sarah. You need a nickname," Tate says.

"I do?" I say, and Andrew hands me a pair of leather gloves with the fingertips missing. I want to ask him if he is aware it is eighty degrees out. I don't.

"What's your last name?" Tate asks.

In this entire time, this entire summer, not one of his friends has asked.

"Levin," I say, panicked that I didn't have time to think of a lie. I haven't mentioned my last name to Andrew since we first met.

"Levin?" Tate says and cocks his head. I'm waiting for it. I can so easily imagine him saying, "Scarlett's last name is Levin." Or that he'll tell me he already knows a Levin, that name is taken and I should know better. Or something.

"Levin needs to know the handshake. If you're about to dune ride with us on the beach, you must know it."

"Then I must know it," I say and widen my stance like I'm about to run a football play. I'm ready.

We shake, we catch fingers, we snap, and he does some weird thing where he shakes his fingers around. I try to mimic it but fail. We try again. "See," he says with a big bear laugh again, "you catch on."

I'm about to ask him to do it again—maybe I should be writing down symbols? For practice? A helmet plops down over my head.

"Come on, *Levin*." Andrew's gentle humor makes my last name sound less like a swear, and I immediately wonder what Scarlett's nickname is with this same group.

"I think I prefer Star Girl," I say from beneath the hot helmet.

"That one's ours," Andrew says and points at a blue buggy with big black wheels. Andrew gets on the bike first then pulls his helmet on, and I climb on behind him.

"It's gonna be really bumpy," he says, turning his head so I see his profile. "Hold on tight." And I do. Our engine revs. One by one, like little gunshots, so do the rest of the buggies. The smoke billows from engines and—*boom*—Curtis is the first to dart off the parking lot asphalt and onto the trails of dunes. We climb slowly up huge sand hills and I dig my helmet into Andrew's back. The whole group yelps, hoots, and hollers as we pop up and down the rolling dunes. Ahead, Curtis revs his engine and his buggy jumps in the air.

The force of the bike is too much over these hills. It's not like a regular bike, there's high velocity. There's force *and* speed. Why didn't I listen more during the aerodynamics lecture? Oh boy. We could go down hard! There's no cushioning.

"Sarah!" Andrew yells over our motor. "Look up! You're missing it."

I raise my head higher. In the distance, the great ocean is sparkling away.

I don't want to miss this. I don't want to miss anything else again.

We race past hills of dunes and tall, green beach grass. The hot summer sunset burns my face. I remember to keep my mouth closed.

The buggies, like toy cars, jump over the last few rolling hills. Whoops and yells sound out around me. Andrew yells too as we jump over a big hill. We hit the sand almost in unison. Curtis rides next to Andrew and me. Through the opening in his helmet, a black ring circles his right eye. His eyes linger on me and maybe—or maybe I just want this to be true—they say they're sorry. He pulls ahead just as we crest another hill and I scream from the loop my stomach is doing when we come back to earth.

More yells and more screams of happiness echo over the dunes as we ride. I love this. All of us, rising and falling, again and again—together.

A couple of hours later, I'm sitting cross-legged watching a bonfire crackling away and I haven't even thought to check my cell. I hold the display up to the firelight: Of course, no one's called. I tuck it back in my pocket. Andrew and a couple of other people have driven the buggies back to the parking lot while the rest of us stay on the beach. He's put Shelby on Curtis "drunk-ass" watch while he's gone. Curtis keeps away from me; I think he remembers more than he lets on. I sit with my beer in my hands as the sun descends over the beach. Shelby sits down next to me.

"You're eighteen," she says, but it sounds like a question.

My stomach swoops like I'm back on the buggies again.

I nod—it's better than saying it out loud. Out loud makes it more like a blatant lie.

"You look younger," she says.

I pinch at the sand and try not to meet her eyes. Empirically, I know this behavior expresses that I am nervous.

"I get that sometimes," I say and take a swig of the beer. A few weeks ago I never would have touched the stuff. It's not like

I'm about to become a beer drinker or anything, but it's nice to relax and have fun. I'm not used to it.

"You know, Scarlett's little sister looks a lot like you. I've seen her before."

"I'm not Scarlett's sister," I say and sip on the beer again.

Shelby raises an eyebrow.

Where is Andrew?

"I've met your aunt Nancy. That woman is a piece of work."

I face Shelby directly.

"Wait a minute. You didn't have dreads last year!" I say and slap my hand over my mouth. Damn.

"How old are you really?" she asks.

"I'll be eighteen in a few weeks. I'm, like, eleven months younger than Scarlett."

"Does Andrew know?"

"No. Scarlett doesn't like to admit we're close in age," I say, really trying to convince her. "And in a few weeks it won't matter." Shelby raises an eyebrow again. I wish I were telling the truth more than I can possibly express.

"I shouldn't have lied. I know that," I add. "But, please keep this between us?"

"Okay, I get it," she says. "I knew I had seen you before."

I can't confess the real truth to Shelby. I want to. I want to tell someone so badly.

Deep down where the truth is hiding I know I can't tell Andrew I am Scarlett's sister. I thought my lie about Scarlett was independent of the one about my age and MIT. I assumed that somehow it would be easier to confess that I was Scarlett's sister—that it was safer somehow. I see now that all of these lies are connected. If Andrew finds out I'm Scarlett's sister, he'll tell Curtis, who will definitely tell Scarlett. It will get back to Andrew how old I am and everything will unravel.

Scarlett won't back me up. She would never protect me.

"Why didn't you tell Dickwad that you're Scarlett's sister? He'd kiss the ground you walk on," Shelby says and nods to Curtis, who's now standing by the shore.

I sip on the beer again. "I've lived in her shadow long enough."

Andrew walks down the steep dune that leads from the parking lot. I turn to Shelby. I am sure my expression reflects that I mean what I am about to say, because my heart certainly does.

"I really don't want to be associated with my sister," I say. "It's hard enough being almost the same age as her. She hates it. She hates me. So, if you could keep this between us, it would be, well, good for me. Me and Andrew," I add.

Shelby's eyes warm. "I have a sister too," she says and pats my knee. "I get it."

Andrew plops down on the sand and pulls me toward him, so I lean against his warm chest.

He kisses the nape of my neck and shivers rush down my arms. Across from us, Shelby joins Tate by the water. She picks up a shell and glances back at me. She winks, and I take this as a sign that she won't tell.

The whole beach is lit in an orange twilight. The tops of the dunes are spotted with stars. I could walk up one, in a dream perhaps, all the way to the crest. I would stand up tall and proud and take one of those stars from the sky. Andrew's arms squeeze around me almost as if he is reading my mind and telling me that yes, we'll do that someday.

We'll take a star from the sky together.

I hope there can be a "we" for a long, *long* time.

That's all I can do—hope.

TWENTY-FOUR

ANDREW'S CAR DOOR SLAMS AND I SLIDE OUT too. The party left me with my head buzzing and my feet light. We're at Andrew's house. I step out of the truck before a traditional Cape Cod house: two stories, small, blue shingles.

"Not Seaside Stomachache," I say.

"Star Girl, you can't make fun of my humble abode. We're not on Shore Road here," he says.

"No. No. It's perfect. Your house is perfect."

I'm not drunk, just warm. Buzzed. Andrew's house has a front porch with a grill sitting on it and a bunch of potted plants—most of which are dead. He unlocks the front door. I follow him inside and plop right down on a floral-patterned couch.

There are stuffed birds, ancient radios, framed vintage news-papers, and creaking floorboards, just like at home. On the walls are aerial photographs of the Cape Cod shoreline and what I assume are portraits of Andrew's family. There are no lighthouses or white wood paneling like at Nancy's house. No invitations organized in shoeboxes, linen patterns, or silver teapots. There are definitely no cupcake dresses hanging in closets.

"This house," I say, "is great."

It occurs to me: There are no parents here, no one telling Andrew what he can and can't do.

Water runs in the kitchen, shuts off, and Andrew joins me on the couch. He hands me a cup.

"How many beers did you have?" he asks.

He smells like sweat and boy, which I can't place my finger on but I think its cologne or deodorant. "You smell like boy," I say aloud.

"Drink," he says. I do and gulp down the whole cup of water.

"Three. Three beers," I say.

Andrew's kitchen is basically a fridge and stove. Above the couch is a picture of Curtis, Andrew, and a tall blond guy with a great barrel chest I haven't seen in their group of friends before. Each of them rests a long lacrosse stick on a shoulder.

"Is that Mike?" I ask and gesture to the photo.

"Yeah," he says. "My dad took that at the BC/Hobart game last spring. He had it framed last summer. You know . . . after."

"I'm sorry," I say and slide to the floor. I turn myself around to face Andrew who remains on the couch. "I'm sorry your friend died."

"Me too," he says quietly.

"I don't know anyone my age who's died," I say.

I place the glass next to me.

"I hope you never have to," Andrew says. He doesn't move his eyes from the floor. I want to take away his sadness and I don't know how.

I pull him to the floor with me and wrap my legs around his hips. Andrew lies on top of me and I kiss him, wanting him, needing him to know how sorry I am that all of this has happened and how much I wish I could take his pain away. He returns my embrace and runs his hand up my back. His hips start moving in a rhythm and I try to match it. His breathing is getting heavier. He slips my shirt over my head.

It's off, it's on the floor, I'm wearing just my bra, and an overwhelming urge takes over me. I want his body near me more than anything in the world. His lips are on my neck, my lips, and on my neck again. I'm fumbling for the button of his shorts and he reaches in and takes out his penis with his right hand. I've never seen anyone do this and all I want to do is hold him, make him feel as good as he does me. He moves his hand and I see how much thicker and larger his penis grows. I hesitate. I don't know what to do exactly. I don't want to be wrong.

"What?" he says gently, his breathing hard. We're both shirt-less, me in a bra and him with his khaki shorts unbuttoned. "Is it—what's wrong?"

"I can't," I say. "I'm not . . . ready. I mean, I am, I just need some time. I want to know what to do." My cheeks must be so red because a flush of heat runs through my chest and face.

Andrew sits up quick and buttons his shorts. "Come here." He opens his arms to me. I lay my head on his chest. His heartbeat is familiar to me now.

"The last thing I want to do is make you uncomfortable," he says.

"You don't make me uncomfortable. Ever."

I say something, which is so painfully true it's a relief to say it aloud.

"It's just that, school and science. That's my life. I've never gotten so close to someone," I say. "Not like this. I don't want to screw it up."

"Never," he says.

He strokes the side of my head again and again. I could fall asleep with our skin on skin, and my cheek warmed by his body heat.

"You don't get into MIT and track comets by dating every guy in the world."

Half of that sentence rings true within me, half of it is the right thing to say. The other half breaks me apart a little. This lie is now in every thread of our conversation. It's everywhere.

"Will you wait a little? For me?" I ask.

"As long as you want, Star Girl."

My bottom lip trembles and I bite at it so it stops. I wish I could tell him everything. Tell him all of it, the whole truth— from the night with Tucker until this moment. Instead, I lie there and when the silence is still nice and the warmth of his body could lull me to sleep, I say, "I think I should get home."

He pulls me up and kisses my head. My hands wrap around

Andrew's and as he leads me outside, I want to tell him the truth.

I want to believe that in some strange scenario we could make it work.

Over the next two weeks, I have to work on the application and every time I start the essay I delete immediately. It's all so cheesy. I want to say something I mean, something true about me. My procrastination is getting out of hand and August 8th is approaching fast.

I came to WHOI today to spend some time with Dad, but also, it's seal feeding day.

I *love* seal feeding day. It's the one day they let Dad and me help the marine biologists feed the seals at the aquarium. We can sit on the edge of the pool with the trainers and help drop fish into the water. One of the seals, Bumper, is blind. I love Bumper. Have since I was twelve.

But for now, until 9:30, I must sit at this desk in Dad's office and finally focus on this stupid essay.

The Waterman Foundation is the oldest astronomy scholarship in the country. Please explain in 1,000 words why your experiment successfully represents who you are as a scientist and how the execution of your experiment reinforces your educational goals.

I don't even know how to begin. Why is tracking the comet part of who I am? Because it's all I think about? Because I've stood outside on Friday nights with long-range binoculars while the rest of my class was out having fun, just so I could see the dusty tail of some silly comet? No. That's not good enough. I don't think the scholarship committee will care about how the comet impacted my social life. The essay needs to be academic and professional. I need to wow them. Who am I as a scientist? Who am I?

I don't want to write this essay right now. Everything else is done. It's the only thing that's left. Fourteen days is more than enough time.

That reminds me. I glance up at the calendar. It's July 25th. That means I also only have fourteen days until Scarlett comes home.

Fourteen days until all my lies come crashing down on me. Ever since I realized that Andrew was invited to Scarlett's party, it comes back into my head on a delayed loop. The last ten days or so I've just been on autopilot. But when I'm alone for five minutes, it will sweep through, unwelcome, haunting me. The beach, the party, Andrew's house—again and again.

Why did I have to pick a boy who knows my sister?

The radio echoes in Dad's office and he turns it up to hear the DJ.

"Tropical storm Lola is heading across the ocean toward the East Coast. It's too early to accurately decipher if she'll be a hurricane. Keep it here for updates on 96.3 the Rose."

There's the squeak of his chair and he stands in the doorway.

"It's 9:45, kiddo," he says. "Make any headway?"

"Tons," I lie.

Dad combs his hair to the side to cover his bald spot. Once he puts the comb in his front pocket, we lock up the office.

"Looks like we might all blow away at your sister's going-away party," Dad says as we walk from Building 40 to the seal aquariums.

"Maybe we can position Scarlett for the strongest gust."

"Come on," Dad says with a laugh. "I'll let you feed Bumper first."

Bumper and Lu Seal turn and spin, uninterested in the walls holding in their tank. I've dropped a few fish into the water, but it isn't holding the same thrill that it usually does. Dad asks all kinds of questions about the temperature of the water and the seals' daily maintenance. Bumper and Lu Seal don't need to do tricks for their food. I love their little whiskers and tiny mouths. Bumper's eyes have a milky film over them—they're not deep brown like Lu Seal's.

In the distance, down the street filled with tourists, the Martha's Vineyard ferry blows its low horn.

You don't get into MIT and track comets by dating every guy in the world.

Lu Seal's little flippers propel her down the long length of the tank. I focus on the ripples in the blue depth of the water.

I am running out of time, I know that. Either I leave early and never speak to Andrew again or I say something. The truth is going to come out at the going-away party. Maybe I can invent some reason for Andrew to miss the party altogether. *I* have to go to the party, what am I talking about?

I groan but cover it up with a cough so Dad doesn't notice. That's ridiculous.

I want to dive in there with those seals. Bumper twists and turns in that water even though he can't see a thing. I wish he knew how beautiful he looked.

Scarlett used to come to seal feeding day when we were little. We would come here and afterward go on the Fort Hill Walk. It is a trail that leads through the Eastham woods. A boardwalk snakes and curls through hundreds of moss-covered trees. It was magical to me then, a place with great but silent power.

We always went every year at the beginning of the summer and then again at the end. That reminds me that I have junior year orientation in a few weeks too. Summer goes by too fast. Everything I've done, all the places I've gone and people I met will slip away soon, just like the warm weather and salty air.

I have to go back to Rhode Island and back to my life. My life where I get my driver's license this year and start prepping for the SATs. I don't want to stand here anymore. Seal feeding day isn't making me feel better like I thought it would. I walk over to Dad, who is still chatting with a couple of scientists.

"I'm gonna go for a walk," I say. "Just go think for a while."

"That essay's got you distracted from Bumper and Lu Seal," Dad says.

"You got it!" I lie, but manage a smile.

"Bean's applying for the Waterman Scholarship . . ." Dad

starts on his whole spiel about the comet and me. Some of the biologists wish me luck.

I say thank you and head out.

"Eleven months of calculations!" I hear Dad say before entering back into the main building. "A hundred percent accuracy."

Even though I know the *Alvin* is not assembled, I head to the tool shop.

I keep thinking about the night of the party at that airport bistro. The night I wore that ridiculous dress. Mom thought I had been home but I had already been out for *hours*. That gnawing doubt I felt that night, that tidal pool churning in my stomach, swirls again.

I make it back to Building 40 and push through the double doors of the tech shop. I walk directly to the spot where the *Alvin* would usually stand, but the floor is bare.

It's only been a minute, but Rodger stands by my side.

"You look like someone stole your puppy."

"Mom's allergic to dog hair."

Rodger's hand gently cups my shoulder. "You know, the *Alvin* is just the vessel," he says. "It's the scientist inside that counts."

He leaves to do something important, like all the scientists do. Was the comet experiment important? Yes, I know in my heart the execution of that experiment was huge. I can track comets. I can track them from millions of miles away.

The Scarlett Experiment was important too. But it's not that important anymore.

I stare at the floor where the ghost of the *Alvin* stands.

Scarlett would never find beauty in the deepest sea. She barely likes sand on her toes.

Jim Morrison said, "break on through to the other side." He said it over and over. Break on through, break on through, break on through. I text Andrew before I chicken out.

ME: I want to try out the Fort Hill trail. Want to come with me?

ANDREW: Never been. Totally game but stuck with work for the next few days.

ME: Perfect.

Andrew will be blindsided at the party. The time has come. And I'm doing it as soon as possible, before I can't, before I break apart and fade away too.

TWENTY-FIVE

"HOW IS IT THAT I'M A LOCAL AND HAVE NEVER been here?" Andrew asks a few days later and slides out of the truck.

My heart is pounding so hard I'm nearly out of breath. This is it. The moment. We stand in the upper parking lot at the entrance to the Eastham, Fort Hill trail.

"I used to come here with my family," I say and lean on the hood of the car. The trail leads through the Nauset marshlands, but across the bay, the ocean waves crash onto the outer beach, Nauset Beach. All I can do is stay focused. *Tell him the truth and don't chicken out.* I'd been practicing in the mirror for the last day or so but could never look in my eyes when I said the words aloud.

"You know," Andrew says, taking his place next to me, "you can drive from the outer beach almost all the way out there." Andrew points to the farthest tip of sand.

"Where we were for our first date?"

"That's a lot farther but the same basic idea," he says and gestures to the path that leads down into the Fort Hill boardwalk. He takes my hand. "Ready?"

"Steady" is on the tip of my tongue, but it feels so silly now. I can't believe that was a "thing" Tucker and I ever said to one another.

We walk out of the marshlands and onto the boardwalk that leads through the forest. The sunlight fades the deeper we get into the woods.

"Wow," he says, ducking under a massive tree trunk that arches six feet above the boardwalk. "You'd never know the beach was behind us."

I inhale the familiar, earthy smell of the moss and bark of the red cedar trees. I just need the right moment or a logical transition. Everything in my body feels tight, from my forearms to my jaw. The pressure to tell him is hardening my muscles. This cannot be good for me.

"So are you going to tell me what's wrong?" Andrew says. "You hardly said anything in the car."

"I'm sorry. Here it is. It's just, my aunt, the one we stay with every summer? She wants me to be just like my sister."

Do it. Say it. Say it. Just say, like my sister, Scarl—

He has that look again, that concerned, "I am here for you" look and I want to scream.

His expression eats away my words.

"My sister has a lot of different interests and I guess I'm more . . ." I search for the word. "One-note," I say.

I can barely stop myself from cradling my head in my hands as I walk.

"You're not that way at all," Andrew says and takes a hold of my hand. "You're the opposite of one-note."

"My sister spends all this time with my aunt during the year. And they can talk to each other, really talk, you know? My aunt doesn't know how to talk to me. She thinks I need to be the same as I was before. . . ."

"Wait, Scarlett! Wait for me!"

Scarlett runs ahead, follows the curve of the boardwalk, and disappears around a bend. Her laughter curls into the air.

"Beanie, look at this tree," Dad says. He stops and Mom follows after Scarlett. Dad touches an ancient limb of a tree. The moss is soft and I run my fingertips over it again and again. "Feather flat moss," Dad says. "It means the forest is old."

Dad holds on to my hand as we keep walking. We finally catch up to Scarlett and Mom. Scarlett pirouettes and leaps down the boardwalk.

"You try it!" Scarlett calls to me, and I try to jump too. I don't land as quietly as she can. Our laughter ripples into the air.

I refocus on the boardwalk. Andrew walks quietly by my side. He doesn't press me to talk. That's a nice change from Tucker, who always told me how I was feeling before I had the words to articulate it.

We're not far from Dad's tree; it's right up ahead. I recognize it from the specific twist of the gnarled branches. This one has a massive branch that arches overhead too. It's much higher than the last one and only the tips of Andrew's fingers can graze the bark.

I stop at the tree and run my fingers over the green moss. Andrew steps behind me and kisses the nape of my neck. Chills rush over me. I'm going to try again.

"My sister is the perfect one," I say. "She's older than me."

"How old?"

"Closer to your age."

Tell him. Tell him now. Frustration gnaws at me. Maybe I can hint at it now and then really explain it to him the night of the party. That way he won't have time to talk to his friends about me and find out about my age. I can contain this a little if I parse out the truth over time. My back aches from holding my breath.

"You should be yourself," Andrew says, and that only makes my muscles even tighter.

"But you," I say. "You're still working out your life too so that's comforting."

"What do you mean?"

"I mean you work for Mike's family. You live his life, you said so on the beach."

Andrew frowns.

"No. I said I'm working for his family because I owe it to him. I'm living my life, Sarah."

"But you're not," I say. "You should be in school pursuing your criminal justice degree."

Andrew stops. "That's not true."

Up ahead is the last bit of the boardwalk, the sunshine beams where the dense trees stop and the dirt lane begins again.

"Yes, it is. You're fishing when I know you want so much more. You're not pursuing your dreams, you're pursuing Mike's, and he's dead."

"What the hell do you know?"

He walks ahead toward the exit and I follow after.

"That's a fact, Andrew. He's dead."

Andrew whips around.

"I know he is!" he yells to the trees, and I jump backward. I'm glad we're alone on the trail. Andrew immediately dips his chin to his chest. "I'm sorry. I shouldn't yell."

I don't say anything. Andrew's face is red and he has both hands on his hips.

"You don't get it. You've never been through anything like *this*," he says and flings his arms out. "I am living the life I want. It's the life I owe to Mike. I should have been there that night and I wasn't. I told you this. You couldn't understand."

"I understand. Believe me. Do you know what I hear every single day? You can't wear that! You should be working on your essay. You should have more interests. You're just a little girl. Get your head out of the clouds. Get a backbone—"

The name "Bean" catches in my mouth and I stop it.

"No one else but you should define the life you want to live," I say.

"Next year, in college, you won't have to worry about that anymore. You'll be living your own life," Andrew replies.

Anger surges through me. I'm angry that I'm not actually

going to college next year and angry with Andrew for believing what he is seeing and not asking any questions. I almost wish he would catch me at this point.

I stride past him toward the exit and once I'm beyond the dense trees, the sun blasts the sandy pathway.

"Sarah, wait," Andrew says, his footsteps padding after me. I stop and look up to the top of the path at the parking lot above. A couple of cars have pulled in, but no one is coming down the path yet.

"I just have to do this for now," Andrew says as he catches up to me. "I can go back to college later in a couple years. We can still be together." I bring my hands to my face. A sob runs through me and it vibrates against my hands.

College. *College.* Damn it. I'm seeing red—seeing blue—seeing nothing but how mad I am.

"You wanna throw your whole life away?" I cry. His hazel eyes seem dark and his jaw is set tight. "Fine. Why don't I do that too! Why don't I take a page out of Andrew Davis's book and I'll skip the scholarship. I'll take more shit from Nancy when she has to pay the tuition. I'll be just like you and throw away my whole future!"

I'm not looking where I'm going and I am thrown forward. I've tripped on a rock and my palms hit the gritty ground.

My skin stings when I push up from the ground. "You don't even know me," I say. "Or what I am capable of."

Andrew takes a step and eyes my red hands. He wants to help me but he, just like everyone else, has no idea how to do that. Only I can. This is my fault. No scenario I've presented will work. I've come to the end of my options.

Andrew follows me up to the parking lot.

"I'm walking home," I say.

"It's, like, four miles."

"I need to be alone," I explain.

"I don't know what to say," Andrew says as he stands by his car. "This is really surprising me."

I turn. Maybe it's dramatic. Maybe it's silly to say, but I'm mad at him for being perfect and for being exactly what I need.

"You wanna live Mike's life, be my guest," I say. "Then you might as well be dead too."

TWENTY-SIX

"TWO TYLENOL?" I ASK MOM THE NEXT MORNING.

Trying to make it through breakfast after a night of no sleep is hell. I imagine this is what it might feel like to be hit by a Mack truck. I think I got about three hours max. I kept waiting for my phone to beep.

I kept waiting for Andrew to respond to my text messages:

ME: Wow. Overdramatic much? I am really sorry for this afternoon.

And the next one:

ME: I had no right to blow up at you like that. Your business is your business and I should keep my big mouth shut.

And the last:

ME: I'm really sorry. I was actually mad about something else. Shouldn't have taken it out on you.

In an effort to do something that wasn't completely sabotag-
ing my relationships, I distracted myself from 5 a.m. to 6 a.m.
by double-checking the Waterman Scholarship application. I
somehow managed to finish proofreading the fifteen pages even
though my headache was slamming against my brain. I still need
to write that damn essay.

Today is not that day.

"Don't feel well?" Mom asks and hands me a couple of Tylenol.

"Not really," I say, after swallowing the pills. I slide on some
sunglasses and head to the stairs. It's dark there and I can be
silent in my room.

"Were you out last night?" she asks, turning to me from loading the dishwasher.

"You couldn't tell?" I ask and back toward the stairwell.

"You're so quiet!" she says.

"I can be loud."

"Beanie . . . ," she says and shakes her head.

When Scarlett goes out on weekends Mom waits at the
kitchen table until she comes home.

I get upstairs and collapse on my bed. I check my phone—I
only have one message, and it's Claudia responding to me about
going shopping for some clothes. I know I'll need some of my
own once Scarlett comes home.

CLAUDIA: Stuck with family today. Tomorrow?
ME: Definitely.

After a quick nap, I can move my head again without a knife digging into the back of my eyeballs. I gather my beach things to head to Nauset alone.

I am about to sling my bag over my shoulder when my phone rings.

I nearly knock all of my Waterman papers off the bed trying to get to it.

"Hello?" I say as casually as I possibly can. I think the decibel of my voice went up too high and I clear my throat. My head throbs and I bring my hand to my forehead.

"Bean."

I rip off my sunglasses, stand up straight, and double check the caller ID just to make sure. I sit back slowly into the chair.

Tucker.

"Bean?" His familiar voice echoes through my phone. Tucker's voice isn't higher than Andrew's, it's just . . . different. Like it isn't totally formed yet. Like it'll be deeper in five years.

"I know you hate me," he says. He's probably sliding his glasses closer to his face.

"I don't hate you," I say, and I'm surprised it's true.

Silence.

"You must be wondering why I'm calling."

"Yes," I say, and I am wondering. "But since quitting the Pi Naries in June, you must be swimming with free time."

He sighs and says, "Can we have a normal conversation?"

"Go for it, Tuck."

"Trish is excited about your sister's party. My mom's been

trying on dresses for weeks."

Ah. The party. I guess I get to finally find out if His Highness is coming.

"Everyone gets to see the famous Nancy house," I say, just to get the conversation to the point.

"Trish went to visit Scarlett in New York."

"Woop-de-doo."

"You don't sound excited," Tucker says.

"I'm sorry. I guess I can't have a normal conversation with you. Let's just cut to the chase. You coming or not?"

"Would you want to go if you were me?"

I don't answer this because I'm not sure what I'm supposed to say. That no, I wouldn't ever want to go to an Aunt Nancy party as long as I lived?

"My mom is kind of making me."

He waits a few seconds before adding, "I know Ettie told you about Becky and me. We're still together."

"Good for you," I say. "Really, that's fantastic. Can't wait to see you guys at school. Oh and p.s.? I have a boyfriend," I blurt out and hit myself on the forehead. My stomach lurches and my headache radiates again.

"That's cool," Tucker replies, but his tone betrays him and I am victorious. Because I know it bothers him. VIC.TOR.IOUS. More silence.

"Who is it?" he asks.

"You'll meet him on the sixth," I say and hang up without saying good-bye.

In the silence that follows, the computer screen stares at

me—it hates me. It mocks me with the question I've been avoiding for weeks. I am not going to pull off the party without getting caught.

My phone rings a couple more times during the day. Ettie, Mom, Nancy—never, not once, is it Andrew. By midafternoon his absence is all I can think about.

He lobsters Tuesday, Thursday, Friday, and he's at the juvenile detention center Mondays and Wednesdays. It's Monday. Maybe he's just too busy?

Maybe?

That night at dinner, I'm stabbing peas again. Andrew still hasn't called.

In the living room the TV weatherman talks about the tropical storm.

"Even if it's a tropical storm," Dad says, taking a bite, "we could have wind speeds up to fifty miles an hour."

"So you're telling me I need to have a tent assembled and disassembled the same night?" Nancy asks and sips on her wine.

I purposefully left my phone upstairs once I started getting the marathon text messages from Ettie, who heard from Becky Winthrop's little sister that I had a boyfriend. She was mortified that she hadn't been briefed about Andrew and me making it official. I imagine how the story went down. Poor Bean has a boyfriend, some loser on the Cape. I'm the butt of some horrible joke and I realize—fork in the air, about to take a bite of Chilean sea bass—Tucker *had* to make that call to me this afternoon.

Becky made him. Becky wanted to make sure that she was in

charge, in control. She wanted me to know that they were still together even though Tucker was going to Scarlett's party where he couldn't bring her as his date. Oh joy. School is going to be super fun this year.

"We'll get Scarlett at ten next Friday morning," Mom says to Nancy. I tune back into the conversation. "You should come along."

"No thanks," I say and sip from a glass of water.

"Oh," Mom replies and lowers her fork. "Okay."

"You should go with your mother if she asks you," Nancy says.

"No," I say, my head swiveling to Nancy. She's dressed in her own grown-up version of the cupcake dress. "We're talking about something that is happening a week from now. And it was an invitation not a command."

I know I stepped over the line. I put my fork down.

"I'm going upstairs," I say. Everyone is silent at the table, and Dad is watching the game in the other room.

"Beanie, you should finish your dinner," Mom says, but I keep going up the stairs.

"Bean!" Nancy calls, but I don't listen. I don't need to.

I don't want to be Scarlett's welcoming committee. Scarlett, who belittles me. Scarlett, who scoffs when she even considers that I might sneak out of the house. How many times has she looked down her nose at me? Heat sweeps over my cheeks. She bought me that Egyptian Musk because she knows that I envy what she thinks is beautiful.

I am at the top of the stairs when I hear whispering from the kitchen table, probably about my behavior.

All that evening I wait for my phone to beep. Andrew usually calls or texts a few times during the day. I blew it. I was a lunatic at Fort Hill. They should just lock me in a cage and let people examine me. I'm like a wild animal.

I finally succumb to the assault of messages from Ettie and confess that I fooled around with Andrew. I don't tell her the specifics, but I admit that we went further than I ever did with Tucker.

ETTIE: You traitor. I am stuck at band camp every day and you are hooking up.

ETTIE: Hello? I want specifics here.

I hesitate.

ME: There's not much to say!

ETTIE: Tell me everything! Please!?

ME: Going to bed, will update in the morning.

I'm not really going to bed. I just want the beeping to stop, so the false hopes stop too. As I lie there, the walk at the Fort Hill trail floats into my mind, but it's not about the fight with Andrew. The boardwalk snakes into the trees and the light filters through the full green leaves in thick beams. Mom and Dad walk side by side. Dad wipes his head with a handkerchief. My feet are clad in pink sandals and the *plunk plunk* sound of my feet echoes over that boardwalk.

That will never happen again.

My phone is silent on the bed. The silence is different in this house than at home. No TV chattering away all night, no whir of the computer, just the central air system cooling the house.

All I want in this whole freaking world is for that phone to beep. And I want it to be Andrew. I want it to be Andrew who says to me *You are amazing. You are wonderful.* Who lets me apologize. Who lets me be me.

Who doesn't call.

AUGUST SCHEDULE

IMPORTANT DATES:

- ❑ *Princess Scarlett returns—Friday August 5th (finish cleaning Scarlett's clothes!!!)*
- ❑ *Party August 6th.*
- ❑ *Organize for Waterman Scholarship: due date August 8th*

LOOKING AHEAD:

- ❑ *Personal Essay.*
- ❑ *Get junior year orientation packet.*
- ❑ *Pi Nary meeting. Projector needed?*
- ❑ *Call Bennett Pool to arrange for lifeguard lessons?*

TWENTY-SEVEN

I DON'T WANT TO MAKE LISTS ANYMORE. I SCRIBBLE out the word "orientation" from my daily planner. I don't need to write and rewrite things a hundred times. It's not making me feel any better. Five days. It's been five days since I talked to Andrew.

My fingers linger over the smooth metal of my cell phone.

Claudia agreed to meet me at the beach and then to go shopping. It'll be good to have someone else to talk to. I can't concentrate on my application anymore and I work well under pressure. Also, it stops me from staring at my phone.

An hour later, we're sitting, my back sticky and hot against the plastic of a beach chair. The sand is well over one hundred degrees. Okay, so I was wrong. The rustling of potato chip bags and the mindless chatter doesn't distract me from checking my phone endlessly.

"Oh my God, Sarah. Stop it."

Claudia takes the phone and buries it deep in my NASA bag.

"Ugh. I know," I say.

"People get in fights. It happens all the time," she says.

"Yeah, but he hasn't even responded to my text messages in five days. It's over. I just have to accept it."

She leans an elbow on the arm of her beach chair.

"Listen to me. Every time you think about calling or texting him, talk to me instead. If he's too much of a jerk to accept your apology then screw him."

It feels better to have a friend nearby.

"Should we head back home a day early?" one tourist asks behind me. All anyone else seems to be talking about is this stupid tropical storm. I wish Nancy would just cancel the party, but I know that's not an option.

"Tropical storm just means there will be rain and some wind," the other tourist says. "I don't want to lose out on the hotel."

A group of girls wearing string bikinis walk by the waterline. They are tourists, or I would probably recognize them. I'm wearing the American flag string bikini for perhaps the last time. I adjust the triangle top; Scarlett will never let me wear it when she comes home. I wear it because in the fantasy version of my life, Andrew is here on the beach. He recognizes the American flag, walks up to me on the beach, and kisses me. He will have some amazing reason for this silent treatment.

But in the reality version, my phone is silent.

"So I think I have to go home on Friday. My parents want to leave because of the storm too," Claudia says later that afternoon at Viola's. She holds a pink bandeau dress up to her frame. "Whatever, at least I'll get to see the renovations at the theater before everyone else."

"That sucks. Did you tell them you desperately wanted to stay for my sister's insanely over-the-top going-away party?"

Claudia laughs. "Of course. But my mom is completely freaked out. When do you start school?"

"September third. I definitely want to see all your plays this year," I add and pick out a black cocktail dress from the rack. It's pretty short with spaghetti straps that crisscross and make complicated interlocking patterns across the whole back.

Claudia plops down in a chair by an oversized window that looks out on to the busy main street. "I'm going to miss you!" she says. "I wish we had started hanging out earlier this summer."

"We'll have tons of time this year and then all next summer," I say. She nods and says, "But I wanted to see your aunt's house. And your telescope."

"Anytime you want. Come before you leave. Nancy will probably cater the event if I tell her I have a friend coming to the house. She might not let you leave. Ever."

Claudia laughs and I step behind the familiar curtain of the dressing room. I change into the dress. It's definitely form fitting. I step out and before the floor length mirror. Only this time, my friend breaks into a huge smile.

"Oh my gosh," Claudia sits up. "You have to get that."

Wow. It's exactly what I've been wanting. It's simple and

elegant and makes my legs look long. This girl in the reflection *is me*—the way I feel inside.

This is who Andrew sees. I can see a glimmer of her here in this mirror.

Maybe when he sees me in this dress at the party, he'll forgive me.

"I guess I'm not getting the blue geode necklace after all," I say.

I get changed and pay.

We walk through town, and I pick up a few more items— some sandals, a couple tops—and when we're done, I have about twenty dollars left from the Pizza Palace fund. I have always gone home with money every single summer. This time, I won't, and I don't feel bad about it at all.

I hug Claudia good-bye at Shore Road.

"If I don't get a chance to come by first, I'll see you when you get home," she says. "And if you don't tell me what happens with Andrew, I will come to East Greenwich and hunt you down."

"Definitely," I say with a laugh.

I watch Claudia walk as she heads back to her parents' house half a mile away. It doesn't feel like good-bye because I'll probably text her in ten minutes. I already imagine her hanging out with Ettie and me at home.

It won't be one of those summer friendships. I think this one might be for life.

That night, even all the way down here in Orleans, I swear I can hear the swells breaking in Truro twenty miles away. I toss and turn in my bed.

Beep. My cell phone chimes twice. I scramble for the cell, but it slips from the night table and I fall to the floor in a twist of blankets.

ANDREW: Surprise.

My heart thuds and I cannot type fast enough. My fingers fumble on the keys and I make twenty typos to write four words. Finally, I hit send.

ME: Where have you been?

The phone beeps again.

ANDREW: Come down to your beach.

I throw off the covers and hop out of bed. I'm wearing sleeping shorts and a Mathlete T-shirt. Ah, who cares? I tiptoe down the stairs. Toe, heel. Toe, heel. My heart is not pounding—it's thundering. Even if someone is awake, it doesn't matter. I can light a bomb off in the front yard, no one will care.

My feet squish on the wet grass.

The moon runs in and out of the clouds and it makes the whole backyard hazy. I tiptoe down the pathway between purple hydrangea bushes. I push aside long branches and lavender petals until I make it to the bay beach. The path opens up and there, standing on the end of the dock, is Andrew. His back is to me, but he turns and when he smiles, the whole moon backlights his head like a halo.

Andrew arcs gracefully and dives into the bay.

He comes up through the water, shakes his hair out of his eyes, and smiles. I hold my arms across my chest. He swims from the dock toward me on the shore.

"Good evening," he says, stepping from the shallow water to

the beach. He wraps his cold arms around me and I nuzzle into his chest even though now my Mathlete shirt is soaked.

"Nice night for a swim," he says.

"What are you doing here?" I whisper. Andrew's little motor-boat sits at the end of the dock.

"I have a surprise for you."

"For me? I don't think I deserve much of anything right now."

He's close. The urge to hold him close overwhelms me. I can barely get the words out.

"I cannot believe the things I said to you," I continue. "You had every right to be mad. Every right not to talk to me any-more."

Andrew's eyes drop to the sand. "I was mad, at first. But after a day or two, I realized that you were right. Everything you said at the trail."

It takes me a second to focus on the actual meaning of the words coming out of his mouth. A line of bay water drips down his chest and I want nothing more than to run my finger along its path.

"I was?"

He nods but to the ground. "Yeah," he says quietly. "Your delivery sucked, but you told me the truth."

Hardly.

"You told me what I didn't want to hear. But I needed to."

His eyes have that sparkle in them again, the glint of light I love.

"Don't you want to know the surprise?" he asks.

"Definitely."

"I registered for school today. I went to BC and signed back up." He smiles huge and the moon backlights him. "We really can start together in the fall."

I jump on him and into his arms. He can't waste his passion or his talent. He just can't. But as he puts me down, the truth dips through me and I want to curl in on myself. For one moment, I believed my own lies.

Andrew leads me to the water.

I know I don't have the strength to tell him about Scarlett right now. The pain of his absence was too much.

"I don't have my suit," I say.

"We find ourselves in this position a lot," he replies.

"I don't know," I say. "What if my parents . . ." But I stop. Mom and Dad would never expect me to be out of bed.

He takes a step closer to me.

"You're a big girl . . ."

He lifts the T-shirt over my head, the air holds a flicker of a chill, and I'm not wearing a bra. Even though the air is salty and humid, a ripple of goose bumps rushes over me. With one tug of his right hand, my shorts are almost at my ankles. I lift one foot and then the other. I am only in my underwear. I throw my hair back over my shoulders.

No Scarlett clothes now.

"You are beautiful, Sarah."

I stand on that secluded bay beach and I'm exposed, open.

"Absolutely beautiful," he says. He leads me toward the bay. Once I am waist deep, Andrew lifts me by my hips, just like that day we jumped in the ocean, but this, this is different. The water in the bay is almost still. It's warm and he is firm under his shorts. And for the first time, I want to take my underwear off. I've never wanted to be so close to anyone before. I want him so close to me that we share our bodies.

He pulls me closer, kissing my mouth and when he pulls my hips to his, I gasp. I run my palms over his chest up to his shoulders.

I can't stay out here as much as I want to. It's too risky with Nancy's bedroom facing out here.

"I should go in," I whisper. Andrew kisses me again, and all I can do is kiss him back because I don't want the night to end.

I do something very, very stupid.

"Come upstairs with me," I say.

A glint of mischief plays in his eyes. Right, I'm standing in the harbor with no clothes on, he thinks I want him to come in for sex. And he's smiling.

"Not for that," I say. "I mean, I do want to, but there're way too many people inside."

"Okay," Andrew says, and his eyes squint a bit. He's confused, but that mischief plays in the raised corner of his mouth.

"Will you come in? Just to be with me. To sleep next to me. I have the top floor to myself."

"Definitely. But I gotta be out by five in the morning."

Perfect. No one will see you.

We trudge out of the water, and when we step back onto the sand I pick up my wet T-shirt and shorts, holding them close to my naked body. We tiptoe together and Andrew stays close behind me. The branches and leaves on both sides of the path tickle my arms. Andrew's breath is quick.

"I haven't snuck into someone's house since high school," he says in a whispered laugh.

"Yeah, me neither," I reply, coming out of the pathway onto the moonlit backyard.

We climb the stairs to the deck. In the reflection of the glass panoramic windows the moon shines down on the patio. My hair drips and sticks to the middle of my back. My pink underwear is nearly see through. Who cares. I turn the handle. The crunch of the sand beneath our feet sounds so loud, I'm convinced Mom and Dad can hear this all the way on their side of the house. Once we get to the third floor, we won't have to whisper. For once, I'm grateful that the Seaside Stomachache is so big.

I reach back, Andrew's wet hand grasps onto mine and something about a boy in just his swim trunks, clutching onto his sandy jeans makes me braver. He is here for me.

For *me*.

I point to the stairs. They creak beneath our feet. We both stop and freeze at one particularly loud crack of the stairs. We dart past Scarlett's floor and soon we're up on mine. I open the door for him and we scoot inside.

His arms slide around me and I shiver, waiting for his body heat to warm me up.

"Come on," he whispers and pulls away. I shiver again as the air-conditioning pumps through the vents onto my skin. Andrew sits down on my bed. "Let's get warm."

"Hold on," I say and lock my door. Just in case. I can't help it. I check to see if the Waterman Scholarship application sits faceup on the desk along with a couple of Summerhill Academy folders. They do and I relish the darkness.

I wring my hair out, bay water sprinkles the white carpet, and Andrew lies across my bed, leaning his head on his hand. I've never been naked in bed with a guy before, not even Tucker.

"I told you this a hundred times, but you're beautiful," he says.

I crawl on the bed toward him and snuggle into the sheets. He stays on top of the blanket. His blue eyes are darker in the night. His shoulders and chest are broad and I want to touch him again, run my fingers over him like I did down in the bay.

Andrew moves the sheets aside and slides his wet body on top of me instead. The pressure of his weight lifts when he holds himself up.

"Tell me something about you," he whispers.

"Like what?"

"I don't know. Something. Anything. I spent a day on a boat with fishermen."

I lift my chin and find his lips—we kiss, and it's salty seawater. There's a tiny ball of light in the center of my stomach and it's radiating up to my chest, to my throat, to my mouth, and I pull away from his lips. I don't want to be anywhere else. *Ever.*

"Okay. Have you ever seen a solar eclipse?"

Andrew shakes his head.

"If it's a total eclipse, the sun and moon perfectly align with the Earth. The moon's disc makes a ring of light around the sun. It's called 'the diamond ring effect.' I mean, it's just a metaphor. You know? Because it's not *really* diamonds," I say.

He considers me as though he's figuring something out for the first time. "Sarah," he whispers, pulling away from me. "Sarah, I—I love you."

Hope—joy—love all explode in me at once.

"There is no concrete scientific proof that love exists," I say.

"Okay . . . but do you love me?" he asks slowly.

"Yes. Of course. I love you." As the three words slip through my lips I know I do not need to test this through empirical data. This is fact.

He dives for me, his tongue parts my lips as we kiss deeper than we ever have before. I pull away and place my hands on his cheeks.

He kisses me again.

And again.

And again.

We talk and kiss and he teaches me about his body. I didn't know the body could pulse like this. Contract like *this*. The stars he makes me see are on the back of my eyes. We don't have sex—I'm not ready, I say. He kisses me as a response and does not pressure me. When the sky starts turning pink is when I fall asleep with my head on his stomach. He's stroking my head, with the palm of his hand. That puts me right to sleep. And I do sleep. Sleep like I haven't a care in the world.

A mouth on mine. Someone's kissing me. Hands run down my shoulders to my arm. I kiss back—oh! I draw in a heaving breath and awake. Andrew is on top of me again, his eyes are now a blue-green in the morning light.

"I gotta go," he says. "Busy day. It's 5:06 and I have to be at the juvie camp at 7:30. I have to get some paperwork to BC, too."

He slides on his swim trunks and he is absolutely beautiful with his unkempt hair and stubble. It's strange. I know what he is covering up with his clothes. I haven't thought about it until now, but it's a special knowledge. One that can only exist when two people really know one another.

"Walk me out?" he asks.

I wrap a robe around me and unlock the door. I make sure to block my desk with my body so he can't see the application in the morning light. We wait in the doorway, listen for any movement in the house, and tiptoe down the stairs. He keeps a hand on my lower back the whole way.

A door unlatches.

We freeze. There are footsteps in the kitchen, heavy squeaky ones, and I know it's Nancy up earlier than she probably ever has been in her life. Of course.

I bring my finger to my lips. Andrew meets my eyes and I mouth, "My aunt."

My fingers linger on the banister. My other hand is firmly grasped in Andrew's. Her footsteps squeak away down the hallway and I nod my head to the patio.

"Let's go," I whisper.

We stop on the first floor near Mom and Dad's room. In the living room, I know there are pictures of Scarlett and me on the fireplace mantle so I need to get him onto the porch and out the door before he has time to really see them and recognize her face. I grab Andrew's hand once we get to the living room and pull him out to the patio.

"I'll call you tonight," he says. And with one more kiss, he's down the patio steps, his feet pad on the path and after a few moments, there's the purr of his motorboat.

He drives a bit out from the dock. From up here in the living room, we're high enough up that I can see the harbor. He's out of my inlet before the sun is fully over the horizon.

TWENTY-EIGHT

LOVE.

Neuroscientists have scanned the human brain in an attempt to understand love and its chemical origin.

Nothing is conclusive.

I know I love Andrew. That is irrefutable. I don't need to peruse pie charts to accurately deduce if I love him or not.

A few days later, after a breakfast of waffles, I gather up all of Scarlett's clothes from my bedroom floor. She'll be home in two days. Forty-eight hours.

I hug her clothes to my chest and head to the laundry room. They smell like coconut oil and suntan lotion. I pass Mom on my way. She writes in a calendar book and I hope it's for an interview.

I toss in the darks. I pull out the short-shorts from the party the night Curtis yanked at me and the T-shirt from the dune buggy ride. I hold up the blue sundress from the night of the comet and I'm not exactly sure I would even want to wear this anymore. The dress is the same. The fabric and the color is too. It's not . . . it's not . . . me. I think it's more girly than I would like to wear. It's more Scarlett. I want to wear clothes that are down to earth. Natural. I would never have known that before the Scarlett Experiment. Maybe Tucker was right. Maybe I had to do the Scarlett Experiment so I could change.

The dress dangles in my hand. The cold water fills the machine and I am about to wash away the sand, the sweat, and the stardust overhead. Once I am done, I will put away all of her clothes and pretend that I never paraded around pretending to be someone I am not. One thing is for sure: I am wearing that cocktail dress Saturday night. I haven't forgotten how I felt when I put it on or that it represents the new me.

I also haven't forgotten that I still need to tell Andrew.

I drop the dress into the washer. It's okay. Andrew loves me. *Me.* The girl he thinks is funny, and smart. The girl who helped him see that he does have a future of his own making.

"Gran mixes her lights and darks too," Mom says from the laundry room doorway. "You two are too much alike," she says with a little shake of her head.

Maybe Mom does see me. Just a little. Even if she can't see

who I am, Mom gets something right.

"Smart, smart, smart. You and your Gran." She steps away.

Mom and Dad love me. I know this, they tell me all the time. But they don't see me. Not really. I watch her from the laundry room doorway. She passes the maid, who is scrubbing the kitchen, and the cook, who is prepping for dinner.

I want to stop Mom and tell her about Andrew. Tell her that someone *loves* me. Loves me for my brain, books, mathematical equations, and so much more.

She calls to me from down the hall, "Beanie, give Dad your essay tonight so he can proof it before Scarlett comes home."

I grip the doorway—hard.

"If I had to smell pee one more time, I swear," Scarlett says when she comes out of the terminal at the Hyannis airport. I didn't want to go, but somehow here I am. "NYC in the summer is pee and garbage."

She hugs Mom and when she sees me, she gives me a one-armed hug.

"You're tan," she says, disguising her jealousy. She takes out her cell phone.

"I've been on the beach a lot," I say.

I grab one of Scarlett's suitcases from the revolving carriage and Mom takes the others. Scarlett gabs on and on about skyscrapers, elevators going up one hundred flights, Juilliard, and the smell of the dorm in summer.

In the car, Scarlett finally takes a break from her stories to turn around in her seat.

"So what did you do while I was gone?" she asks.

"Nothing much. Tracked the Comet Jolie." I am about to mention that I think she'd like some of the necklaces I've seen in town and that maybe we could go together to pick one out. Scarlett brings her hands up to her mouth like a chipmunk and sticks her teeth out.

"Did you get your acclimation and detention?" she says in a funny, deep voice. Is that supposed to be me? She laughs at herself and spins back around.

"Right ascension and declination," I mutter.

"Come on, Scarlett," Mom says as we get back on route 6 heading toward Orleans.

"What? Beanie is our eager beaver."

"That's enough."

"God, Mom. We've only had to hear about her tracking that damn comet for a *year*. If I don't ask, she'll die. It's her whole life."

I lean forward, heat rushes through my cheeks.

"Did you gain weight?" I ask. I know it's a nasty thing to do. I know it's the one thing in this house we *do not say*.

"No, she didn't, Bean," Mom says, and her eyes are daggers in the rearview.

"No, I'm pretty sure she did," I say.

"You're a bitch," Scarlett says and twists to me. "I have a trainer at Juilliard. In fact, I weigh exactly a quarter pound less than when I left." She spins to face forward so all I can see is her tight bun wrapped on the top of her head.

The word "bitch" hangs in the air and I sit back in the seat.

Scarlett's never called me a bitch before. I've never called her fat before. She doesn't have an eating disorder—*yet*, as the dance teachers say. One time Mom and Dad caught her with a bottle of diet pills and made her go to a psychiatrist.

"You shouldn't call your sister a bitch," Mom says to Scarlett in a low tone once we get back to Nancy's. "I don't ever want to hear that from you again."

"Did you hear what she said to me?" Scarlett asks.

"Well, you're not the easiest person to talk to sometimes, dear."

I can't decide if this is progress or not.

The next morning, the morning of the party, I stand in the backyard.

A huge tent has been put up and takes over almost all of the lawn. Though in true Nancy fashion, she's positioned it so there is still a fantastic view of the ocean.

The band has come with piles of tarp in case it rains. The party planner that Nancy hired screams at a higher decibel than Nancy, if that's even possible. She is currently hollering into her cell phone while checking uniform sizes.

Beneath the massive pavilion are piles upon piles of tarp in case the rain starts early. Glassware has been delivered too and it's sitting there in plastic containers.

I'm not staying to help.

I am telling Andrew today. If he knows I am Scarlett's sister, I can contain it before the party. He probably won't find out my real age by nightfall. I need to go to the docks before Andrew goes out on the water.

I walk back in the house to grab my cell but stop at the patio doorway. At the kitchen table, Mom, Scarlett, Dad, and Nancy sit together, laughing and smiling at Scarlett's photographs from her month in New York. Some new costumes hang from the countertop, they glitter and sparkle under the track lighting. They're a tapestry of color compared to the whiteness of everything else. Mom holds on to Scarlett's arm.

"Look at that! Look at that grand jeté!" she says, showing Dad a photo, and he raises his eyebrows. He isn't distracted at all.

I'm wearing a chocolate-colored peasant blouse I picked out on Main Street with khaki shorts, and some sandals with a blue gem on the toes. The blue is a great detail that compliments my tan.

But they don't notice.

I turn right around and walk down the wooden steps of the patio and to the backyard. I keep walking, past the garage and the hidden shingle with Scarlett's and my name scrawled in the wood. I walk down the shell drive to the street—to tell Andrew about Scarlett.

When I get down to the docks it smells like my first date with Andrew: fried fish and seawater. I walk across the parking lot, replaying the memory of my skinny-dip in the ocean. At the docks, tourists take pictures of a couple of seals poking their little whiskered noses out of the shallow water.

Andrew jumps down from the boat to the dock and kisses me quickly.

"Attention whores," Andrew says about the seals.

"Shameless," I reply. *Just tell him. It'll be easy. You can stall on the MIT thing for just a bit longer.*

Sweat beads on the top of his lip and he takes off a baseball hat covering his matted down hair. He wipes his forehead.

"We're taking off in a few minutes," he says. On cue, there are a couple high-pitched beeps, the motors go, and engine smoke billows from the back of the boat. "Just going in the local harbor. With the tropical storm we have to reinforce some lobster traps."

Across the docks, the seals have ducked back under the water. I hope they swim out into the harbor where it's safe.

"About tonight," I say. "The party at my aunt's house . . ."

"Oh, yeah, I have to go to that girl's party tonight too. You just reminded me. I lost the invitation in Curtis's Jeep, like, a month ago."

"Yes, about that. My sister—"

"Andrew!" one of the guys calls from the boat and raises his hands in the air. "Come on!"

The boat pulls forward and a couple of the guys throw the line from the dock and jump aboard.

He kisses me quickly on the cheek. "The lobsters are calling. I'll come by your house after this other thing. Ten thirty? I'll sneak you out if I have to."

I want to tell him so badly it makes my throat ache.

"Ten thirty," I whisper.

He jumps from the dock to the boat, just making it within seconds.

"Good-bye!" Andrew calls out dramatically. He hangs off the

boat like a guy in a Broadway musical. A chorus of male voices mock Andrew.

"Good-bye, fair lady! Good-bye, Maiden Sarah! I shall see you when I return to port," some of the fishermen screech. A couple others hold their hands over their hearts. Six or seven guys, all in fishing gear, call my name and for the moment, I'm the princess of the docks. The princess who did not tell him what she needed to, the girl who has a mouthful of truth that she couldn't say.

TWENTY-NINE

FOR THE REST OF THE AFTERNOON, I WALKED throughout town practicing all the ways I was going to tell Andrew about Scarlett. None of them sounded right.

Already a couple varieties of catering trucks and the usual smattering of BMWs and Mercedes make a small line in front of Nancy's house. As I walk up the steps of Seaside Stomachache, I recount my plan. First, I am changing into the black dress.

Second, I will get Andrew cornered and tell him about Scarlett. The party should be too busy for him to find out my age. I can keep him distracted from that conversation. Yeah, that sounds perfect. An hour should be enough to make Nancy happy and—

"Bean!" Mom says when I walk in the door. "Oh good. You're here." I'm amazed she noticed I was gone, but this isn't a typical day for Mom. "We need to take pictures in ten minutes."

It smells like garlic and cooking spices.

In Mom's hand is the cupcake dress.

Nancy steps up behind her. "I cannot believe how late you are." Nancy wears a white dress that resembles a huge marshmallow.

Mom shoves the cupcake dress in my hands and the tulle scratches at my arms.

"Go up and get ready!" Nancy says and waddles away into the kitchen.

Waiters dressed in white button-down shirts and black pants shine the silver in the kitchen.

Mom puts a pair of gold studs in her ears.

"Your sister is getting dressed now; check on her, will you?"

I nod and look at the time. Six o'clock. The party is due to start in thirty minutes.

I climb the rest of the stairs to my room. I don't want to check on my sister. She can take care of herself.

I lay the dress down on my bed—thar she blows. The tiered pink dress with enough tulle and padding to protect me in a motorcycle accident. I lift it from the hanger and stop at the full-length mirror behind my door. I let flashes of last night ooze through my mind. *Our bodies under the warm sheets. Andrew touches me until I am writhing on the bed. Tugging and touching and placing my mouth all over him until I have to get a towel from the bathroom.*

309

Now here I stand in front of the mirror in a strapless bra and panties.

This body. This girl. I am not who I was when I got here at the beginning of the summer. I am the girl yelling to the sky on the back of a dune buggy. The girl accepted by a group for the first time. I am the girl who wants to try the world outside of the biology lab. I still want to be in that bio lab, of course. I just want *more*. I want both.

"Bean!" Mom calls. I can barely hear her over the music and voices now echoing throughout the house. I leave the cupcake dress on the bed and slip on my new dress and delicate black heels.

I draw black liner that I bought from the makeup store down on Main Street along my eyelid. I sweep some bronzer over my already tanned cheeks. I click off the light and just when I step out, the doorbell rings for the first time. It keeps ringing as more and more guests arrive. Chatter and orders from the cooks make all the sounds jumble together.

I close my eyes. I can do this. The dress and Andrew. No problem.

"Mrs. Levin! This house!" Trish's voice screeches up the stairs.

Tucker is here. My stomach fills with ice.

"We just have to take some pictures first, but Scarlett is waiting on the patio," Mom says, and the door opens, letting in the live band's rendition of Sinatra and the party chatter.

As the door closes, Scarlett cries, "Oh my God! Trish, I missed you!"

Step by step, I descend the stairs. I run my hands down the black cotton and lift my chin high. I step into the kitchen just as Nancy calls my name. I stop at the kitchen island and even though I am ready for it, my heart pounds.

Mom is outside with Dad, and I can't see Tucker with all of the people moving around.

Nancy shuffles through the RSVPs and whines, "You're annoyingly punctual. To the minute. Must you be late for the one evening I actually need you to be on time? It's time for pictures. And—" She glances up.

I clench my jaw, cross my arms, and don't move from next to the island.

"What is this? What the hell are you wearing? Maeve! Maeve, what is your daughter wearing?"

"My dress," I say.

"Go change right this instant."

Nancy walks away and when she realizes I'm not heading dutifully upstairs she turns.

"I am not going to be in a family photo in that dress," I repeat. "I'm not going to be at this party in that dress."

Nancy turns fully all the way around.

"What? We went over this."

"*You* went over it," I say and lean a hand on the counter. I don't even see Nancy. I am the heat in my cheeks and the rapid zoom of my heart. "*You* always tell me what you think I need. You never actually ask what I want."

"You don't know—"

"Yes. I do know!" I yell and smack my hand on the granite

countertop. It stings and radiates up to my wrist. "I know exactly what I want. Maybe you don't like it or it doesn't make sense to you, but it makes *perfect* sense to me."

Nancy steps very close to me and the kitchen staff pretends like they don't see this very public fight. Nancy breathes so hard through her nose, she's like a bull.

"You will get up there and change," she says and punctuates each word, *"right now!"*

"No!" I yell. A waitress stops filling a silver tray of puffed pastries when I yell but immediately goes back to what she was doing.

"Nancy! Bean!" Mom calls from outside. "The photographer has started taking pictures of the . . ." Mom's words trail away and she stops next to Nancy. Her jaw drops when she catches sight of me.

Nancy brings her hand to her oversized chest and keeps shaking her head at me.

"I don't understand you," Nancy says. "You barely say thank you for what I do for you."

I'm trembling.

"Why?" I ask and have to breathe heavily through my nose. "Why do you insist on telling me who I am?"

"Bean? What's going on?" Mom asks.

"Damn it," I continue yelling at Nancy. "If you would just *listen* to me you might know what to talk to me about!" I feel unhinged, like a telescope I can't quite focus. I want to bite something until it makes my teeth break. I just want them to *hear* me.

Nancy looks to my new dress, then the floor, and when her eyes land on me, her expression softens. She's not a bull; she's hurt and I'm a jerk. Nancy shakes her head slowly this time and says quietly, "I don't know how to reach you. I try to suggest new things for you to do. The teen dance, trips to the salon with me, but you always fight me on it. I can't connect with you."

I don't know how to follow. I'm expecting Nancy to be angry, so this softer reaction is confusing.

"I've tried all summer. I bought you this expensive dress, I am giving you my car, I—" Her voice squeaks and she grabs a napkin from the counter and dabs at her eyes. "You just talk to my sister. You barely ask how I am. You don't come visit me and now Scarlett is leaving and . . ."

I can't believe this. This does not compute.

Nancy's full-on crying now, and I step to her, grab a couple of napkins, and hand them over. She collapses onto a bar stool and wipes her nose.

Mom continues to be silent. Her eyes are wide and I don't think she has ever looked at me like this in her entire life. Scarlett, sure. But me? Never.

"You really want me to visit you?" I ask Nancy.

"I don't expect you to understand me like you do your grandmother. You two are cut from the same mold. But . . . that beautiful dress."

"I'm sorry," I say. "I just couldn't be humiliated. It's for a baby."

She looks me up and down.

"Oh," she says with a sniff. "Maybe it was."

I could hug Nancy right now. I almost want to tell her about Andrew. In one fleeting second, it passes through me. Maybe for just this one instant she'll understand.

"I want to like more than just science and the stars," I say. "But I can't do it the way you want me to. You have to just let me be me."

I get it. Maybe for the first time ever. Nancy *needs* us. She needs to bother me, rag on me, and stay on top of every little choice I make. We're all she has for family. Gran is in California and Nancy is alone. I didn't care or I didn't know how I could play a role in her life that wasn't a burden. I assumed, just like I had with many, many people that Nancy didn't like me. Nancy loves me. Maybe too much.

"Did you spend your birthday money on this?" Mom asks.

Outside, on the patio, Carly calls Mom's name. Her voice is close, which means Tucker isn't far behind.

"No. I bought it with the rest of the Pizza Palace money."

"Maeve?" Carly calls from the patio again, and Mom needs to sweep out to join her friend.

Nancy pushes up from the island stool. She sniffs again and wipes her nose. Before she walks away, I add, "I saw a picture of you," I say. "Of you and Gran in bathing suits. You were really young."

She dabs at her eyes again. "I think that was our last summer before I went to college."

"Can I keep it? I mean, I took it, but I can put it back. I really want it."

Nancy looks at me, her head slightly cocked.

"I am sure we can cut me out of it if you just want the picture of Gran."

"I want it because both of you are in it."

Nancy sniffs with a little smile.

"Sure," she says. "You can keep it."

She reaches a hand to me but drops her arm and I wonder if she wanted to hug me like she does Scarlett. Instead, she just nods.

I don't want her to be alone in this house all fall and winter.

She turns to join Mom outside.

"Nancy?" I say.

She glances back with a small, "Hmm?"

"I'll come visit this winter. If you want me to. As long as you let me bring my telescope and show you some things on the beach."

I think I see another smile curve at the corner of her mouth.

"You got it," she says. She points at me and adds, "Just don't bring that algae, I don't want it staining my carpet again."

I want to laugh but don't.

"You got it."

THIRTY

I HAVE *TO FIND ANDREW. I'LL FIND TUCKER* eventually, but this is step one.

Down on the lawn, Trish and Scarlett grab some shrimp off of an appetizer plate. Tucker hangs out with his dad. I can't help but pause when I see him. He's tan, which I haven't seen in a long time. He's filling his tux out too. I guess he worked out this summer.

There's Andrew! I don't know how long he's been here or what he already knows. He crosses the lawn, stopping at the bar outside the tent. He spins around a couple times and searches the crowd, I assume he is looking for me. I have to get to him *now*. I'm down the patio stairs in seconds. Mom and Dad are in the tent, and Nancy is near the band. They are also far enough away from Andrew. Perfect.

"Andrew!" I cry. He nearly spits out his drink when he sees me.

"Sarah. How do you know Scarlett? I didn't know—"

"I'll explain all of that."

"Wow, you look great."

"I have to talk to you."

I take him by the hand and lead him away from the tent and down near the entrance to the bay beach. Scarlett is on the beach already. She's taken her hair down so it flows over her shoulders. She's laughing open mouthed and touching the arm of—oh my God. She's touching Curtis's arm.

I can't breathe so well. I really do have to do this. Don't I? It's darker here and the sky has faded to a light lavender gray.

"What is happening, Sarah?" Andrew's voice pierces my thoughts. "This is your aunt's house. I'm so confused."

Shelby stands next to Scarlett too. This is it—the moment.

"Listen, I have to tell you something. I tried telling you at the docks today."

"Sarah!" Curtis calls and peers down the pathway at Andrew and me.

"It's about Scarlett," I add quickly.

"Is that Sarah?" Curtis calls out again. I want to cringe at the mention of my name.

"What about Scarlett?" Andrew says.

"I know her. I didn't tell you, but I do and—"

"You know her?!"

Curtis runs up the pathway and leads Andrew by his jacket

sleeve down to the beach. Andrew keeps a hold of my hand.

Scarlett turns from some guys I recognize. Her eyebrows furrow and she looks like a confused bird seeing me next to Andrew. She keeps looking me up and down.

Andrew's hand falls away from mine.

"How do you know Scarlett?" he asks again.

They're all here: Shelby, Tate, and all my new friends. A small bonfire is crackling. I swallow hard. I know most of the people beyond the bonfire too. Trish flirts with one of the guys I met this summer—I can't remember his name. But these are my friends and it'll be only moments before they *know*. I won't be Sarah, I'll be Bean, sixteen and a liar.

"That's my sister," Scarlett says.

"*This* is your sister?" Curtis says. "What are you? Twins?"

"Sister?" Andrew's disbelief is so soft. I want to run us both out of here.

"I wanted to tell you," I say quietly. His eyes meet mine and I want to take away the confusion in his gaze. "At the docks today. Lots of times. I never quite got it out."

"Twins?" Scarlett says with a cock of her head. "Please. Do we *look* like we're twins?"

I swallow hard. She'll never defend me. She's going to ruin everything. I was completely stupid to put this off for so long. All I need is for Mom, Dad, and Nancy to come down here too. Scarlett opens her mouth. Everything I built this summer is about to blow away and I'll be nothing but Tucker's old scraps.

Curtis throws an arm over Scarlett's shoulder. He's already

drunk so he sways a little. He's rolled up the pants of his tuxedo so he has sand all over his ankles. "MIT and Juilliard?" he says.

He hangs on Scarlett. Andrew is by my side; I can feel his body heat.

"Two geniuses in one family?" Curtis says. "How come you never told us you were Scarlett's sister? Why did you keep it a secret, buddy?" Curtis throws his arm over Andrew's shoulder. He remains silent. "How old are you, little sis?" Curtis asks.

Scarlett and I are locked eye-to-eye.

Scarlett . . . please . . .

With a flip of her hair, Scarlett says, "She's going to MIT. You figure it out."

I want to double over from the relief that rushes over me.

Scarlett defended me. She lied for me.

"Scarlett! Sarah!" Mom calls from up near the tent. "Pictures."

"I'm sorry," I say to Andrew. "I'm really sorry I didn't tell you that Scarlett is my sister," I say quickly. Across from me, Shelby smirks, but it's not evil, it's knowing. But not even she knows the real truth. My lies are so layered that I have to keep track of which ones are consistent with specific people.

Scarlett sips her champagne flute and nods for me to follow her up the path.

"Scarlett!" Nancy's voice now squeals over the party music.

Andrew keeps his hands in his pockets.

"You should have told me," he says. "That was a big secret to keep."

"Huge," I say while walking backward to my sister. "I'll be right back."

He lifts his gaze to me and stops me by gently touching my forearm.

"It's what I said about her, isn't it? I called her," he lowers his voice, "I called her a bitch at that party."

"Hardly," I say, even though I could use that justification easily. I can't lie anymore. I just can't say one more untrue thing. I step to Andrew and squeeze his hand. "There's something else I have to tell you. I'll be back," I say and hurry after my sister toward a collection of photographers up near the tent.

The truth about MIT and my age won't change *who* I am to Andrew. The truth of who I am when I am with Andrew is absolutely real.

Once we get next to the tent, the main photographer maneuvers us around so Nancy is sitting in a white chair in the center. Behind us is the bay and the setting sun. The sky is scattered with hazy gray clouds and the fall of twilight makes the sky the color of a bruise. I can't meet my sister's eyes but I can feel her watching me. I pretend everything is normal.

"Let's get this in before sunset, guys. Let's get the sisters on each side of Mom and Dad. Dad, you go on the right; Mom, the left."

I stand next to Dad, and Mom is next to Scarlett. Thankfully, Andrew doesn't come up from the bay beach. The happy jazz music doesn't make sense given how hard my heart is pounding.

Scarlett *defended* me.

"And . . . smile!"

Flashes explode and we move positions twice. Scarlett still glares at me while Mom and Dad pose with Nancy.

I need to tell Andrew about my age. *He knows me. He does. He'll understand.* When Scarlett is taking pictures with Nancy, I glance down the long path back toward the beach. I don't see Andrew.

Through the space between the spiky branches and jagged leaves, Scarlett's friends dance around the bonfire. The moon should be high in the sky but the clouds cover the stars and move even faster than they did a few moments ago. Soon they won't be visible at all and the rain will come. There, on this strange nature night, are all the people who I coveted this summer. There's Shelby and her dreads. Curtis, who seems to have given up on Scarlett and is all over some girl I don't recognize. They're all together under the crescent moon like abstract angels. Too perfect for real life.

I turn to the tent to try to find Andrew there. There is a long line for food now. I stand at the edge of the tent and lawn and search for Andrew in the crowd.

"Your aunt has . . . the worst taste ever."

Tucker has stepped next to me. His clipped humor is familiar. Even the way he talks when he's trying to be funny; he starts out slow and then finishes his sentences fast. I forgot how much I liked his delivery. We stand a foot or so apart. We don't hug or embrace. Shaking his hand seems weird, so I nod.

Waiters walk with trays of food and stand at various stations. The twelve-piece band has moved on from classics and is now playing music from the turn of the century that's authentic to the *Titanic* disaster. I only know that because the party planner screams into a walkie, "*Titanic* music. *Titanic*, go!"

"Who are you looking for? That guy you were with earlier? Is that your boyfriend?"

"Yeah, that's him."

The wind makes Tucker's hair skate over his eyes. The clouds are moving fast but break apart just enough for the moonlight to trickle through.

Mom and Dad's friends stand in their fancy tuxes and eat appetizers off square cocktail napkins with the symbol of the White Star on the corner. Nancy is back from taking pictures and is clearly over the moon describing to everyone the prestige of the ice sculpture artist. Her arms flail everywhere and her many gems sparkle when they glint off the candlelight.

"School starts soon," Tucker says. I'm not surprised this is what he talks about first. I used to think being predictable meant we were perfect for each other. I shrug.

"Sorry again for what happened," he says. "With Becky. I wanted . . ."

"To tell me?"

"You were always so busy."

"Please," I say, and scoff. "You were shady. You could have told me a hundred different times. It would have sucked, but I would have understood."

He shrugs but doesn't tell me I'm right.

"What was the phrase you used? I 'watch the world'?"

I can't help it. That phrase still burns.

"I never said that."

I laugh so hard it nearly makes me cough.

"You don't know half as much about me as you think you do,

Tucker. Did you know that I decided not to do Bio Club next year?" I raise my chin in the air.

Only as I say it do I know it's true. But I know a lot of things are true that I didn't before.

"And I probably won't tutor," I add.

"Why?"

"Because I want to volunteer at Ninigret Observatory. And I think I'm going to take up lifeguarding."

"Wow, except it'll be freezing in a couple months."

"Indoor pools, Tucker. You have, like, zero perspective," I say and flip my hair over my shoulder in a very Scarlett move. Tucker doesn't reply. We're silent a moment and I need to circulate back down to the beach to find Andrew. Though Scarlett is down there.

"I gotta—" I start to say.

Tucker leans forward and interrupts, "Is that . . ."

"What?"

He points. In the center of the tent is the enormous ice sculpture. I saw it, I just didn't really pay attention at first. Tucker cleans off his glasses to make sure what he's seeing is real.

"I think it's a mini re-creation of the *Titanic* leaving port," I say.

Under it, in blue lights it says, BON VOYAGE, SCARLETT.

I shake my head and laugh. Tucker starts laughing too. I can't help it. I laugh because Scarlett defended me. Because I'm in this new dress that's all mine, and because Nancy has an ice sculpture shaped like a large ship about to sail to its doom. Tucker is laughing so hard he's crying and wiping his eyes on his jacket sleeve.

My stomach clenches, I bend over, unable to stop it. Oh, it hurts. I'm laughing too hard. My face hurts, I massage at my cheeks.

"Everything from the table linens to the waiters' uniforms is meant to replicate the *Titanic*," I say.

"That's awful!" he cries.

"Isn't it?"

The brass band plays and I turn, wiping my eyes again. My laughter stills. Sunset has fully fallen over the party, but it is muted behind clouds. The tips of hydrangea flutter. Maybe Nancy will get her wish—the tropical storm will miss us after all.

"I do want to be friends," Tucker says now that our laughter has faded. I look away from the hydrangea. Tucker's been watching me.

"One day," I say. "Just give me time."

I don't wait for him to respond; I walk away. I don't need to get Tucker's response or his approval. It's okay that he's here. I've changed and so has he.

So many people are dancing that I have to walk around the perimeter of the backyard. The first whip of wind makes the sides of the tent snap with a loud *thwap*.

From down the pathway, on the beach, Andrew waves at me. I head toward him. This is it—I draw a deep breath. I will lead him from his friends to somewhere quiet.

Scarlett barrels toward me from the direction of the driveway. Her face is redder than I've ever seen it and the wind lifts her hair from her shoulders. Her nostrils flare and she shakes her head. She looks like Mom when she's *really* angry.

Scarlett digs her nails around my left shoulder and drags me away to the area underneath the patio stairs.

"Ow!" I say as her fingernails poke into my skin.

We are alone here, even though the party continues on behind us.

"I just heard. Are you crazy?" she whispers.

I stand up tall and turn my nose in the air. I have to rub at my arms and I'm sure she made me bleed or close to it. Fine. I'll confess. I'll tell her about the hundreds of outfits of hers I wore this summer.

"Bean. Andrew Davis is too old for you."

"He's nineteen."

I don't mention that's it only for a few more weeks.

"God! Don't you get it?" Scarlett yells, and I take a step back from my sister. "Andy hasn't been in high school for two years. He's had experiences you can't even imagine yet. You live in two different worlds."

"Not *that* different."

"Yes, that different. And you've been lying to him this whole time."

I know that but I'll never own up to it in front of Scarlett.

"I can't believe you would do something like this. You're Miss Logical. Miss Math Club. Miss Scholarship. You overthink your entire life."

"Exactly!" I cry. "That's exactly right. And for once, I didn't, and I loved who I was!"

"You always do what *you* want. You're so selfish, you don't even care about Andy."

I gasp and my cheeks flush.

"It's *Andrew* and of course I do. I know what I'm doing."

Scarlett puts her hands on my shoulders but I don't want to look her in the eyes. "He's a really nice guy. Do you—"

Scarlett takes a breath, seemingly steeling herself for this conversation.

"Bean, do you have any idea how unfair this is to him?" Scarlett puts her face in her hands. "I can't believe this. Thank God you're leaving in a week."

Thunder smashes around us. Both Scarlett and I flinch. Scarlett even hunches a bit and covers her head.

"Is that why you defended me? Is that why you lied for me to your friends? For Andrew?"

Scarlett doesn't answer. I know she's right about lying—it's wrong, *of course*. But that's why she defended me, so Andrew could save face. It wasn't even for me.

"They're all talking about it. Andrew and your sister. Inseparable this summer. It's so wrong. I shouldn't lie for you. I'm not a liar."

"You're no saint, either, Scarlett. You go out with Curtis and he's a murderer."

Her porcelain face seems to crack. Her blue eyes soften. The wind whips again and tiny specks of rain fly through the air.

"The least you could do is defend me. Your sister. I'm flesh and blood, remember?"

"I didn't defend Andy, I defended you," she says, and her eyes lift to me, her mouth turned down in a distinct frown. "But you made up this whole life that isn't real."

"It feels real," I say quietly. "It's me he's with. And I'm going to tell him. I was about to when you came to get me."

"Oh right."

"I actually was. Not like you care or believe me."

"No. I don't."

A crash of thunder explodes again. People around us scream and then break into laughter. The guys holding the tent start ushering people to the house.

The rain does not hesitate. There is a blast of lightning and the water comes down in a thick sheet.

I turn on the spot, leaving Scarlett by the side of the house. I walk directly into the fray. The band races past me, nearly running me down with their rain-soaked instruments. Guests make a dash for the stairs so quickly. The various catering managers steer people inside, and the party planner holds an umbrella for some of the ladies from the DAR.

"Tell him the truth, Bean," Scarlett calls after me, though it is a soft warble through the rain, like a bird song. I turn back and Scarlett hasn't moved. She doesn't even hide her face from the rain. Her hair is already stuck to her skin and mascara is running small lines onto her cheeks. "Tell him."

"Sarah!" Andrew's voice calls out to me from the chaos.

Dad helps Nancy waddle to the house before me. She cries out, "Don't light the candles, you twit! Get some of those brute waiters to bring the ice sculpture inside!"

The valets help to run platters of desserts to the house. The caterers have to walk in teams of four as they balance silver platters of food. The precious apple meringue cakes Nancy paid top dollar for are soaked. One apple, which I think was garnish, falls from a silver platter to the ground and rolls by Curtis and Tate, who jump over it and race up the patio stairs.

"Sarah!" Andrew's voice calls out again. Mom, Nancy, and Dad are already on the patio. Scarlett must have gone inside because the space under the stairs is empty.

Andrew runs up the path to me; he is completely soaked.

The wind and rain crash onto the party. I snatch my bag from the back of Dad's car where I had left it earlier in the night.

"Let's go! Let's go!" Andrew cries. Without a glance back, we escape out onto the street.

THIRTY-ONE

ANDREW PARKED ALMOST AT THE END OF SHORE Road. He's unbuttoned his bow tie and his shirt clings to his body. We jump into the truck. The rain is so strong it runs down the windshield and blots out anything on the street.

I hold my bag in my lap. Inside is a much-needed change of clothes. I keep shivering. Andrew starts the car but doesn't go anywhere just yet; he drops his hands to his lap.

"So the party tonight," he says, "was for Scarlett. Because she's going to Juilliard."

"Yep."

"But not for you."

"No. Not for me," I say.

"Why didn't you have a going-away party? You're going to college in the fall," he asks.

"Oh," I say, working up my nerve. "I guess I'm not really a party person." We drive toward Andrew's house. Lies are like water. They ripple out, the details slip through; they're hard to contain.

Shame keeps my eyes to the floor. The guilt is so easy to push aside when the love I feel for Andrew is so real. I can't imagine him knowing the truth. Who am I kidding? I can't imagine even saying the words: I am sixteen.

Andrew doesn't say anything else about the party and I suppose he's just trying to be polite. We pull up to his house and run to the patio. The rain has lightened up momentarily, but a flag on the top of the house makes the same *thwap* sound as Nancy's too-expensive tent.

He turns from unlocking the door and lifts an eyebrow. "I bet I can convince you to get out of that wet dress."

"I would take that bet," I say with a smile, but it's hollow inside. That uneasiness I haven't been able to place settles over me again. As I step into the house, I finally identify the feeling. It took me all summer, but I can finally confirm the emotion.

Disappointment.

I am disappointed.

Andrew flips on the lights and places his keys on the table. I run through Scarlett's party in my mind: the delicately scrawled place cards, the twinkle lights, and brass band.

I step past the kitchen and Andrew's question runs through my mind a second time: *Why didn't you have a going-away party?*

Why *didn't* I have a party? I was number one in my class; I never received anything less than an A in my life. I turned sixteen this summer. Why didn't I ever ask Mom and Dad to celebrate?

Andrew makes himself a drink in the kitchen, and there are two clinks of ice in a glass. He is making one for me too. I walk to the window. Outside, it's dark but the leaves on the trees whip and snap.

Andrew stands at his computer, scrolling through some music. Out the window—the leaves make tiny cyclones. I imagine Nancy's backyard and the decadent linens swirling and spinning over the perfectly manicured lawn.

A melodic but slow acoustic song trickles out of the computer speakers.

"Do you know what dorm at MIT?" I hear from behind me. But it's a punch to my gut.

"No," I sigh.

Words from the summer, voices from fights, and discussions filter through my mind.

You stop me, Star Girl. You make everything I see . . . better. More interesting.

Let Dad proofread your essay.

Backup your back ups.

It's all so clear to me now: why I'm not allowed to have my cell phone on the table. Why I'm lying to this perfectly beautiful boy who has no idea I'm sixteen. Why I told the lie in the first place.

And why, all summer, there was never a light left on for me.

I place a palm on the glass and I'm surprised how cool it is.

"Sarah?"

In my mind, Mom checks her cell phone, wondering and worrying about Scarlett.

Dad's reading. Dad's working. Dad's watching TV. Dad's constantly absorbed with an article.

I am not there.

I am not there.

I wanted them to see me, understand me, but they haven't been paying attention. They haven't *wanted* to see me. I found myself all on my own, here in this house and on the beach with Andrew, but they haven't even paid attention.

"Sarah? Are you okay?" Andrew asks.

A flush of heat circles in the apples of my cheeks. Andrew stands before me, but in my mind, he is at the water's edge. The sunset falls over him and he's about to dive into that icy cold ocean, where we first kissed, where it all started.

"You know, tonight at the party," I say, "I watched my life from the outside. I walked through those people; I'm not one of them."

My palm drops from the window smearing long finger lines against the foggy glass.

Andrew's lips are tight; he lightly touches my shoulder. "I don't think anyone really knows the real me," I say with a shrug, "I let them tell me who to be. I let them dress me up." My voice cracks and I try to hide it by clearing my throat. "But you," I say, though it's hoarse. "You see me."

He lets his hand drop from my shoulder.

I clear my throat again, shaking my head and the threat of tears away.

"Want to know what my nickname is?" I ask.

"Sure . . . ," he says gently.

"Bean. The little small thing you push around on your plate that you don't even really want."

All these truths are not the right one. They aren't the one he needs to hear.

Andrew takes a step to me, reaches behind my head, and unclips my barrette. My hair falls, the clip drops to the floor, and Andrew kisses me deeply. He's kissed me like this all summer. At the beach, at parties, in my driveway. I kiss him back. This kiss is to say I'm sorry. Sorry that I had to construct a whole false life, to create a stage where I could stand.

"Come on," he says once he pulls away. We move down to the carpet. He lies on his back in the middle of the floor. We lie side by side and listen to the music. Andrew holds me and I wonder: why is Scarlett so angry with me all the time? Is it because Mom and Dad are never worried about me? Does she envy my invisibility? I would give anything to have them consider me dangerous, a kid they have to worry about.

I refocus on the aerial photographs. Jagged geography trapped inside a frame. *I'm like that.* Most people aren't close enough to see all the parts of me. Or maybe it's Scarlett I'm thinking of. Before I can think anymore Andrew's hand is running up my side and soon he's pulling me back up. Andrew takes my hand and we're dancing.

A new song plays on the stereo, another slow acoustic. The guitar strums a melancholy melody. We spin ever so slowly. His chin is close to mine and I breathe deep, inhaling him. He's salty and smells a little like suntan lotion. His hands run over the straps on the back of the dress, up and down, again and again. We keep dancing.

"Sarah," he whispers. I lift my eyes to his. "I love you." This just makes my face hot and my lips tremble. "I love you," he whispers again. The song picks up and it's so sad—the guitars, the drumbeat—and I know that I absolutely love him. I run my thumb over the tattoo I was so obsessed with all summer long. Swimming to the moon, swimming through the stars; it's just a wish. Like all of the lies I told this summer.

His finger loops under the strap of my dress—he slides it down my arm. His eyes fix on the other strap. His index finger hooks under the fabric and he pulls ever so slowly, down. He unclips my bra so that my shoulders and breasts are bare. The air in the room is warm, but I shiver anyway. My teeth chatter like I'm back on Nauset Beach in June. He lifts me up, my legs wrap around his waist and my chest presses against his chest. Only this time we're not in the water. Up the stairs we go, step by step, I kiss him, legs wrapped around his waist.

Thunder crashes outside and the wind howls against the side of the house. He places me down and we're standing in the middle of his bedroom with the shades drawn and the queen bed unmade.

The dress drops down around my ankles. My feet sink into the soft carpet. I curl my toes into it. I slip off my underwear. I want him to see me, know me.

Andrew comes down to his knees. I come to my knees too.

"I really want to do this," he whispers. We still don't touch yet—we're so close. I can feel his breath on me.

His expression darkens in concern.

"You're shivering," he says and touches my shoulder.

"I think it's because I'm happy," I say, though my teeth chatter.

"I'm going to take your hand," he says. "Then I'm taking you to the bed."

Shudder.

Only tiny snippets of thoughts run through my head once Andrew pulls me on top of the bed. He slides off his dress pants and boxers so he is completely naked.

He extends a hand and together, we lie down. His head moves from kissing my lips to my breasts to my thighs. My legs spread, his mouth moves to me.

No comet can touch this.

When he moves back up and kisses my mouth, he pulls away. "I love you," he says it again and again.

Love.

Love.

I repeat the word over and over in my head until the hollow slide of a wooden drawer brings my eyes to the bedside table.

He takes out a condom. Andrew leans back on the pillow.

How many ways are there to stare?

Blond hairs run over his knees. There's a sheen of red, a burn from where he's missed suntan lotion. I want to run ice over it. I see these details in the bruised moonlight. The thin condom wrapper splits so easily in his hands. Andrew lifts his eyes to mine. He sits back against the wall with his knees bent a little.

His penis is hard and it's not science telling me, it's me. I want his body, want to put my mouth all around him, and I do. There's a pulse through me. A star racing across the sky.

He touches me on my shoulders, stopping me, and I lift my head up. My lips pulse with my heartbeat.

"Is it okay?" I ask.

"Yes, I just need you to stop. Or . . . ," he says.

"Oh!" I say, and we share a smile. I know what he means.

"You want to do this?" he asks.

"Yes," I say in an exhale. "Yes."

The condom remains poised in his hand. I wonder if he wants me to reach out and put the condom on him myself. But he does it; a slow roll. He crawls toward me. Every time his palms touch the sheet it leaves an indentation like a handprint in the sand.

He slides on top of me, his hands curl over my shoulders, and Andrew breathes softly on my lips. When his mouth is on mine, he enters me. I open, I widen. Andrew thrusts his body and something deep inside me tears just a little. I gasp and my hands tighten on his shoulders.

"Are you okay?" he says, pulling back.

The pain dissipates, rippling away. Andrew's eyes move from my parted lips to my eyes. "Sarah?"

Andrew leans forward and runs his lips over mine. He doesn't kiss me. He skirts over my mouth with his own so an electric wave rolls over me all the way down to my toes.

"Are you okay?" he asks again.

"I'm perfect," I whisper. Andrew starts to move again.

And only as his mouth touches mine, tasting of salt and

sweat do I realize that yes, I am fine. *I* am fine. Me. The girl he has grown to love is here. I'm here, I am here, I think, as his body moves with mine again. I'm here and I love you.

I love . . .

"Don't leave in a week. Don't leave . . . ," Andrew whispers in my ear.

He cups the back of my head with his palm and whispers it again. These whispers are the bay breeze in the morning through an open window.

"Don't leave," he says again.

They are tiny waves rippling onto the shore.

Oh, Andrew, I want to say as the rhythmic timing of our bodies quickens.

I'm already gone.

Sixteen—eighteen—isn't it all the same? Boston College, Scarlett, bonfires, lawn parties, and beaches.

Andrew is on his side, stroking my hair. Sweat slides down my temple and my heart beats between my legs.

They say that the light from a star takes four years to reach Earth. Four years ago, I was twelve. I liked my bed. My toys. The Boston Planetarium. Four years from now, I will be twenty, Andrew's age. When the light leaves the nearest star, right now, from the moment Andrew and I made love, it will take four years to reach me again. Somehow, this comforts me. This amazing moment can be relived.

"What am I going to do without you until school?" he says in a growl. The early morning makes his voice hoarse. "I know," he says with a lift to his voice, "I'll move you into MIT. It's like twenty minutes away from me on the T."

Something cracks apart inside my chest. Like a bone or a muscle.

"I'll show you around Boston. We can do it together."

I take a breath. "Yeah . . . ," I say. "That sounds perfect." And it does.

He pulls me toward him as the tropical storm blows everything around outside and the branches knock on the windows. I curl my body into myself and rest my head against Andrew's chest. He immediately brings his hand to it and strokes me lightly. We let the storm do the talking, the rain lashes the windows and the wind rattles the house.

Scarlett's words swirl through my head.

You're sixteen!

I grip gently onto Andrew's forearms. I hate being sixteen.

But that's not really true. I hate wanting to be going to MIT in the fall and knowing that there would be this whole life for me if I actually were. And this here, this moment, is just another part of that life.

There was so much more to me. I never knew. So much more than that American flag string bikini. More than a closet full of clothes that weren't mine and a telescope pointed up to the sky and away from the earth.

I grip Andrew's forearm even harder, not to hurt but because I fear he'll slip away like the outgoing tide, undetected, and I'll never feel him again.

THIRTY-TWO

ANDREW'S CHEST RISES EVENLY AND HIS BREATHING
is quiet; I've been watching him since he drifted off. When a rim
of light outlines the two windows across from the bed, I know it
is at least five thirty in the morning. My arm aches from holding
it in one position for so long. Andrew's shaggy blond hair skims
over his closed eyes.

I'll move you into MIT.

I try to close my eyes and drift off. Just relax, I tell myself.

Star Girl.

I stare up at the darkened wood ceiling. The rafters make
horizontal lines.

Lines make sense. Left to right, I stare at those rafters. I count the lines in the wood until I lose count.

Don't leave. Don't leave.

Who was he talking to? Bean? Sarah? Which one? My breath catches in my chest and I hold it. I turn on my side so my back is to Andrew. His hand cups my hip and sadness flies through me like a steel weight on a fishing line. I touch my hip, let the warmth of my fingers rest on the skin.

When Andrew made love to me, I was Bean. I was a girl who loves astronomy. Who can't wait for the science fair at school, and who is looking forward to debate team. But I was Sarah, too. I was proud, confident, and funny. I am unafraid to dance in a crowd now and I can tell jokes to strangers without fear. I don't know how to choose, or how to be just one or the other. I find comfort in facts, but the only fact I know as I lie here staring at the wall is that I am sixteen.

And a liar.

This isn't about the lie I told on the beach that day. This isn't about an experiment that made me feel better about myself. I brought Andrew into this with me. This is about who I have become—the kind of girl who would completely manipulate someone.

I have to go home. I have to walk in that door and be Bean. I exhale, but the breath is rattled.

I have to get out of this house. I am a liar.

I slide off the bed very slowly and sweep the dress from the floor. I hesitate, holding the black material to my chest. Andrew's back muscles clench and he moves so he's stomach down. He grips his pillow and hugs it.

He reached inside my heart last night.

I tiptoe downstairs, scrawl a note, and leave it on the table.

Last night was one of the most important nights of my life. So important, I didn't want to wake you up. See you later.

—Sarah

I stuff the black dress into my bag. I slip the T-shirt over my head, change into my denim shorts, and try not to make a sound.

Shoes . . . shoes . . . where are they? I shove my party shoes in the bag and dig out my flip-flops.

I bend over and slip them on, just as the mattress upstairs creaks. I freeze.

Wait. Don't move. Wait . . . silence. I sling my bag over my shoulder, tiptoe over the carpeting, and open the front door.

Without a word, I sneak out.

I had almost forgotten there was a tropical storm. When I step outside, I see that a couple of oversized branches have fallen on Andrew's porch. They haven't done much damage, but one cracked a flowerpot. I step over the scattered soil, off the patio, and down to the street. A few overturned trash cans litter the road.

I walk from Andrew's street and quickly turn onto Main. The shops are empty, dark, and the sun is barely a glimmer in the sky. As I walk, I pass the empty Goosehead Tavern. Many of the shop owners had taped their windows, so large X's cover the massive glass fronts. I pass the still unopened Bird's Nest Diner. Inside, one waitress places a filter in an oversized coffeemaker. I stop just past the diner and look up the long street where I first talked to Andrew. Mike's jersey still hugs the tree.

I know the intimate details of Andrew's life.

He will never get to know mine.

I close my eyes, just for a second.

Andrew's hands run over me in languid movements, up and down my body as though he is sweeping up from the bottom of the ocean. He could be swimming, taking long strokes to break the surface. He kisses my mouth and says my name again and again and again.

I open my eyes to the empty street.

The thought of Andrew's face makes a rusted hook pull at my belly, sending a jab through me. The hook snags and makes my stomach uneasy and I try to swallow a couple times. I need to get home. I pass by the library, Viola's Dress Shop, and the penny candy store.

I can't count periodic tables anymore.

Or the constellations, either.

I keep walking to the end of Main Street, where a truck of town workers arrives to clean up debris from the storm, but it is just some leaves and branches.

I stop in the middle of the street again and something occurs to me that hadn't occurred to me at the beginning of the summer.

Jim Morrison didn't just *die* in that bathroom in Paris. He overdosed on drugs. Or he died because of years of abuse to his body. Maybe the French coroner was right, his heart really did just give out. Maybe. But that's just a wish.

I'll never get to know. The truth died in Paris.

When I get to Shore Road, I stand at the end of the street with my hands hanging by my side. Branches and leaves are scattered across the lane. Sand is pushed up against the base of trees.

I swallow hard, something hurts in the back of my throat. I lick my lips and they're salty from last night's sweat.

Scarlett was so angry with me last night. She seemed horrified that I could be with someone like Andrew.

No big deal? Bean! Do you have any idea how unfair this is? I can't believe this. Thank God you're leaving in a week.

It's like a punch to my gut.

I fall to my knees right there in the street. I bow my head. I know what she means.

I just never thought about it; I never allowed myself to.

Andrew works at a government facility. Sure, I'm sixteen and it's legal, but they wouldn't look too fondly on a relationship between a twenty-year-old and a sixteen-year-old. Oh God. I am disgusted with myself. I was fifteen when we met. I could have gotten Andrew into real trouble if anyone from his job found out. That's what Scarlett meant about how bad it is. Not that I lied, but what my lie can do.

The Scarlett Experiment was just the selfish excuse. I put on the clothes and walked the walk and it gave me confidence. But I didn't need any of it, not really.

I push up from the middle of the road and walk down the road to Nancy's house. Before tiptoeing onto the front lawn, I glance at the street. The ghost of Andrew's car waits for me in the street just like it did all summer. I see myself bounding onto the pavement and jumping into his arms. The fishing hook inside me widens the crack that's opened in the center of my chest.

I step onto the lawn and walk past the house toward the backyard.

"There you are!" Scarlett says in a harsh whisper. She's on the patio outside her bedroom. Her hissing words are nothing compared to how horrible I feel. She'd probably gotten up to practice yelling at me and saw me walking. She would never expect me to stay out all night.

I don't stop to talk to Scarlett. I keep going toward the backyard.

How could I risk Andrew's future? How could I do that to someone? Even last night at the party, I kept thinking about myself. I just kept pushing the truth away so I didn't have to accept the severity of what I have done to Andrew.

I walk down the little path between the house and the garage. I turn behind the garage and stop next to a hydrangea bush with the great purple flowers. Behind these flowers is the shingle where Scarlett and I carved our names. I come to my knees again.

It was *me* Andrew shared laughs with, *me* who talked about probability and living life the way you want.

It was me all along.

I just couldn't believe that someone would see in me what I felt deep inside my soul.

I rest my forehead on my knees and sit next to the hidden shingle and hydrangea. My back shudders and tears run down my legs toward my shins. I wonder right there on the grass about survival. How we become the adults we're meant to be. We all start off small, we all start off here. Don't we? I can't bring myself to lift my head.

My sister's footsteps walk gently down the patio steps.

Maybe I could stay here forever? Hide in the bushes and grass. It's dark here. It's safe. Or maybe I could go back to the *Alvin* and take a trip down to the deepest part of the sea. I would like to creep and crawl along the bottom of the ocean. I know there are some fish that can make their own light because it's so dark where they live. Lanternfish. That's their name. Maybe I could go there too.

I shudder again, surprised that I'm crying so hard. But the pain feels good and that scares me too.

I wonder . . . I wonder what would happen tomorrow, if all the stars in the sky burned out and the world went dark—would the Lanternfish survive?

THIRTY-THREE

SCARLETT LETS ME CRY FOR A WHILE. SHE FINALLY asks, "What happened?"

"Go away," I say to my knees.

"I waited up all night for you."

I squint when I lift my head; the yellow light of the sunrise is blinding.

"You. You waited up?" I can't help the distrust in my voice.

"It's five forty-five in the morning," she says and removes a stray branch blown from the storm from the top of the hydrangea bush and places it on the ground.

She pushes the leafy bushels aside and there, between the shadows, is our shingle. It's barely been weathered from the years.

Our names—*Scarlett and Bean*—are almost black compared to the gray of the wood.

"That was the day you tripped and skinned your knee on the boat dock," she says.

Her hands cup the flowers so as not to damage the buds. The tenderness in her voice makes my bottom lip tremble.

"You took a bobby pin from your hair," I say and my nose prickles.

I have to look away from our shingle and the memory of my burning knee and sticky cheeks. The tears are different this time, but she is still here. Maybe Scarlett has always been with me.

"Why did you lie to everyone all summer?" Scarlett asks quietly.

I shrug. "Why do I do half the shit I do?" I ask.

"Bean," Scarlett says, almost scolding me.

"What?" I ask, sitting up and linking my arms even tighter over my knees. "Can I curse? Can I do anything normal? Can I wear a dress that isn't a fucking doily? Can I, Scarlett?"

Her eyes are gems to me. Blue marbles framed by blonde lashes. She looks down at her hands when I hold on to her gaze.

"I don't know, can you?" Her voice is frayed around the edges.

The tears burn my sun-warmed cheeks. "Do you want to know what I did last night?" I ask.

She doesn't answer; she wants to know.

"I had sex with Andrew."

Scarlett's lips part. A cloud passes over us, dimming the halo of light over her head. She slides a hand over her mouth and it's so white, I can see the tendons and bones. I turn my head slowly back to the water. Tiny waves lap against Nancy's private beach. I smell the coconut of Andrew's skin and taste the tangy bite of his lips after swimming.

"It all started with this ridiculous lie," I say. "I met him on the beach and he had no idea I was fifteen. I lied, told him I was eighteen . . ."

The whole summer comes spilling out. I tell her about The Doors, about the comet, what happened on the beach that night. I tell her about all her clothes that I stole, about the bikini, Mike's death, and about Curtis being an alcoholic.

"And last night. He, *we* . . ." But the words trail away. I meet her steely eyes and my face collapses. I cry into my hands. "He held his hand behind my head. He told me he loved me. *Me.*" Tears fall over Scarlett's cheeks too, which only makes me cry harder. "But it's all a lie. He doesn't know. He doesn't know the truth."

Scarlett does what I can't remember her doing since we were babies.

She scoots closer and hugs me. She doesn't let go, either. Her grip is stronger than I thought. She squeezes and it's like a tiny fist clenching around me. Something circles in my chest. A whole universe—a constellation. The hook, which has been pulling at me, drawing me to the surface, has brought me all the way to the stars.

"I love him," I say and collapse, crying even more hot tears.

"I know," she says and grips me harder. "It's okay."

I close my eyes and let Scarlett pull me to her chest. I let her heart beat against my ear.

I let it dance.

I close the door to my bedroom. The silence evens my breathing. I was intending to shower but stop at my desk. I clench my jaw and run my fingertips over the Waterman Scholarship application. I understand the elemental construction of paper: cellulose, fibers, and water. Facts still comfort me.

I slowly sit down in the chair. My palm rests flat on my many stapled pages of data. I know this place. I take pride in meticulous reports. I wait for the relief to wash over me at the sight of an experiment well done. But it doesn't come.

Beside the desk are mounts, three types of LED flashlights, and four models of telescope lenses. The top of my application says: Sarah Levin. She is the girl who can work all this equipment. She is the girl who knows the way to academic success.

She is split in two.

I think I might know how to bind her back together.

My fingers wrap around a pen and I slide forward a notebook. The ballpoint hovers over the blank lines and I reread the Waterman Scholarship essay question.

Please explain in 1,000 words why your experiment successfully represents who you are as a scientist and how the execution of your experiment reinforces your educational goals.

I press my pen to the paper.

Local astronomers told me I was being "silly."
They asked in various forms: Why track a comet by

hand when there are plenty of reliable, computerized sources to accurately project the right ascension and declination of a comet? Why bother calculating this yourself?

I tracked this comet successfully from its initial discovery at the University of Hawaii to the day it reached its perihelion, July 3rd 11:13 p.m. As you can see from my attached reports, my calculations were exact.

Much to the surprise of my mentors at Summerhill Academy in Rhode Island, I only used electronic sources to program my telescope and confirm my calculations.

I pride myself on the persistence and meticulous observation I pursued in order to accurately track our fast-moving friend. After all, it makes me who I am. I am fully committed to my experiments and never once in the year that I spent tracking the Comet Jolie, or P/1413, did I waver from this commitment.

Not until this summer.

You might be wondering why in an academic paper such as this I would bring up my social life. You see, before this summer, I didn't have one. I sat in bio lab or at the observatory, looking at the stars. I loved being a Mathlete and deconstructing fractions and percentages. I missed school dances, games, and parties, just to observe the night sky.

I was living a fraction of my life. A half-life. I watched the world.

Nietzsche says, "One must have chaos within oneself to be able to give birth to a dancing star."

This summer, I stopped watching the world. Instead, I dove in the ocean, danced in crowds of people, and laughed at jokes that I otherwise would have heard from the outside. Those who never once looked up at the stars and wondered what it all means embraced me. They let me in. I was part of their world. Suddenly, I was the one with my feet planted on the earth. I wowed my new friends with my statistics and commitment to the pursuit of truth about our beautiful universe. My stars always led the way.

So, you ask, why does my experiment successfully represent who I am as a scientist? Regardless if I get this scholarship or not, I will pursue the workings of our universe for the rest of my life.

Because I am a keeper of the stars.

In my heart, in my soul. Forever.

They have guided me back to myself.

I know how to live a full life now because of this incontrovertible and very simple fact:

Each atom is made up of protons, neutrons, and electrons. The number of protons in a nucleus determines the identity of an element. The many plants, animals, and beaches of the world have different equations for these protons and neutrons—but we all have them. Even humans. We are all linked by the power of the infinitely small.

So, am I a scientist? Yes, but I am so much more. I know now it is not only the experiment that counts but also the scientist inside. I don't just watch the stars. I don't just watch our world anymore.

I am the stars.

I am the Comet Jolie that shot across our beautiful sky.

I am the universe.

THIRTY-FOUR

LATER THAT AFTERNOON, I COME DOWN THE STAIRS and the smell of tomato soup meets my nose. There's the clink of silverware against bowls and the TV chatters away in the living room.

No one noticed I was gone all night. No one except Scarlett.

Mom's going home on Monday. I stop just to the side of the laundry room door. The honeysuckle scent of fabric softener wafts into the empty hallway. She hasn't said anything about my new dress, but she must have come to get my laundry this morning when I was sleeping. It's pressed and hanging above the dryer. I want to ask her if she thinks I looked pretty at the party, but before I open my mouth, she runs a hand down the front of the dress. She shakes her head a little but she's smiling. She hums when she's happy and it takes me a second, but I think she might be singing The Doors, "Light My Fire."

I hold the finished Waterman Scholarship in my hand. It is sealed. I did not let Dad proofread it. The essay I wrote was typed up fifteen minutes later and then sealed within the official Waterman envelope. Even though it's only Sunday and there is no mail service today, I will drop it in the mailbox anyway.

This experiment is complete.

I have spent the whole summer worrying about Andrew. Worrying about how to make him like me. Worrying how I could protect myself and guard the lie. I will go back to school and start over. Start on a new astronomy scholarship. And I will work on it without the lie weighing on my heart.

This new heart.

Earlier that morning, as I sealed up my envelope for the scholarship, I held my cell phone in my hand and hovered over Gran's ten-digit number. I couldn't bring myself to call her and listen to Gracie's voice sing out of the receiver. I didn't deserve her advice or her comfort. But one fact is certain, when I visit her on Labor Day weekend, I'll tell her the entire story.

I walk past Nancy, Dad, and Scarlett. They are sitting and talking at the kitchen table. I hesitate at the foyer, where they can't see me, and listen in on the conversation.

"She didn't want me to read her scholarship essay," Dad says.

"Maybe she doesn't need you to," Scarlett adds, but it's flat, closing the discussion.

"Maybe you're right," Dad replies.

Nancy huffs.

"I liked her dress," Dad says.

"I kinda did too," Scarlett says. "I mean, it was a little tight, but it looked nice."

"She's finally a teenager," Dad says with a big sigh.

"She has been a teen for a long time, you just haven't noticed," Scarlett says to Dad playfully.

"You seem to know everything," Dad says.

"She's my sister. I'm supposed to know more than you."

I smile at this and slip past them, out the front door, and into the sunlight.

Fishing Pier. Tourists walk across the hot pavement making direct lines for the fishing boats. It's just before noon. Even though it's Sunday, Andrew texted earlier to tell me that the crew had to go out around one to clean up after the storm. Because of the tropical storm it'll be a longer trip than usual. I try to distract myself with these thoughts as I walk from the parking lot, past Hatchman's Fish Market, and toward the docks.

I take a deep breath: I'm wearing Scarlett's white sunglasses. She wouldn't let me leave the house without showering first.

The water rolled down my body, collected the sand and salt that lingered from Andrew's skin. The water circled around the drain and washed away.

"Wear these," Scarlett said. "Your eyes are bloodshot."

"It's just because the skin is reacting to the excess moistu—" I tried to explain.

"I don't care why, dork," she said and held them in front of my face. I took the glasses, but hesitated before putting them on. I thought about that picture of Nancy and Gran in their bathing suits.

"Scarlett?" I asked.

"Yeah."

"Do you think we'll be like Nancy and Gran? Living on other sides of the country, barely speaking to each other?"

She kept our gaze and shook her head. "No way," she said. "We'll figure it out."

I believe we can.

It's bright at the pier even with Scarlett's sunglasses. I stand off to the side of the parking lot. Just ahead of me, dozens of tourists snap pictures of the fishermen in their yellow gear. Andrew's boat is there too. He's hammering something into a metal pole. The hammer makes a clanking sound that echoes over the fishing pier. He's wearing a gray T-shirt, but he's sweating through it. I try not to follow the line of the muscle of his forearm, but it's pronounced because he's straining so hard. I can't help but think it—the line of the muscle looks like the tail of a conch shell. I want to run my fingers along the skin.

"Hi," I call. Andrew's head turns to me. The shadow of his baseball hat darkens his eyes.

He smiles a little and I know that smile, I've seen it hundreds of times this summer. He grabs a water bottle and jumps down from the boat, meeting me on the parking lot.

His arms envelop me and he pulls me to his chest in a tight embrace. I smell Andrew in one deep salty breath.

"I won't be back until tonight," he says. "But I can get you after, go to dinner if you want."

"I just need a minute," I say.

"Okay . . . ," he says.

I move the sunglasses to the top of my head.

He takes a step toward me, water bottle in hand, and the concern passes over his eyes.

"Have you been crying?" he asks.

I take a deep breath, blinking away the spots of sun reflecting on the harbor behind Andrew.

"I . . ." I take a breath but stop.

I have to do this.

"I'm going home on Monday," I say. "I have to get ready for school. Start packing up."

"We have a few weeks until school."

"I need to prepare."

"But college bookstores have half the stuff you need. I want to help you move in. I don't want you to assume—" He sighs. "Look, this isn't just a summer thing for me."

"Me either," I reply, and it hurts deep in my gut.

"I love you," he says. "I didn't just say it. And—"

Whirlpools churn within me as he speaks.

"I really do have to prepare," I interrupt.

Why am I continuing to lie?

"I have the truck. I'll come talk to your parents."

Bigger waves now. Stronger.

"Talk to my parents?" I say.

"About helping you move in. I'm strong," he says and flashes his biceps like it's some big joke.

"I know a lot of strong guys. . . ." He keeps talking. About all the people I will never meet and all the things we'll never get to do. "I'm serious."

The waves are huge inside me, hurricane huge. I'm drawing in breath, but it's not breath, it's salt, it's brine. I have to say it.

"Like, three or four dudes," he continues. "They will love you."

Say it, Bean!

"I'm sixteen!" I cry.

My voice carries so I lower it. "I turned sixteen on the night of our first date. I'm going to be a junior. In high school."

"What?" Andrew says with an edge of a laugh. He must think this is some big joke. In the back of his eyes is that beacon of light I love. I know that light; it called to me all summer. The black asphalt below me is cracked in thousands of tiny fractures. "What are you talking about?" He says with a chuckle.

"Not even seventeen," I say. "I haven't taken my SATs yet."

He laughs yet again, but there's something bitter on the edge of it this time.

"You're going to MIT," he says.

"No. No, I'm not."

There's a silence between us. Seagulls cry, there's the background noise of the cars and the boats.

"I had to tell you. I couldn't lie anymore."

The shadow of the hat hides his eyes at first. When he lifts his chin, the hard stare makes something tighten in the back of my throat.

"Scarlett is my older sister. By two years."

"What are you talking about?"

"I'm sixteen years old," I say very slowly. "I—I lied."

"You're serious?"

"I'm sorry," I croak.

He backs away from me. His hand comes up to his mouth. He stops and stares at me again.

"I'm so, so sorry."

"Holy shit."

He bends over, his hands on his waist. When he stands back up, he's grimacing, his teeth clench. "I think I'm gonna be sick."

"I'm sorry," I repeat.

"You're *sorry*?" His voice cracks. "Oh my God," he says and squats down with his face in his palms. "Oh my God," he says to his hands.

The moon tugs at the waves, at the sea. I want to tug Andrew back to me. Tell him it's just a joke—a different science experiment. Bring him back and tell him about the comet. Startle him with all of my knowledge.

But I cannot find the lighthouse in his eyes.

"You don't *look* sixteen," he says.

I swallow hard and say, "I've only been sixteen a few weeks."

He shakes his head. "All that shit about MIT."

"Andrew," I say and take his hand. He's frozen to the spot. His hand is cold in mine, he doesn't squeeze back or caress my skin. His lips are tight. "I did this," I say. "I did it. I didn't know what would happen when I met you. I never thought you would want to be with someone like me. And then you did. And it was too late. You didn't do anything wrong."

His eyes flicker across the pavement, he does not look at me as he says, "Sarah . . ."

I wish he wouldn't say my name. My real name.

"I'm so sorry."

"Don't say you're sorry. I could lose everything I've worked for. Everything I—"

"I know. I know that now. I didn't realize."

He drops my hand.

"Stay away from me," he says. He points at me while backing away. "Stay the fuck away," but it's a hiss of a whisper.

"I love you," I say. "That was true."

He turns on the spot to walk back to the dock. I watch him for a few paces. He takes long strides and the small burn on the back of his calf is still red. He stops and turns back to me. Hope. Horrible, unfair hope prickles in my chest.

"I can't," he starts to say, but it comes out as a sigh. "I can't tell anyone why this is over. I have to live with what you've done."

He walks toward the dock. With a whip of his hand, he chucks the water bottle against the ground so hard that it explodes. I jump, surprised by the force of the water splashing everywhere.

I have to watch him walk away. I have no choice.

I watch him get on the boat.

I watch him pick up the hammer and begin hitting whatever it was he was hitting when I walked onto the parking lot. He pulls the brim of his hat down over his eyes even more.

The girl who I wished I was, the one going to MIT? She would have told him the truth from the beginning. She would have let him go because it wasn't her time yet. He slams the hammer now and Andrew's lips break from a thin line into a grimace for the barest of seconds. He's crying.

My pain burrows deep inside where I know the first person who I ever loved was someone I manipulated.

So I do what any scientist would do. I study his frame for a few minutes. Then the curve of his muscles, so I won't forget. I try to remember the glimmer in his eyes too. Science can't explain a glimmer. Can it? Can science explain the soul?

I do what I have to do.

I turn and walk away.

THIRTY-FIVE

One Year Later — Late June

ETTIE, CLAUDIA, AND I MAKE A CHAIN WITH OUR hands. We run out of the Seahorse and onto Main Street Orleans to my car, Nancy's old Volvo. We admire our purchases—on sale from last year's shipment. We bought three of the geode slice necklaces I admired in the window last summer, before I met Andrew.

Before the lie.

Ettie snatches the keys from me. Claudia gets in the back and I slide into the passenger seat. Ettie got her license a month before me, which means that she is more experienced. Or so she says.

We've been in Orleans for two weeks and all three of us are

bronzed from the days on Nauset. I have searched for Andrew on the beach but haven't seen him. It's not like I would know what to say if I did. Ettie starts the motor and we pull out onto Main Street. We don't make it very far—a couple feet. It's packed and we immediately sit idling in traffic.

"We could have just sat in the parking spot," I say.

"Hey!" Claudia says, pointing at my necklace. "Yours is bluer than mine."

"No, yours is bluer than mine!" I say with a laugh.

"Mine is the bluest!" Ettie cries. She reaches behind her neck to unclasp her necklace, but the car rolls forward. We break into hysterics. We'll be waiting a while for the many tourists to figure out how to go through the rotary at the top of Main Street.

"Let's swap," Claudia says, and her black hair shines in the sunset that fills Main Street. All three of us laugh, unhook the clasps, and swap to the person to our right. We hold our hair up and admire our rightful necklaces.

"Much better!" Claudia says with a smile.

"I love this song!" Ettie cries and leans forward to turn up the volume. She turns the music up so loud that everyone on the street looks in our direction. We don't care; we sing at the top of our lungs.

And that's when I see him.

I stop singing, my lips part.

Andrew's been watching me from the doorway of the Bird's Nest Diner. He is wearing the same baseball hat from that last day on the docks. Our eyes lock. I've been dreaming of this moment for months.

Then the strangest thing happens . . . I'm thinking, suddenly, about the Zuckermans' boulder on their lawn. For years I believed it was a piece of the moon. Last summer, the summer with Andrew, my life was like that. A little piece of the stars—a little piece of something I could never touch.

I wait for Andrew to turn away, to grimace, and to remind me of all that I did to hurt him.

The traffic inches forward, it's now or never—we'll pull away.

We're moving ahead, I have to turn my head to keep eye contact. Just as the tires roll past, just as I expect him to scowl or look away . . .

He breaks into the smallest smile.

And it's a smile just for me.

ACKNOWLEDGMENTS:

THANK YOU TO JOCELYN DAVIES. THERE IS NO ONE I would rather hash out story lines and character with! Working with you has made this book even better than I could have envisioned. Thank you for your collaboration, respect, and for showing me just how lucky a writer can be.

Thank you Margaret Riley King at WME for loving this book and understanding just how much Bean's story needed to be told. And, of course, to Chelsea Drake for your patience and support!

To Jacqueline McCleary, Brown University astrophysicist, for your unparalleled wisdom. You know it's not fair to be that smart *and* that pretty, right? Bean's story is stronger because of you.

To Bryant Grigsby, SETI scientist, for multiple annoying phone calls in which you had to explain way too complicated science to me. I attempted to keep up while you gave me your valuable expertise and time.

Thank you to Kate Madin and Hovey Clifford, WHOI staff. You are generous and without your expertise my story would have suffered.

To A.M. Jenkins and the power of "feeling it"—your mentorship means more to me than I could express.

To Franny Billingsley—you changed my understanding of character for not just Bean but Penny too (but more on her later)! Thank you, thank you, thank you.

Thank you to An Na, who read an early version of this book and pointed me in the right direction.

Thank you to Sarah Ellis—who reminded me that the hard stuff is the least sentimental and who taught me about the power of subtlety and subtext. I am trying to give up ellipses . . . I swear.

To the VCFA community, especially the faculty—you are magic.

Of course—to the CCWs: Rebecca DeMetrick, Linda Melino, Mariellen Langworthy, Claire Nicogossian, Maggie Hayes, Tracy Hart, Laura Backman, Hannah Moderow, Kristin Sandoval, and Matt Hudson.

And, for my sister, Jennie—for all the tamago, "head things," and trips to the Cape we can stand.

Thank you to Mom and Dad, who brought me to the Cape for our wonderful vacations. You showed Jennie and me the best place on Earth and always encouraged us to reach for the stars, no matter how high.

I discovered Jim Morrison and The Doors on the Fourth of July, the year of my thirtieth birthday. I heard *Moonlight Drive* on the beach and within weeks had sped through the entire catalogue of albums and read four biographies. The poetry, the music, and the sheer passion that The Doors embodied weaved itself into the fabric of my life. I got to see Ray Manzarek and Robbie Krieger play live in 2011, just two years before Ray passed away. It has been my honor, even in some small way, to continue the legacy of The Doors through Bean's story.

For me, this quote is the heartbeat of *Between Us and the Moon*:

"I tell you this. No eternal reward will forgive us now for wasting the dawn."—Jim Morrison

Thank you: Jim, Ray, Robbie, and John—for all of it.

JOIN THE
Epic Reads
COMMUNITY

THE ULTIMATE YA DESTINATION

◄ **DISCOVER** ►
your next favorite read

◄ **FIND** ►
new authors to love

◄ **WIN** ►
free books

◄ **SHARE** ►
infographics, playlists, quizzes, and more

◄ **WATCH** ►
the latest videos

◄ **TUNE IN** ►
to Tea Time with Team Epic Reads

   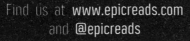